Praise for

New York Times and *USA Today* Bestselling Author

Diane Capri

"Full of thrills and tension, but smart and human, too. Kim Otto is a great, great character. I love her."
Lee Child, #1 *World Wide Bestselling Author of Jack Reacher Thrillers*

"[A] welcome surprise... [W]orks from the first page to 'The End'."
Larry King

"Swift pacing and ongoing suspense are always present... [L]ikable protagonist who uses her political connections for a good cause...Readers should eagerly anticipate the next [book]."
Top Pick, Romantic Times

"...offers tense legal drama with courtroom overtones, twisty plot, and loads of Florida atmosphere. Recommended."
Library Journal

"[A] fast-paced legal thriller...energetic prose...an appealing heroine...clever and capable supporting cast...[that will] keep readers waiting for the next [book]."
Publishers Weekly

"Expertise shines on every page."
Margaret Maron, Edgar, Anthony, Agatha and Macavity Award-Winning MWA Grand Master

JACK ON A WIRE

by *DIANE CAPRI*

Published by: AugustBooks

http://www.AugustBooks.com

ISBN: 978-1-942633-99-0

Original cover design by: Cory Clubb

Jack on a Wire is a work of fiction. Names, characters, places, and incidents either are the product of the author's imagination or are used fictitiously, and any resemblance to actual persons, living or dead, business establishments, events, or locales is entirely coincidental.

Published in the United States of America.

Visit the author website:
http://www.DianeCapri.com

ALSO BY DIANE CAPRI

The Hunt for Jack Reacher Series

(in publication order with Lee Child source books in parentheses)

Don't Know Jack • (The Killing Floor)

Jack in a Box (*novella*)

Jack and Kill (*novella*)

Get Back Jack • (Bad Luck & Trouble)

Jack in the Green (*novella*)

Jack and Joe • (The Enemy)

Deep Cover Jack • (Persuader)

Jack the Reaper • (The Hard Way)

Black Jack • (Running Blind/The Visitor)

Ten Two Jack • (The Midnight Line)

Jack of Spades • (Past Tense)

Prepper Jack • (Die Trying)

Full Metal Jack • (The Affair)

Jack Frost • (61 Hours)

Jack of Hearts • (Worth Dying For)

Straight Jack • (A Wanted Man)

Jack Knife • (Never Go Back)

Lone Star Jack • (Echo Burning)

Bulletproof Jack • (Make Me)

Bet On Jack • (Nothing to Lose)

Jack on a Wire • (Tripwire)

Tracking Jack • (Gone Tomorrow)

The Michael Flint Series:

Blood Trails

Trace Evidence

Ground Truth

Hard Money

The Jess Kimball Thrillers Series
Fatal Distraction
Fatal Demand
Fatal Error
Fatal Fall
Fatal Game
Fatal Bond
Fatal Enemy (*novella*)
Fatal Edge (*novella*)
Fatal Past (*novella*)
Fatal Dawn
Fatal Shot

The Hunt for Justice Series
Due Justice
Twisted Justice
Secret Justice
Wasted Justice
Raw Justice
Mistaken Justice (*novella*)
Cold Justice (*novella*)
False Justice (*novella*)
Fair Justice (*novella*)
True Justice (*novella*)
Night Justice

The Park Hotel Mysteries Series
Reservation with Death
Early Check Out
Room with a Clue
Late Arrival

Short Reads Collections
Hit the Road Jack
Justice Is Served
Fatal Action

CAST OF CHARACTERS

Kim Otto
Carlos Gaspar
Charles Cooper
Reggie Smithers
Lamont Finlay
William Curry
Marilyn Stone
Nora Ramsey
Iniko Makinde

and
Jack Reacher

Perpetually, for Lee Child, with unrelenting gratitude.

JACK
ON A
WIRE

TRIPWIRE
By Lee Child

She eased to a stop in the drop off lane and waited, motor running.

"Well, thanks for the ride," Reacher said to her.

She smiled.

"Pleasure," she said. "Believe me."

He opened the door and stared forward.

"OK," he said. "See you later, I guess."

She shook her head.

"No you won't," she said. "Guys like you never come back. You leave, you don't come back. … Good-bye, Reacher. I'm glad I got to know your name at least."

He kissed her, hard and long.

"So what's your name?" he asked.

CHAPTER 1

Saturday, June 4
Rural Vermont

TWO HOURS AGO, THE shooter had set up his rifle in the back of the van parked on a hill overlooking the grave site. He had a panoramic view of the well-tended country cemetery.

Through the high-powered scope, he saw gently rolling hills covered in deep, verdant green. Damned grass was more plush than private golf courses favored by obscenely wealthy professionals.

Only the privileged rested beneath that grass. Most had been greatly admired in life and deeply mourned after death.

No one the shooter mourned was buried here. Or ever would be if he had anything to say about it.

A large lilac bush in full bloom shielded him from view even as its sweet fragrance filled his head with his mother's memory. She had loved lilacs like crazy.

The scent conjured his childhood home surrounded by the huge green bushes heavily laden with sweet purple blooms. Until the end, he'd foolishly imagined the lilacs served as a thick blockade keeping danger from his family.

He'd believed, 100 percent, that his family was safe inside the compound where his dad, ever vigilant, could always protect them.

Dad said people passing by couldn't see anything through the heavy bushes.

Even if they could have seen inside the family compound, they couldn't execute a successful attack through the thick foliage.

There was only one way in or out of their property and dear old Dad had insisted the home was completely defensible.

Which turned out to be both true and irrelevant.

He'd been a child. And a fool.

The shooter shook his head to clear the memories threatening to lead him astray. He returned his full attention to the task at hand.

Through the rifle's scope, he watched Congresswoman Sheryl Tardelli as she stood before her father's headstone, bathed in the soft morning light. She was a good-looking woman at fifty, even with her shoulders bowed by the weight of unrelenting grief.

Tardelli had experienced great loss. She knew how it felt.

The shooter chewed on his lower lip, the pain keeping his mind focused.

Tardelli would have been better served by a heart full of righteous anger.

He understood the power of anger.

Anger pushed him to action.

He was in charge.

Never a victim. Not then, not now, not ever.

Anger could have done the same for Tardelli if she had embraced it.

She hadn't. She'd embraced the enemy instead.

That window of opportunity had closed. She'd lost her chance.

He watched Tardelli as she stood amid the cemetery workers bustling about, tending to their duties. The caretaker, a kind, elderly man, approached her with a bunch of lilacs in his fist. The shooter imagined he could smell them from across the distance. The caretaker gestured toward the vase of wilted flowers beside the headstone. He said something the shooter couldn't catch through his earpiece.

Sheryl's father, Bert Tardelli, had loved vibrant, growing things. He'd been raised on a farm before he went off to fight the Vietnam War at eighteen.

Sheryl often said that she wished her father had never volunteered. But his older brother had died in the war, and he'd felt obligated to finish what his brother started.

When Bert Tardelli returned, older, wiser, and worn out by his war experience, he'd been too debilitated to work the farm. But he'd nurtured the flower gardens with care despite his limitations.

Sheryl reached for the vase at the base of her father's headstone, intending to replace the withered flowers with the caretaker's fresh bouquet.

The caretaker offered a gentle smile as he spoke. This time, the shooter heard the caretaker's words, transmitted to his ear from the tiny listening device he'd planted earlier.

"I can dispose of the old ones for you, Ms. Tardelli."

Sheryl nodded gratefully. "Thank you, Mr. Turner. That's okay. There's very little I can do for my dad now. I can handle this. I want to."

Mr. Turner stood aside as Sheryl bent to gather the dead flowers.

The caretaker's gaze lingered on Sheryl's face and the pronounced scar above her lip. The surgeon's failure had left a permanent mark that had drawn piteous glances from strangers most of her life. She had to be used to the curious stares after all these years.

Mr. Turner touched his upper lip gently. "If you don't mind me asking, what happened?"

Self-consciously, Sheryl covered the scar, her fingers tracing the imperfection. "Cleft palate repair surgery when I was a child. Army surgeon. He was new. Not as skilled as some."

Mr. Turner's eyes softened with sympathy. "I'm sorry to hear that, dear. Can the scar be improved now? They have better techniques these days."

Sheryl shook her head, her gaze drifting toward her father's headstone. Tears welled up in her eyes and her voice trembled with emotion. "After Mom died, it was just me and Dad for many years. I keep the scar to remind me of the sacrifices he made for his family."

The caretaker's gaze flooded with understanding as he gently patted her shoulder. "I'm so sorry for your loss."

Sheryl nodded as if her throat, tight with the weight of her grief, prevented sound for a moment. She cleared her throat before she said, "He suffered so much. He's in a better place now."

"I see," Mr. Turner replied.

It was just the sort of thing people said to be kind when there was nothing they could do to help. He patted her shoulder again and left her to grieve in peace.

The shooter's vigilant eye remained on his scope.

After Turner walked away, Sheryl carried the vase of dead flowers to a nearby trash bin.

Her fingers brushed against the withered rose petals, and she took a moment to inhale their faint, lingering scent.

With a firm hand, she lifted the vase and tipped it to dispose of the fetid water and lifeless blooms.

The shooter growled low in his throat from his nest in the back of the van, still peering through the scope. "Get on with it."

He needed the situation to unfold while the witnesses were there to see it happen in real time.

Otherwise, he'd be forced to shoot her.

Which was okay because she'd die today either way.

But a quick bullet to her head wasn't the plan.

Stick to the plan, he murmured.

The mantra his driver lived by.

Sheryl had dawdled too long.

The shooter was losing the light. And she'd exhausted the last ounce of his patience as she ran out the clock.

Five more minutes and he'd take her out. He set the timer on his watch.

Sheryl continued to linger over the dead flowers until she eventually realized there was something stuck to the bottom of the vase. She tipped the vase and reached inside to loosen the bent flower stems he'd carefully positioned there.

Which was when the tripwire activated precisely as he'd intended to release the poison.

A hissing sound pierced the quiet country stillness.

A heavy green cloud rose from the vase and settled over Sheryl like a shroud.

The sticky green substance covered her skin, her eyes, her nose. Her eyes closed tight and then widened. Her nostrils flared. Her mouth widened to scream.

Taken together, her face resembled a moldy Halloween pumpkin carved for horror.

The shooter smiled.

"Finally," he muttered under his breath.

Dousing Sheryl in a thick blanket of oily, cold, and utterly fatal toxins wasn't as easy or quick as shooting her. Which was totally okay.

Speed was not the goal. Only the result mattered.

"Never confuse effort with results, son," his father had often said.

As the shooter watched through the scope, Sheryl's eyes widened further with terror. The green cloud entered her eyes, mixing with her tears, and turning the whites to a sickly yellow.

She clutched her throat as she gasped for breath, inhaling more of the poison, while the chemicals assaulted all of her senses at once.

The shooter knew what was coming next. He'd watched this particular poison perform many times before. He smiled as the scene unfolded exactly as planned.

Sheryl dropped the vase and stumbled backward, eyes stinging, vision blurred, heart racing, gasping to breathe.

She fell to the ground in a heap of flailing limbs, writhing on the ground like a dying lizard.

Blindly, Sheryl reached for her phone and her trembling fingers struggled to dial 911.

The shooter's grin widened.

Her throat would be tight now, making it difficult to speak or to be understood.

"Poison...help...," she managed to whisper, the words barely audible.

Sheryl's body collapsed as panic and confusion gripped her.

At this point, she must have realized that she would never live another day.

The shooter resisted the urge to laugh. His eyes crinkled when he laughed, making it difficult to see clearly. He wanted to witness every last nuance.

In the distance, the cemetery workers and Mr. Turner heard the woman mewling for help like a newborn kitten. They rushed to her side, faces contorted with concern.

Of course, they were too late. From the moment the tripwire triggered, they were defeated. Whether they knew it or not.

The shooter watched closely from afar until Sheryl took her last, gasping breath even as the old caretaker made frantic but feeble attempts to revive her.

"Mission accomplished," he muttered, pulling back from the scope.

No need to shoot. He could save the bullet.

He watched another satisfyingly long moment. Then he drew the rifle deep inside the van, closed the back doors firmly, and moved to the passenger seat.

"Time to go," he said as he snapped his seatbelt into place. "She's done."

"Good work," the driver replied, rolling the van slowly along the rugged fire trail deeper into the trees.

"I had a clean shot. Would have been easy to end her suffering." He shook his head slowly. "Could have done that old guy and the four worker dudes, too."

"No reason to do that. We don't want that much heat coming down on our heads, either. We've got too much left to accomplish. Stick to the plan."

"Yeah, yeah. Stick to the plan. That's always your answer," the shooter groused angrily. "That's what my old man used to say. Stick to the plan. We both know how that turned out."

The driver gave him a fierce scowl in response as the van bounced into a deep rut in the gravel road. He gave it more gas and struggled with the steering wheel.

When the driver managed to clear the ruts and they were moving forward again, he said, "You want to grab a bite and catch some sleep?"

The shooter gave him a terse nod. He slumped down into his seat and closed his eyes. "Let's wait until we cross the state line. Just in case Vermont's local yokels are smarter than the others."

CHAPTER 2

Two weeks later
Friday, June 17
Detroit

FOLLOW THE MONEY WAS a solid strategy for any investigator. FBI Special Agent Kim Otto and her partner, Carlos Gaspar, had certainly tried to do exactly that when she was assigned to find Reacher. No luck. For a variety of reasons.

Yesterday, after eight months of looking, she'd found a breadcrumb. More digging last night had persuaded her that the breadcrumb shouldn't be dusted off into the trash.

Gaspar had retired a while back, and she'd been working the off-the-books assignment on her own since then.

Still, she made a fresh pot of coffee, settled into the most comfortable chair in her apartment, and called him at home in Miami.

"What's up, Sunshine?" he asked when he picked up.

"I may have a lead," she said, getting right to the point. They were both too busy for chit-chat.

"You've found Reacher?" Gaspar joked, slurping something like a kid. Some sort of Cuban guava dessert, probably. The man lived on caffeine and sugar, as far as Kim could tell.

He had taken a job working with a high-end investigations firm in Houston. Whatever free time he could carve out went to his family. But he always took Kim's calls, and he was more than willing to help when he could. She tried not to abuse the privilege.

"And once I find Reacher, what will I need you for?" she teased in return. He rewarded her with a hearty chuckle. "Seriously, I've found a possible place to start looking. Down in your neck of the palms. Key West."

"Damned hot down there this time of year, Suzy Wong," Gaspar warned. "Don't forget your sunscreen."

"No point in 'splainin' you all this if you're just gonna blow me off when I'm done, Ricky Ricardo," she said with a mock Cuban accent, offering a bad imitation of the classic character. "You gonna help me or not?"

Gaspar laughed again, as expected, and it warmed her heart. She missed him. Simple as that.

Gaspar was as reliable as a comfortable old shoe. He was an excellent husband to Marie and an even better father to his five kids. Of course, he'd been a great partner, too. Her go-to guy on the Reacher assignment from the beginning. They'd been through a lot together.

"Okay. 'splain it to me, Lucy," he replied, amused.

"I finally found a money trail. Possibly."

The big question they'd tried to answer initially was just how Reacher was supporting his off-the-grid lifestyle. Even loners who lived in caves had to buy food now and then. The laws of nature applied to hermits, too.

In theory, the money trail could lead them to Reacher. But it hadn't worked out that way.

They had assumed Reacher was receiving some kind of pension. A quick look at the existing Army files revealed he wasn't eligible for any of the normal Army pensions.

He didn't serve long enough for regular retirement. He'd been wounded and battered, for sure. But unlike Gaspar, Reacher was not disabled. Not even remotely. Which meant no disability pension.

One by one, they'd chased down the options and none of them fit Reacher's particular situation.

They soon discovered that he had a bank account. Which led to even more questions and few answers. One confusing issue was where his money came from.

"You know how Reacher's been receiving regular monthly payments into his bank from Uncle Sam?" she asked.

Gaspar must have moved his chair back because she heard the loud screech from unlubricated casters against the tile floor. "Not a lot of money. Not enough to keep a normal American afloat all these years later."

"Right. But he gets paid, and the money comes in as regular as clockwork," Kim insisted. "It's gotta come from somewhere specific. Money just doesn't pop into my bank account every month by magic."

"We've been down this road before. It's a dead end. Move on."

Kim closed her eyes and counted to three, for patience. "Hear me out. Like everything else about Reacher, the situation is not what it should be."

"Not hush money or blackmail payments or gambling money or anything like that," Gaspar said. "We checked all those options a while back."

"He left the Army really quick. Nothing the government does happens that fast." Kim swiped a palm over her black hair, which was still smoothly in place, as always. "Only thirteen years of service, too. Not enough for any of the pensions, as you know."

"Yeah, but so what?"

"He could have negotiated some kind of stipend or payoff, somehow," Kim was unwilling to let this go. She'd found something. She could feel it all the way down in her toes.

Gaspar's patience was wearing thin. She could tell by the incredulous tone. "You think Uncle Sam is sending him money on the regular from Key West? What the hell, Otto? There's no Army payment processing in Key West as far as I know."

She tried a different approach. "Reacher's bank is in Virginia near the Pentagon. It's been bought and sold a few times over the years, but it's the same bank. Same building. Same everything."

"Right."

"Which means his bank should have had records. Archives or something. We should be able to trace everything."

"But?"

"But we can't. Turns out, banks don't actually keep everything on file forever."

"Who knew?" Gaspar deadpanned, slurping the last of whatever he was drinking.

Kim ignored the sarcasm. "Not even in old archives in some dusty vault somewhere. Neither does Uncle Sam. Not even the IRS stores tax returns indefinitely."

Gaspar's grin came through loud and clear. "So if I just wait it out, I don't have to worry about the IRS hunting me down for tax fraud?"

Kim scowled and ignored him. "So Reacher's old banking records are nowhere to be found. At least, not in the usual places."

"Is there a point here, Sunshine? At this rate, the baby's gonna be in college by the time you get to it."

After months of searching a few minutes a day when she had the time, she had finally located some of Reacher's old financial records. It was like finding a wad of twenty-dollar bills in an unused coat pocket. Totally unexpected, but very nice, indeed.

Where did the money come from?

Before she was recruited by the FBI, Kim worked as a forensic accountant. The work was similar to a tedious scavenger hunt. Days and days hunched over spreadsheets until she thought her eyes would bleed. Mostly finding nothing. But every now and then, she'd hit the jackpot.

When she applied the right methods to Reacher's old bank records and discovered what could be a lead, she felt like she'd won the Powerball. She had the winning ticket right in her fingers. Now all she had to do was claim her winnings.

"Okay. I've been working on this, off and on. And like I said, I found something." She paused to give his ears time to perk up. "You already know Uncle Sam's deposits to the account were made routinely by a wire transfer from some government computer somewhere."

"And?"

"Reacher's relationship with the bank is totally inconsistent."

"I know. He withdraws money from locations all over the country at irregular intervals and in varying amounts. Sometimes, he uses an ATM machine. Sometimes, a Western Union office. Every now and then, he gets cash back from a grocery store or the post office," Gaspar said in a sing-song way to show his patience was barely hanging on. "Yada yada yada."

"So there's no discernable pattern to the withdrawals and no way to predict his location from that data alone, right?" She tried to lead him along with her tone.

Kim refused to give up. She'd kept digging, looking for irregularities. Patterns. A period of stability.

Eventually, she'd found something.

A breadcrumb. Not the whole loaf.

And the bread crumb was thirteen years stale.

But it was more than she'd had before. So she'd kept at it.

"I've grown a two-inch beard here waiting for the punchline," Gaspar said snidely.

"Okay, so nothing goes into Reacher's bank account except those government deposits, and nothing comes out except those irregular withdrawals by Reacher himself."

"Got it."

Again, she ignored the long-suffering tone. "Until about two years after Reacher left the Army. When *he* began to *send* regular *deposits* to his bank account."

"What?" Gaspar said, like he'd just awakened from a very long nap.

"For about three months. And then he stopped."

Kim paused, waiting to let him come to the same conclusion she had reached.

It didn't take him long. The answer was clear now that she'd already done the tedious parts.

"Day-um, Sunshine. You mean Reacher had had a paying job?" Gaspar said, clearly impressed by her results, at the very least.

Kim smiled like a canary eating a Siamese cat. "Makes sense. Not just an occasional gig, either. A regular job that earned more money than he'd ever made before. Probably got paid in cash. Enough money to require bank deposits."

"You mean he was saving for a rainy day. The kind of thing a normal American male would do," Gaspar said. "Problem is, Reacher has never been a normal American male. Not even remotely."

"And what the hell kind of work was he doing back then? Corporate security? Private investigations?"

"Only two years out of his job as a military policeman, he was certainly well qualified for both. His skills hadn't had time to get rusty," Gaspar said, warming up to the idea.

"Another thing. Reacher's bank deposits were made by money orders."

"Money orders? That's the old school alternative to checks. Fits his usual pattern, I guess," Gaspar said. "Money orders are harder to trace than checks. But still possible to trace if you know where to search."

She grinned again and knew he could feel it. "Reacher purchased and sent money order deposits for *three months* from a Western Union office in Key West to his bank in Virginia. Which might mean that Reacher was living and working in Key West back then."

"What does Cooper say about all of this?" Gaspar asked, meaning her boss. The one who sent her down the rabbit hole looking for Reacher in the first place, and then seemed to stymie her efforts at every opportunity.

"Don't know. Didn't ask. Don't care," she said tersely, like a six-year-old sticking out her tongue. Which made Gaspar laugh, if nothing else.

"Okay," Gaspar said, drawing out the word. And then he paused, and she knew he was checking her theory for holes. "So you're thinking you'll go down to the southernmost point of the United States and find Reacher's former employer?"

"Or, failing that, someone who knew him. Maybe I can get another lead," she said.

"Okay. Why are you calling me?"

"I never want to get on a plane if I don't have to. Is this too crazy to pan out? What do you think? You know the place. Am I wasting my time?"

"Probably. But this is the best lead you've had in a while. You have to chase it down," Gaspar said reasonably. "Meanwhile, I'll do some digging for you. See if I can find employment records or hotel records. I mean, he had to be living somewhere. Hell, he's bigger than the whole island. A guy like Reacher would stick out down there like a raisin in a loaf of white bread."

"I was half hoping you'd say the trip is a waste of time," she admitted, shoulders slumping.

She was determined to find Reacher, no matter what. But she hated flying.

Every flight was an opportunity to die prematurely. Some people said her views on that were irrational. But they were wrong.

Aerial craft were mechanical. Everything mechanical could and did fail. Eventually.

Each time a plane or a helicopter or, hell, a hot air balloon went up could be the last. It was like playing Russian roulette with your life.

And she'd checked the weather reports, too. It was hotter than Hades in Key West in June. Storms every damned day, and way too close to hurricane season for her taste.

Reacher wasn't there now, surely. He rarely returned to a place he'd spent time before. No reason to believe he'd changed his quirks.

And what about Cooper? If Reacher were in Key West now, Cooper would know about it and he'd have sent her there, whether she wanted to go or not.

Which he had not even hinted at doing. Why not?

The only reasonable answer was that the trip was a fool's errand. Cooper knew it. He also didn't have a better idea, or she'd be headed somewhere else right now.

Still, Gaspar was right.

She had this one slim lead, and she had no other brilliant options.

Which was why she'd already bought the plane ticket to Key West before she even called Gaspar.

At least it was a short flight. Two hours and thirty minutes, give or take.

Maybe she could get in and out before midnight tomorrow.

CHAPTER 3

Friday, June 17
Rural Virginia

"TIME IS A FUNNY thing," Jimmy said as he carried his bourbon outside onto the screened porch. "One day is pretty much like another and the years just keep rolling by. Terrible things happen that you think will surely kill you. Sometimes they do. But when they don't, the pain sits there like a hard lump in your chest forever."

His son and his grandson followed him out, each with their own glass of the bourbon they drank only on special occasions. They seemed pleased with themselves, as if they'd accomplished something special. They'd been wearing the same look for two weeks.

Jimmy settled into his rocker, so old and well used that the seat molded to his body. He gazed across the field. "Why are you two so excited?"

His grandson clapped a reassuring hand on Jimmy's shoulder. "It's your birthday, Gramps. Ninety-two years is a good, long life. You've had some good times, too. Look around you."

This house, the porch, and even the rockers had been Jimmy's home for most of his life and his father's life before that. Generations of ancestors had lived here since they came down with little more than the shirts on their backs.

Land was cheap and plentiful back then. If you could claim it and defend it, you owned it.

The land had been a cattle farm back when Jimmy was young. Acres of empty dirt dotted with cattle and barns as far as the eye could see. It had been a fine life for a boy. Plenty of room to ride and hunt and chores to keep him exhausted enough to sleep well at night, he often said.

Some days his grandson knew Jimmy wondered why he'd ever left for Boston.

Jimmy had been young and full of piss and vinegar, wanting to make his own way in the world. His father had been furious. Cut him off without a cent. Told him he'd be back with his tail tucked between his legs soon enough.

Jimmy got a job, found a fine woman, married, had a few kids.

Which was when things began to fall apart, near as his grandson could tell.

Families were expensive and Jimmy's job prospects were limited, it turned out. They struggled to make ends meet, like a lot of American families did.

His older boy had been a handful, sure, but he didn't deserve what happened to him. When he died in Vietnam, it nearly killed Jimmy and the boy's mother, too.

Then his second son ran off and joined up, aiming to finish what his brother had started. Grandma had a breakdown and never got over it. Grandpa knew it was time to swallow his pride and go home to Virginia with their third boy while they could.

When Grandpa looked westward now and squinted, he could barely make out the interstate. Sometimes, when the wind was blowing from that direction, he could hear the big rigs rushing along the pavement past the open grasslands.

Grandpa said he'd always wondered where the rigs were headed, but he'd never been tempted to join them. The grandson understood the feeling. Who would want to be stuck in a truck for days on end?

Despite his troubled family life, Grandpa was a wealthy man in some ways. His family had plenty of money all his life. Which his grandson counted among Jimmy's many blessings, even if Jimmy didn't.

But every last cent of Grandpa's money could not save his family. Great wealth had never insulated Grandpa from heartache.

"People who think money is the answer have never faced the hardest questions," Grandpa often said.

His first son was killed in the Vietnam War. His second son was killed by the war, too, even if it took years to finish him off. And his third boy, well, he was no prize, was he, the grandson grinned?

Sure, being wealthy was a wonderful thing more often than not. Of course, Grandpa would rather be wealthy than poor. He'd seen firsthand how devastating poverty could be when he'd served in Korea. Grandpa was grateful for the privilege and flexibility wealth had created for him and his family, he'd always said.

But Grandpa would die one day, just the same as everyone else. And in his case, that day wasn't too far down the road anymore. All his money wouldn't keep him alive.

Grandpa often wondered aloud whether the money had ruined him and his boys. Maybe if they'd had to work harder to provide for themselves, they'd have made different choices.

Which was what his grandson had overheard Jimmy talking about to his lawyer last week. He wanted to change his will.

"Have you discussed this with them, Jimmy?" the lawyer asked.

"No. And you're not to tell them until after I'm gone. It's my money and I can do with it whatever I want," Jimmy replied as stubborn as ever. "My son and my grandson have been pampered. It's long past time for them to be self-sufficient."

"What do you want to do with your money, then?" his lawyer had asked.

"I want all of it to go to the veterans' charity I've been supporting since my sons died. With an endowment for my museum. The charity can use my fortune to help vets so they don't end up like my second boy," Jimmy said. "It might be too late for my third son. But my grandson is young enough. He still has a chance to live a normal life."

The lawyer promised to draw up the documents and come back for Jimmy to sign.

But his grandson couldn't let that happen. The conversation enraged him. The money was his. Jimmy had no right to take it away from him. Not now. Not ever.

Which was when he'd settled the timeline and decided Grandpa's ninety-second birthday would be his last. The more he thought about it, the more he liked the idea. Ninety-two was plenty old enough.

He watched as Grandpa took a long sip of bourbon, letting the smooth burn slide down his throat. Beside him, his son gazed quietly across the field too. Each of the three men were lost in their own thoughts.

Grandpa's son shifted in his rocking chair. Even in profile, the deep lines etched around both sets of eyes were visible. Lines that told of a lifetime of sorrow, loss, and regret.

They were both too old now. They'd wasted their time. The grandson still had a chance to live a full life. All he had to do was move them out of the way.

"How's the bourbon, Dad?" the son finally asked, breaking the heavy silence.

Jimmy turned slowly, as if coming out of a trance. He attempted a smile that didn't reach his eyes. "Hmm? Oh, it's fine, son. Fine. Thank you for remembering my birthday."

His rugged jaw clenched as he nodded and drained his glass.

"Let me get you a refill," the shaggy-haired grandson offered, taking the glass before Grandpa had a chance to object.

When he handed the glass back, he watched intently, icy blue eyes flickering with a secret excitement. Two weeks of laying low and no blowback. The rest would start tomorrow.

"There's so much history in this place," Jimmy said with a nod of thanks for the second whiskey.

The grandson had heard these stories most of his life. He knew the tale by rote at this point.

The family had stopped cattle farming when Jimmy was a teenager, after his grandfather struck oil in Australia. That discovery had funded the family's wealth originally and forever more.

Now the land held Jimmy's true passion. His airplane museum, with vintage aircraft and a well tended runway that made good use of the acres.

But with all his wealth and success, a profound emptiness still haunted the old man. They all felt it as they gathered on the porch to look out over the legacy Jimmy's family had built.

His son swigged the last of his bourbon and stood. He squeezed Jimmy's bony shoulder.

"Well, early day tomorrow. You can sleep in. We're going hunting at first light."

Jimmy shook his head, swallowing a large swig of the warm whiskey. "That seems foolish, hunting dangerous animals. One of those wild hogs gores you and you'll be as good as dead."

"It's a public service, Dad," he replied. "Boars are multiplying faster than the state can control them. They're becoming a real threat. We need to cull the numbers, make it safer."

"That right?" Jimmy replied doubtfully.

"I'll keep the boy safe, don't you worry," his son assured. "If we stay away from the piglets and out of the path of the daddies running from threats, we're more dangerous than they are."

"I know you're both good hunters," Jimmy cautioned. "But do an old man a favor and keep yourselves alive out there."

"That's the plan," his son said as he headed indoors.

His grandson flashed the sly grin that was so like the uncle he'd never met. The smart one, the clever one, the ruthless one. He imagined they were genetically linked and more alike than different. He often wondered how his life would have turned out if Carl had been his father.

A long shiver engulfed Jimmy's body from head to toe.

"Que sera, sera," his grandson said in the same way Grandma used to say the same words. *What will be, will be.*

The old man sighed and kept rocking as the sun dipped below the horizon, unaware that his grandson watched him from the kitchen.

Jimmy also didn't know, as he enjoyed the lingering moments of his birthday and the end of the sunset, that this night would be his last. Ninety-two years was plenty long enough.

When the grandson returned, the hunt would be finished. His enemies vanquished. This place and Jimmy's fortune would be his.

Follow the plan.

CHAPTER 4

Saturday, June 18
Key West, Florida

FROM HER WINDOW SEAT on the plane yesterday, she had
had a bird's-eye view of the island as they landed. Key West was
surrounded by the Gulf of Mexico. Beaches were within walking
distance from everywhere on the entire island. Residents and
tourists alike could enjoy the invitingly warm waters day or night
on a whim.

She'd heard that Key West was a crazy place, and she was
prepared to believe it. Bohemian and unconventional. Wild and
dangerous. Everything she'd learned suggested Reacher would
never be caught dead here.

Such as, despite easy access to the beach, many homes had
installed backyard swimming pools. Sparkling turquoise pools
surrounded by lush tropical landscaping. Banyan trees, towering
schefflera, palms of all sorts, and more.

The tranquil scenes were beautiful but totally frivolous. Who
builds a swimming pool in such a paradise?

The largest of the pools she'd seen was behind the museum that had been Ernest Hemingway's home. According to the brochure, he'd built the first in-ground pool in Key West back in 1938 at enormous personal cost. It was an engineering marvel of sorts, too.

No way a backhoe could get into some of these yards. The lots were too small, streets too narrow, trees too low. Key West sits on sheer coral almost as hard as bedrock. Removing the earth was fraught with all kinds of difficulties. Once they dug out the hole, where did they put the dirt?

Gaspar called shortly after the plane's wheels hit the tarmac. When she picked up, he joked, "Key West International Airport. The only airport in the world where the name is longer than the runway."

Kim smiled and put amusement into her voice. "What can I do for you, Chico?"

"Quick update before you start pounding the pavement."

"Okay," she replied. "But make it quick. We'll be deplaning soon."

"Confirmed a few things for you. Reacher lived on that island for three months. Longer than he's lived anywhere since he left the Army," Gaspar said.

"As far as we know," she cautioned.

"Right. And the population of Key West hovers around twenty-seven thousand, give or take." Gaspar paused for her to connect the dots.

"Meaning he was here a good long while and not likely to get lost in such a small crowd."

"And that suggests you might actually find at least one or two residents who knew him back then," Gaspar wrapped it up for her.

"Got it. What else?" The plane had taxied to the gate.

"As for Reacher's regular bank deposits," he replied.

"Yes?" The captain had turned off the seatbelt sign and passengers were standing to collect their bags.

"You know the deposits stopped abruptly. Given his touchy nature, he probably walked off the job at some point."

"But why? That's the issue."

"Could have been anything," Gaspar said. "Maybe he ran up against some trouble."

"That wouldn't be surprising," she grinned, even though he couldn't see her. "Or maybe he had somewhere to go, and the boss wouldn't give him time off."

Kim had traced the rough timeline she'd been putting together. She'd realized the bank deposits stopped right around the time of Leon Garber's funeral. Which could have been coincidental but probably wasn't.

"Somewhere to go like Leon Garber's funeral, you mean," Gaspar deadpanned. They'd reached the same conclusion, which made Kim feel better about the logic, at least.

Kim had tracked down Reacher's connection to Garber six months ago, before Gaspar retired. Which is how they both knew about the funeral already.

From all accounts, Garber had been both a decent human being and Reacher's mentor. Reacher seemed to have a tighter connection to Garber than to his own father.

When Garber died, he'd bequeathed his home in Garrison, New York, to Reacher. Which more than Reacher had inherited from anyone in his actual family.

Garber had one daughter, Jodie. Reacher sold the house to her.

Kim had met Jodie Garber Jacob back in January. Interesting woman. Strong, independent, clever. Very attractive.

More to the point for Kim's purposes, she might have been the love of Reacher's life. Like all of Reacher's women, Jodie was no longer with him.

As if he'd read her thoughts, Gaspar said, "Forming lasting relationships with women is not a solid plank of Reacher's skill set."

"No kidding," Kim deadpanned. Jacob had disappeared six months ago, and Kim hadn't been able to find her again. Not yet anyway.

"The facts are starting to form a picture here, Sunshine. Stay with me while I summarize. Then I have a point to share," Gaspar said.

She pulled her travel bag from the overhead and slung the laptop case across her shoulder. "Make it quick. We're deplaning."

Gaspar gave her a quick summary to confirm. "Two years after he left the Army, Reacher was working in Key West. He left the job and the island and the regular bank deposits stopped. He went to Leon Garber's funeral. He rekindled a relationship with Jodie. He inherited a house. He broke up with Jodie and sold the house and disappeared again."

"That's how it looks." She followed a tall woman down the aisle toward the exit door.

"All of those things could have been related. Or not," Gaspar said. "But they happened closely in time."

Warm air wafted into the cabin through the open doorway. "Yeah. Which means what?"

"If we put this all together, then Cooper could, too. He probably did. A long time ago." Gaspar stopped for a deep breath. "You're wasting your time. You won't find anything down there. If there's anything to find, Cooper already found it."

Kim nodded. "Possibly. But I'm here now. Might as well confirm what I can while I'm on the ground."

"Copy that. But then, get the hell out. Reacher's not there," Gaspar paused to be sure she was following along. "You're dithering. Losing your window."

"What window?"

"Your chance to find Reacher wherever he is right now," Gaspar stated flatly.

"And where is that?"

Passengers ahead of her were filing off the plane. Kim juggled her bags and her phone and struggled with both.

A guy stepped out of his row and hit her in the head as he slung his backpack behind him, knocking the phone out of her hand.

She waited until he was a few feet ahead of her to kneel and pick up the phone. "Look, I gotta go. We can talk more later."

She disconnected and dropped the phone into her pocket. When she deplaned into the solid wall of heat and humidity, she tried to call Gaspar again, but the call went to voicemail. She hung up. They could talk later. She had work to do.

After that, Kim had stashed her bags and pounded every inch of pavement on the island. She didn't meet a single person who could confirm or dispute any of the facts or theories she and Gaspar had developed.

Which meant, after several hours of trying, her shirt plastered to her body with sweat, she'd learned nothing useful at all.

What had she missed? Whatever it was seemed out of her grasp. For the moment.

The town was busy despite the oppressive heat and humidity. Tourists wandered the streets under the relentless midday sun. Milling through the crowds was a job in and of itself.

Street level bars and eateries were overrun with cruise ship passengers making more noise than a schoolyard at recess. Nobody could possibly hear their own thoughts in such a place.

If she'd learned anything at all about Reacher, it was that he'd hate the crowds and the noise and the unruly behavior. What the hell had he been doing here?

By now, she was hot and thirsty and frustrated by lack of progress. She needed a break.

She'd walked into a nice hotel on Duval Street. There was a sign out front that said *Jimmy Buffet Never Comes Here*, which was one way to keep the tourists at bay and made her smile.

She took the elevator seven stories up to a quieter venue. Tony's Rooftop offered stunning views from near the center of Old Town in Key West's historic district.

When she settled into a comfortable seat under an oversized umbrella, only two tables were occupied, and one of them was hers.

Sipping cold club soda with lime, Kim watched the streets below from behind oversized sunglasses, mulling things over.

Her recon mission hadn't panned out. She'd found nothing and learned less since she arrived.

If she'd interpreted the banking records correctly, Reacher had lived and worked here for a short stint thirteen years ago. Which, she now realized, was a lifetime in a place as transient as Key West.

She'd come here because she had no other leads. She still didn't.

Now what?

Kim wasn't expecting company, so when a tall shadow fell over her, she glanced up.

"Mind if I join you, Agent Otto?"

The man was about fifty, give or take a few years. He looked vaguely familiar. Not personally, but as a type. She'd never met him before.

His lightweight jacket was some sort of polyester blend, which was okay because it didn't wrinkle, but it didn't breathe, either. Had to be hot as hell.

He wasn't a conch, which was what the residents called themselves. No Key West local would be wearing a jacket like that in this heat.

He shrugged the jacket off and draped it over the back of his chair. Which left him wearing a sweaty white polo shirt and khaki pants with cordovan loafers and no socks. He definitely wasn't from around here. He'd flown in from somewhere up north, for sure.

"I'm not looking for trouble," he said, handing her a business card. "William Curry. Formerly NYPD detective. Now private."

Which was why he'd seemed familiar. Cops were easily recognizable, even out of their element. Kim should know.

"You can take the man out of the NYPD..." she mumbled, leaving the rest unfinished as she examined his card.

How did he know who she was and what the hell did he want?

CHAPTER 5

Saturday, June 18
Key West, Florida

WILLIAM CURRY. PRIVATE INVESTIGATOR. Offices in New York City. Nothing to worry about. Kim relaxed slightly and slipped his card into her pocket as she gestured toward an empty chair.

A waitress came over and Curry ordered an iced tea. Kim studied him, wondering why he had sought her out.

"What do you want?" she asked finally.

"Same as you. To find Jack Reacher."

Kim shook her head, staying cautious. "I'm on vacation."

"No, you're not. And I can help you find him because I know what I'm looking for. I've crossed paths with him before." Curry smiled and took a sip of his drink. "Reacher was in Key West working a while back. He had a couple of jobs. One employer was a local swimming pool contractor. Digging pools by hand and the like."

Which sounded preposterous. Then again, Reacher certainly had the physique for manual labor. And she'd seen plenty of swimming pools on this island that had been here for a while. Assuming Curry wasn't full of bull, Reacher could have dug a few.

"You're saying Reacher was actually digging swimming pools by hand with a damned shovel?" Kim kept her face neutral, giving nothing away.

His comments aligned with what little she knew. He could be telling the truth.

Curry seemed to read her thoughts. "I figured you might be talking to Reacher's old bosses. Getting their take on his time in Key West. Probably looking for a lead you can use to find him. I've already done the leg work. I can help you."

Kim countered. "Why do you care?"

Curry hesitated and she waited.

"I've got a client looking for Reacher, too," he finally offered. "She thinks he might help her solve a murder."

Kim's curiosity was piqued. She wanted details. "A murder?"

Curry nodded, perhaps acknowledging he needed to offer more. "An NYPD buddy told me the FBI's looking to locate a man matching Reacher's description. Big guy, about six-five. Fair hair. Blue eyes. My buddy said to get background from you."

Kim froze. Curry had her full attention now.

She was working under the radar. She'd revealed her cover story several times during her assignment. The idea that the intel was being passed around freely caused her stomach to churn. She reached into her pocket for an antacid and slipped it into her mouth.

Curry knew she was hunting Reacher and he'd wrangled that information from NYPD. That much alone was concerning.

Cops tended to help each other out. Being NYPD for a couple of decades himself, Curry's contacts probably went pretty deep, too. What else did he know about her or have access to?

Before she had a chance to follow up, he spoke again.

"Here's my offer," Curry said, folding his hands and leaning forward. "I'll share everything I've got on Reacher if we work together. An extra set of eyes and hands could help both of us. Two heads are better than one, and all that."

Kim weighed the proposition. Curry's knowledge of Reacher's history here in Key West could shorten her work. But she couldn't trust him until she understood his stake.

"What's your interest in Reacher?" She cocked her head to listen closely.

"Fair question." Curry sipped his tea. "My client is convinced Reacher can help."

"Why?"

Curry quickly summarized the situation. "Guy named Bert Tardelli apparently left a suicide note before hanging himself a few years ago. Tardelli's daughter, Sheryl, is a friend of my client. She died recently."

Now he had her full attention. Kim widened her eyes. "Sheryl Tardelli? The congresswoman?"

"That's the one." Curry nodded. "Neither she nor my client believed the simple suicide story. They thought Bert Tardelli was murdered. Now, with Sheryl gone, my client wants to clear things up."

"Who is your client?"

"Marilyn Stone. She hired me to find Reacher, uncover the truth, and fill in the gaps."

"What's Marilyn Stone's connection to Reacher? Why does she think he'd help her with this?" Kim narrowed her eyes against the bright sunlight slipping under the umbrella as sunset approached. "Death of a congresswoman's father sounds a long way out of Reacher's wheelhouse to me."

"Possibly. But I owe Marilyn a favor. She saved my life once. She believes Reacher can do things the cops can't. She gave me a couple of names to track down." He confirmed as he sipped his tea. "I wasn't making much progress on my own. Until I caught wind of you asking around about Reacher down here."

"Tell me what you know and then we'll see," she suggested, without making any promises.

Curry nodded and launched into a brief but detailed account of Reacher's time in Key West. "He was digging swimming pools by day and working as a bouncer in a strip joint by night. Kept himself to himself, mostly. Good worker. Productive. Stuck around for about three months and then he left."

"Where did he go?" Kim asked, although she thought she already knew.

He'd gone to Garrison, New York. For Leon Garber's funeral. To see his house. And to hook up with Garber's daughter, who might have been the love of his life.

To the extent Reacher was capable of loving someone.

"My guess is he hitched a ride to Miami and flew out. Not sure where he went. I'm checking the airlines, but it was a long time ago. Airlines don't keep records forever," Curry said, gulping the last of his tea as if the speech had him totally parched.

"You mean he simply disappeared?" Kim asked without surprise.

"Probably not. He's no magician. But after all this time, that trail is stone cold," Curry replied.

"How'd you find out all of this?" Kim wanted to know. He'd certainly made more headway in a short time than she'd have expected.

"Cops stick together. I can trust you?" Curry lowered his chin and pushed his lips around as if he were thinking about what to say next. "Former NYPD Detective Costello. He was asked to find Reacher back then. He uncovered the banking stuff I already told you. The same stuff you found. Told me about it."

Okay. That tracked. The intel would have been easier to find thirteen years ago. "And what else?"

"He came down here. Talked to Reacher."

Kim raised her eyebrows. "Yeah? How'd that go?"

"Guy lied. Said he wasn't Reacher. Costello believed him. Few hours later, Costello was dead. Beaten to death and dumped on the street. And then Reacher disappeared," Curry said flatly.

"You think Reacher killed your friend?" Kim widened her eyes to suggest she thought the idea preposterous.

Truth was, it could have happened that way. Reacher did things for his own reasons.

Curry shook his head. "Matter of fact, I don't think he killed Costello."

"Why not?"

"Because Costello's body was mutilated."

Privately, she agreed. Kim had plenty of experience with Reacher's activities over the past eight months. She'd seen the bodies. Mutilation of a corpse was not Reacher's style. Not even remotely.

"Mutilated how?"

"Fingers were cut off. All ten of them. Cut off with something sharp and efficient. Like a linoleum knife, maybe. Probably trying to eliminate fingerprints and slow the identification," Curry said quietly. "I don't figure Reacher for a guy who kills cops or does crap like that. He was a cop himself once upon a time. Of a sort. Why would he do that?"

Curry was partially correct. Reacher actually had killed a few cops along the way. But never a righteous one. Not so far, anyway.

If Costello had been a straight shooter, Reacher wouldn't have taken him out. Not intentionally.

"How is all of this related to Congresswoman Tardelli?"

He shrugged. "Might not be. But my client thinks Reacher can figure that out."

"Why does she think that?"

"You'll have to ask her yourself."

"She'd be better off talking to the investigating officers on Sheryl Tardelli's case. I know nothing about that." Kim checked her watch. "I want to see this stripper bar, though. The one where Reacher worked nights. You know where it is?"

"Yeah. Nobody there who knew Reacher back then. I already asked."

Kim hesitated while she made up her mind.

Curry could be useful.

As long as he didn't get in the way.

"Come on." She dropped a twenty-dollar bill on the table to cover her club soda and his iced tea and stood.

"There's a woman Reacher was casually involved with back then," Curry said as he stood and slipped his jacket on. "She still lives here in Key West. Owns that stripper bar now. Wasn't there when I checked in before. She may have useful intel."

Kim said, "Okay. Lead the way."

CHAPTER 6

Saturday, June 18
Bristol, New Hampshire

THE DRIVER HAD PARKED the van across the street from the courthouse in North Haverhill, New Hampshire. The street was busy at the end of the work week and the van blended well with other vehicles in the area.

The target couldn't see them from this distance, but other witnesses might notice. They wore dark clothing, baseball caps with the bills pulled low, and oversized sunglasses. Easy disguises they could ditch later.

In the passenger seat, the shooter had a clear view if Judge Matthew Gunston left the courthouse promptly at five o'clock as he usually did.

Gunston was a man defined by his habits. He was the coach of his eight-year-old daughter's soccer team, and they had a game tonight. Which meant he would leave the courthouse promptly and drive straight to Bristol.

The game started at six-thirty. The easy forty-minute drive allowed him time to go home to change clothes and make it to the field by six-fifteen.

Gunston walked through the courthouse door into the bright sunshine exactly as expected. Tall and lean, wearing an expensive charcoal gray suit, striding like a man with a purpose. He carried himself with authority. Power fairly oozed from his pores. He pulled sunglasses from his breast pocket and settled them onto his face like a television advertisement for the latest eyewear.

The shooter was disgusted. Gunston had abandoned his responsibilities. He deserved to die. Which would happen soon enough.

He approached the sleek black sedan parked in his reserved parking space. His briefcase dangled from his left hand. Gunston pressed the key fob to unlock the doors and stashed his briefcase in the backseat alongside the soccer gear.

When Gunston's sedan was on the way, the driver rolled the van onto the road behind the judge.

"Relax," he said. "We've practiced this. We'll have plenty of time."

"Yeah, I know," the shooter replied, watching the sedan speeding smoothly several vehicles ahead on the winding pavement. "He'll get home, run inside to change clothes and pick up the kid. I'll hit him on the front lawn when he comes back out."

"It'll be tricky with the girl," the driver said.

The shooter shrugged. "If she stays out of the way, no problem."

"Make sure it's not a problem." The driver gave him a quick stare. "We don't hit kids. We've got a long way to go before we're done. Stick with the plan."

"I'm getting pretty sick of you saying that all the time," the shooter said calmly, as if he weren't delivering a deadly serious warning.

The driver shook his head slowly but didn't reply. Which was a good thing. The shooter's nerves were taut. He felt the pressure rising throughout his body. Wouldn't take much to set him off.

But the trip unfolded smoothly, allowing the shooter's blood pressure to stabilize.

Gunston drove through Bristol to his property on the other side of town without a hitch.

The judge's home was set back on a wooded two-acre lot on the outskirts of town. When he pulled the sedan into his driveway, the van's driver continued another mile and turned into another wooded parcel.

Quickly, the driver found the elevated location they'd selected during the recon mission last week. In winter, the van would be visible through the trees from Gunston's front porch. But today, the boxy vehicle was camouflaged by lush green New Hampshire foliage. The same mature maples and oaks that would burst into autumn splendor later in the year.

The shooter hurried to the back of the van to set up his rifle. Quickly, he settled into position.

Breathe in, breathe out.

One shot, one kill.

The sniper's credo.

Exactly as his father had taught him.

Success required control and stillness and calm.

Breathe in, breathe out.

He felt himself relax and come home.

And then he waited, ready, watching through the powerful scope trained on Gunston's front lawn.

Soon enough, Gunston emerged from the front entrance. He'd changed into khaki shorts and a bright pink polo shirt, which painted an easy target.

His daughter wore her soccer uniform and carried the black and white ball in both hands as she skipped joyfully ahead toward the sedan. She went around the vehicle where she disappeared from view. She must have opened the front passenger side door and slipped inside.

Gunston would be dead before the girl saw him again.

The shooter waited until he was certain the girl was well away from the path of blood spatter and then he squeezed the trigger.

The first shot hit Gunston in the head and killed him instantly.

The gunshot was loud and there was a *crack* from the bullet and a blast of pink burst from his head and he went straight down like a puppet with the strings cut.

For a split second, no reaction.

The quiet was surreal. It probably lasted less than half a minute, but it seemed like an hour.

Then the girl jumped out of the car leaving the passenger door open and ran around the front of the vehicle. When she rounded the bumper, she had a clear line of sight toward her father. She screamed like the damsel in a horror movie.

The front door of the house opened and Gunston's wife ran outside toward her husband.

The shooter could have taken the mom and the girl out in a hot moment. But he didn't.

We don't shoot kids.

Stick to the plan.

The shooter pulled the gun inside and closed the doors to the van.

"Go! Go!" he yelled to the driver, who put the van in gear and sped backward down the hill and farther along the path. The shooter hurried to the passenger seat and buckled in while the driver got the van to the pavement.

They drove as quickly as they dared, heading away from the Gunston house.

From experience, they knew it would take a few minutes for the neighbors to notice what had happened.

A few more for chaos to reign and reactions explode.

Maybe five full minutes before the police were called.

A few more minutes before the sleepy town cops could rush toward the judge's home.

By the time the locals gathered a team, the shooter's van would be almost to New York.

When they cleared the first corner and turned south, the shooter fist-pumped the air. "Yes!"

The driver smiled in response. "Nice job."

"Dude never saw it coming," the shooter grinned widely as the van picked up speed. "Good infiltration. One shot. One target down. Easy exfiltration. Doesn't get any better than that."

"Damned straight."

"You hungry?" the shooter asked.

"Starved. How about a big steak and a cold beer?"

"Damned straight," the shooter echoed, resisting the urge to whoop again. "Followed by a long nap. We've got more to do tomorrow."

CHAPTER 7

Saturday, June 18
Key West, Florida

KIM AND CURRY WALKED off toward the garish neon lights of the strip club. Even in the heat of broad daylight, Key West streets were alive with people looking for fun and entertainment.

"What do you know about the crime rate here?" Kim asked, one cop to another.

Curry shook his head. "Nothing. But I know that with this many people around, there's bound to be trouble. You're carrying, right?"

"Always."

In Kim's experience, the recipe for crime in a place like Key West was pretty simple. Serve the tourists enough alcohol and normally vigilant people became easy targets. Where there's opportunity for crime, scumbags come out of the shadows like cockroaches.

Kim's internal threat meter moved into the red zone.

As they approached the club, thumping bass could be heard coming from within. The bar was a long, narrow upstairs room with a runway and a small stage with a shiny pole. Mirrors lined the walls and music pulsed loud and hard enough to reverberate through your body.

The entrance at the top of the stairs was blocked by a small desk where one of the dancers collected the cover charge. Curry gave her a hundred-dollar bill and she waved them inside without comment.

An oversized man, probably the current bouncer, leaned his back against the bar about a third of the way inside. His muscular arms crossed intimidatingly.

Kim imagined Reacher standing there in exactly the same pose. He was the same size, the same build.

It would take more than one bullet to stop this guy, even if she hit him right in the center of his huge, oil barrel chest. Same as Reacher. An involuntary shudder ran through her body.

Curry nodded as they entered, and the bouncer nodded back. She wondered what Curry had already learned from him.

The dark room was illuminated by pink and purple neon lights. Three nearly naked women danced on the stage, gyrating to the pounding music. Patrons, mostly fully clothed men, ogled the women hungrily while downing overpriced drinks.

Curry led Kim through the crowds to a smaller bar in the back. The bartender, a tough-looking woman with short spiky pink hair, gave Curry a wary look.

"She's here," the bartender said curtly, jerking her head toward a door marked "Private."

"Thanks," Curry replied, passing her another of his apparently endless supply of C-notes. Which made Kim wonder again about his client's financial status and why she was willing to fund this lavish search for Reacher.

Curry led Kim through a dark, narrow corridor to the back room, which turned out to be an office strewn with paperwork. Security monitors lined the walls casting an eerie blue light. Behind the desk sat a strikingly beautiful woman with long dark hair and sharp green eyes. She held a vape pen in her teeth. Sun-damaged skin had aged her, but Kim guessed she was about forty-five.

She looked up as they entered, her gaze quickly assessing the situation.

"Hello, Crystal," Curry said. "This is Agent Kim Otto with the FBI. We'd like to ask you a few questions about Jack Reacher."

"I heard you were in here asking earlier." Crystal's eyes narrowed and then she shrugged. "It's no secret. Reacher worked here years ago for a short time. Before I owned the place. He left. Haven't seen him since. End of story."

"When exactly did he leave?" Kim asked.

"Hard to say. He worked off the books. Can't check the records or anything like that." Crystal shrugged again. "Worked nights as a bouncer for a few weeks. Kept to himself mostly. Never caused any trouble."

"Did he say where he was going?" Kim pressed.

"Said he was moving on. Told me he never stayed in one place for long. Something about wanderlust. Sticking around made him twitchy." Crystal took a long drag on the vaping pen and held it in her lungs for a bit. "He was efficient. Didn't hit on the girls like some bouncers do. Right from the start, he made it clear he wouldn't stick around. No surprise when he took off."

Kim nodded. Reacher's banking records matched Crystal's story and the way she described him tracked.

"One more thing," Kim said. "Did Reacher ever mention a guy named Costello?"

Crystal froze, the vape pen halfway to her lips. Barely a moment, but noticeable. She knew something.

"It was a long time ago. Costello..." She took another long drag, exhaling slowly. "Yeah, there was a guy came around asking about Reacher. Next thing I hear, he turned up dead. Could have been Costello, maybe."

Kim and Curry exchanged a glance. "Reacher have anything to do with that?"

"No." Crystal suddenly looked anxious. "Listen, I told you what I know. I need to get back to work. I'd like you to leave."

She stood up abruptly, making it plain they wouldn't get anything more from her tonight.

Kim handed her a business card. "If you remember anything else, call me. We need to find Reacher. It's important."

"I've told you everything I know." Crystal took the card without looking at it. "We're done here."

Kim and Curry left the office and headed out of the club into the warm air. The neon glow of the strip club sign cast garish colors on the sidewalk. Drunks stumbled in and out of the bars that dotted both sides of the street.

"Have you interviewed the local police chief?" Kim asked Curry as they walked along the crowded sidewalk toward Mallory Square.

"Tried." Curry kept his arms by his side, hands loosely ready for trouble. "The chief back then died a few years ago. Small department. Murder case is still open, but nobody remembers Costello. Or Reacher."

"You said Costello was a friend of yours. Didn't you try to find out what happened to him?" Kim asked, skirting a puddle of something disgusting blocking her path on the sidewalk.

"Of course I did. He was murdered. Reacher didn't do it," Curry said. "That's the end of the road."

"So who killed Costello?"

"Couple of guys working muscle for a psychopath. All three are long dead now. Nothing more to do," Curry replied, his tone making it clear he'd say no more on the subject.

Which told Kim all she needed to know.

Reacher had solved Costello's murder and delivered his own brand of justice.

It worried her a little that she'd come to understand how he operated.

Or at least, to recognize his handiwork when she saw it.

Even if her oath of office meant she couldn't condone or excuse his behavior.

Reacher was no longer an officer of the law.

But Kim was.

"Okay. So tell me about your client, Marilyn Stone," Kim said.

"How about I do better than that and introduce you to her," Curry replied.

"She's here? In Key West?"

"And she wants to talk to you." Curry extended his hand toward a crowded bar at the end of the street overlooking the intracoastal waterway. A three-piece band was playing the ubiquitous Jimmy Buffet songs tourists expected to hear, which added to the chaos.

A slender well-dressed woman wearing a wide brimmed straw hat was seated alone at the weathered railing. She was staring straight at Kim.

When they approached. She stood and removed her sunglasses and leaned in to be heard and offered her hand, all in one smooth motion like she'd practiced it. Which she probably had.

"I'm Marilyn Stone. You must be Agent Otto." Her hand was pampered and polished, the grip firm and decisive. "Thanks for meeting with me."

CHAPTER 8

Saturday, June 18
Key West, Florida

KIM SLID INTO THE chair across from Marilyn Stone. Even with the harsh sunlight revealing every inch of her exposed skin, Marilyn was a stunning woman who knew how to make the best of her assets.

In one quick glance, Kim noticed her artfully colored and styled shoulder-length hair. Makeup expertly applied to conceal that she was wearing it. Casual couture outfit resembling Ralph Lauren, but better cut and cloth.

Even her luxuriously understated jewelry was remarkable. Only the most sophisticated observers might recognize it as rare and unique *Haute Joaillerie*.

Stone's back was ramrod straight. Ringless hands loosely clasped in her lap betrayed nothing.

"I'm sorry for your loss," Kim said, offering reassurance like gentling a wild horse before it stomped on her.

"Thank you. I appreciate you taking the time." Marilyn's mouth tightened. "Bert Tardelli was a decent man. He had his demons, but Sheryl never believed he'd killed himself. And now she's dead, too. Accident, they say. I don't believe that for a moment. It's just not possible."

"We never know what's truly inside another person's head," Kim replied kindly.

"Sheryl's grandfather, Bert's dad, died in Korea. During the war. Bert was a teen at the time. Left him an orphan. He never got over it. He wouldn't have left his only daughter an orphan. Not a chance," Marilyn said with firm conviction.

"Okay." Kim's pulse quickened. Marilyn Stone was a straight talker, which Kim always appreciated. "Tell me what happened."

"Sheryl died two weeks ago. She was poisoned. Covered in toxic gardening chemicals. The police say she slipped and dropped a vase, and its contents spilled all over her." Marilyn gave her a sardonic stare as she said snidely, "At the cemetery where her father is buried. She was throwing away some dead flowers to replace them in the same vase."

"Sounds plausible, doesn't it?"

"Definitely not." Marilyn shook her perfect hair angrily, magnificent eyes flashing. "I've known Sheryl a long time. She was a successful real estate agent before she became a congresswoman. She wasn't some clumsy child. She wouldn't have spilled a gallon of poison all over herself. That's ridiculous."

"You think her death was somehow intentional, then." It was a statement, not a question.

"Absolutely. No doubt at all." Marilyn's luxurious mink eyelashes widened to reveal flashing smoky eyes and held Kim's gaze unflinchingly. "Especially considering her father's supposed suicide. Sheryl never believed he killed himself and I supported her because she was my friend. But now I'm certain she was right."

Kim pulled out her phone to review her hastily jotted notes. "Bert Tardelli. Died by his own hand according to the police?"

"So they claim," Marilyn said bitterly. "But he loved Sheryl, and he loved life. Even with all their health issues."

"What kind of health issues?"

"Bert was exposed to toxic chemicals during the Vietnam War. And yes, you're starting to see the point here, aren't you? When Bert first came home, Sheryl said he seemed okay. But over the years, he developed several cancers. Every time he'd beat one, another seemed to take its place."

"Bert Tardelli's father died in Korea, and he still volunteered for Vietnam?" Kim asked.

Marilyn shook her head. "Of course not. Bert was drafted. One of his cousins, too. The cousin died. Bert came home. But the war killed them both, one way or another."

Kim frowned, trying to make sense of things. She had followed Sheryl Tardelli's career because she'd known her back when Kim was in law school and lived in DC.

Sheryl Tardelli was a powerhouse. And a decent human being, too.

"I'm so sorry. That's a lot of tragedy for one lifetime," Kim said. "Some people just can't catch a break."

"Yeah, well, Bert and Sheryl were convinced that his health was destroyed by that defoliant. R1 they called it. That's why she ran for congress. She wanted to get involved and get help for her dad and others like him," Marilyn said in her straightforward way.

Kim made a few notes because Marilyn seemed to expect her to. "I think I recall hearing that exposure to R1 impacted Sheryl as well?"

Marilyn nodded. "She was born with a severe cleft palate, which several doctors said was caused from her father's experience with R1. But her initial surgery was delayed by lack of funding. Which meant she went through years of speech therapy, too. It all left her with scars both on her face and on her psyche. And motivated her work for vets' rights."

"Which was why she served on the House Veterans' Affairs Committee," Kim said, nodding. Kim had done an unpaid internship with the committee in school. It seemed light years ago now.

"Yes. But recently Sheryl told me she was beginning to doubt R1 was really to blame." Marilyn shook her head angrily. "We argued about it. She was under relentless pressure from interest groups. Chemical companies who don't want to make restitution and budget hawks who simply want to keep spending down. But families who are in denial, too. No one wants to believe that they made such bad decisions. Decisions that caused so much harm."

Kim's mind whirled with the implications even as she stayed focused on Marilyn. "Did Sheryl say who was pressuring her to recant her views?"

"She was rattled by the protesters when she started questioning things. There were hearings coming up. She asked me to visit because she needed help figuring out what to do next."

"Sounds intense." And probably dangerous.

"These last few weeks, she'd been searching for someone. I'm not sure who it was. She said she didn't want to say yet. She asked me to hire Curry to help her, to keep him under the radar," Marilyn wiped away a tear trailing down her cheeks. "I was planning to go see her, like she wanted. But by the time I could get free and get Curry on board, Sheryl was dead."

"You couldn't have known." Kim tried to reassure, but Marilyn was not having it.

"I wish I'd made her tell me who she was searching for. Why she needed Curry," Marilyn said harshly, jaw clenched as she gave Curry a hard glance. "But I thought we had time to cover all of that."

What could Kim say? Guilt wouldn't bring Sheryl or her father back to life. Or erase the use of R1 from history. But Marilyn already knew that much.

Marilyn used her knuckle to dab her eyes. She cleared her throat of the emotion blocking her vocal cords. "You know, you have the look."

"The look?" Kim asked curiously.

"Someone who does whatever it takes. Reacher was like that. Is like that, still, I'm betting." Marilyn paused and cleared her throat again. "Powerful people wanted Sheryl silenced. Which is why I need Reacher. He'll figure it out. He's smart enough and big enough and strong enough to handle anything."

Kim felt the electricity run through her as she met Marilyn's warning with a steady gaze. "So you've met Reacher, then."

She nodded and fixed a steady gaze on Kim's face. "Years ago. My husband and I were in real trouble. Serious, life destroying trouble. Reacher fixed it."

The electric jolt had subsided, leaving the feeling of a thousand ants crawling along her body. "Reacher fixed it how?"

Marilyn shrugged. "He…eliminated the threats to us. He was like a one-man wrecking crew. Got seriously hurt in the process. But he just would not quit. We needed him then, and he came through for us. He's what Sheryl needed. Still needs. Reacher. We need to find him."

Kim understood exactly what Marilyn implied. Heard it loud and clear.

Why didn't life come with a rewind button? Kim needed to rewind and erase everything Marilyn Stone had just said.

She cocked her head and inhaled deeply, wondering what the hell to do next.

Without saying the actual words, Marilyn conveyed that she knew for sure Reacher was guilty of cold-blooded, premeditated murder.

Which was a capital crime in every state of the union and most civilized countries in the world.

A crime that carries the possibility of the death sentence.

Which was something no one had said out loud before.

It was also intel Kim absolutely did not want to know.

Kim was a law enforcement officer and there was no statute of limitations on murder.

Which meant she'd be required to follow up on this crime and, if true, to arrest Reacher when she found him.

With an eyewitness as reliable as Marilyn Stone, a murder case against Reacher would be nailed shut with a sledgehammer not much more than a nanosecond after his arrest.

He'd be shipped off to prison forever.

Or worse.

Which would be an absolute disaster.

Not only for Reacher, but for Kim.

Kim's assignment was to find Reacher and bring him to her boss. Reacher was being considered for an essential classified assignment. One he couldn't perform if he were locked up or dead.

Implied in her orders to find Reacher was also an order to keep him out of custody at all costs. Absolutely.

CHAPTER 9

Saturday, June 18
Key West, Florida

MARILYN STONE DIDN'T KNOW where Reacher was now. That much was obvious. She wouldn't have hired Curry or be here talking to Kim if she'd known how to locate Reacher on her own.

So Kim steadied her nerves, ignored the implications, and changed the subject. For now. "Did Sheryl confide her concerns to anyone else? Other than you?"

"Maybe." Marilyn cocked her head, considered the question, but couldn't come up with a name.

"If you think of anyone, just call me," Kim said. "We'll take it from here. Try not to worry."

"I'm not worried. I'm pissed off. And I intend to do something about it." Marilyn nodded. "I need Reacher. Do you know where he is or not?"

"Not right at the moment, no," Kim replied. "But I will. Right now, I do need to get going."

Marilyn grasped Kim's arm as she slid off the high stool and turned to leave.

"Sheryl sacrificed so much to help veterans and their families. She didn't deserve this." Marilyn's jaw tightened. "If you can't find Reacher, you make them pay for what they've done to her. And to Bert and the other vets. For Sheryl. That's what Reacher would do."

Kim held Marilyn's desperate gaze and gave her a firm nod, which implied more than she could actually promise.

She didn't want to lie to this woman.

What happened to Sheryl Tardelli and her father, whether foul play was involved or not, were cases that were being handled already.

Even if Kim had the time and resources to handle them herself, she wouldn't be able to do more than an entire law enforcement department.

Truth was, Kim wasn't totally persuaded that Congresswoman Tardelli's death was anything other than accidental, either.

Oh, she believed Reacher had killed to save Marilyn Stone's life. Defense of others was righteous. Kim had done it herself. More than once.

Reacher was different. He'd become a vigilante. A one-man judge, jury, and executioner. The limits of the law had become irrelevant to him. People like Marilyn Stone were glad of it.

If he wanted to, Reacher would avenge Sheryl Tardelli, no questions asked.

Still, the Vietnam War had ended long, long ago. Toxic chemicals like R1 had been removed from the market and the government had acknowledged the health dangers.

Veterans and their families were being treated and compensated for the exposure. Had been for decades.

Which was of little comfort to the injured, but it was the best the government could do after the fact.

A congresswoman pressured to deny the dangers of toxic chemicals, a Vietnam vet's suspicious suicide, his crusading daughter murdered years later? What could Kim do about any of that?

And why dredge all of this stuff up now? Kim's dad had fought in Vietnam. Her mother was a Vietnamese war bride. Her parents rarely talked about the war or how they met or why her Vietnamese family never came to visit. Her dad was a proud veteran and patriot, as were many of his closest friends. But he didn't live his life in the past.

Besides, the world had moved on. Tourism was a booming business in Vietnam these days. Wasn't the aftermath of war better left to the pages of history?

Kim walked a couple of blocks up Duval Street before Curry caught up with her. "What do you think? She's a compelling witness, isn't she?"

"Witness to what? She doesn't really know anything about what happened to Tardelli. She's a grieving friend who wants answers that may never be found," Kim said plainly, one cop to another.

Curry gave her a hard stare. "Sheryl Tardelli stumbled into something. Marilyn's convinced that what she found got her killed."

"Marilyn Stone's your client. You'll do a good job for her. And there will be other jurisdictions investigating Tardelli's death. I've got my own work to do," Kim said.

"Oh, come on." Curry wagged his head as they walked along making slow progress. "Sheryl's old man? The supposed suicide always looked fishy. I checked the records from years back when it happened. Talked to the investigating detective, too."

"And?" Kim prompted, threading through the drunken tourists wearing flip-flops and Hawaiian shirts while strains of island music wafted from every open-air bar on both sides of the street.

A belligerent redhead wearing a coconut bra fell off her flip-flop and landed against Kim, knocking her sideways. Which was okay because the redhead's beer splashed all over the spot where Kim had been standing instead of all over Kim.

She regained her balance and gave the redhead a hard shove toward her staggering boyfriend. The redhead toppled sideways and landed on the guy's beer, which spilled all over both of them.

They guy glared at Kim and yelled, "Hey! Watch where you're going!"

The redhead slipped her arms around him and stuck like Velcro to his sweaty body.

Kim sidestepped the puddles on the sidewalk and kept moving.

Last thing she needed was to get in the middle of a drunken brawl. She wasn't even supposed to be here in Key West.

"Medical examiner's report was sloppy. Ruled Bert Tardelli's death a suicide fast. Barely looked for other causes." Curry shook his head as they moved away from the sodden couple.

"Then you can lean in even harder to uncover the truth." Kim watched the slow-moving traffic on Duval looking for a cab. "You don't need me to tell you how to do your job."

"We're both looking for Reacher. I've got some ideas about where to look. I'm not giving up until my client's money runs out. She's loaded, you know," he cajoled, suggesting Kim could make a bundle on the case, too. "We both keep trying separately, we'll just get in each other's way. Reacher will slip right through both our fingers."

"Sorry. I can't." Kim shook her head and refused to take the bait. "You find Reacher, let me know. We'll talk again."

"Okay. But I've actually met the guy. So has my client. Met his girlfriend, too."

"Reacher's girlfriend?"

"Jodie Jacob. Tried to find her, but she's disappeared, too. But I know what he looks like. How he behaves. What drives him. You've never even seen Reacher, have you?" Curry said, refusing to give up as he kept walking beside her, parting the throng of tourists with his bulk. "Come on. It's not like you're making a ton of progress, is it? What have you got to lose?"

Before she could politely decline again, Kim's cell phone vibrated in her pocket. Fishing it out to check the caller ID gave her a good excuse not to engage with Curry's questions.

"This is Otto," she said when she picked up.

"What the hell do you think you're doing down there?"

Cooper's angry tone on the other end of the call suggested he wouldn't be satisfied with her answers, so she said nothing. When the boss was that angry, no response would suffice.

"You've got exactly three hours to get your ass to DC. You're booked on a commercial flight in an hour. Don't miss it."

Kim didn't bother to object. No point. He'd already hung up.

"Sorry, Curry. I'd like to help you. But that was my boss. Vacation's over. Duty calls," she said as she slid the phone into her pocket.

She stepped into the alley out of the throng of sidewalk traffic and turned to hail a bike taxi.

She figured a guy on a bike pulling a rickshaw along Duval would make it to the airport faster than a real taxi could fight its way through the traffic anyway. She saw one coming alongside the line of vehicles and raised her hand to flag him down.

Which was when she caught an odd movement deeper inside the alley on her left side. Squinting into the shadows, she saw a knot of men standing loosely gathered. Their demeanor was too cautious, glances too furtive for a casual meetup. Something about the men felt menacing.

"What is that?" she asked Curry, tilting her head toward them, gaze narrowing as she observed a heavy briefcase change hands.

The anxious glances and the weight of the briefcase set off her internal alarms as the two groups shuffled apart.

"Gun deal?" Curry replied as his hand reached for his weapon.

Half a moment later she saw an unmistakable muzzle flash followed quickly by a return flash from the other side.

CHAPTER 10

Saturday, June 18
New Hampshire

THE SHOOTER STRETCHED OUT in the passenger seat, but he was too wired to rest. As he often did to relax, he closed his eyes to visualize the remote campground and the rented cabin by a tranquil lake. He imagined the warm breeze and the sparkling stars, willing his heartbeat to slow.

Broken Lake was the time and place his heart returned to when he was anxious or annoyed or worried. The night he'd never forget.

It had been very late. The campfires were extinguished, and the other campers were asleep in their darkened cabins. A full moon spotlighted the picturesque setting in the clear night sky like a greeting card.

Stars sparkled in the distance. An easy cool breeze carried gently rustling night sounds.

In movies, they might have called this part of the memory as the establishing shot, although he had learned the term much later in life. The opening sequence that sets up the context of the scene. Designed to show the people and the objects and establish the geography.

He zoomed in on his father, Rupert, alone in the darkened kitchen, drinking whiskey steadily from a bottle that was now almost empty. He'd been drinking all day for several days, trying to work up some courage.

Rupert had chosen the setting with care. The remote campground and this particular cabin removed from the rest. He'd explained to his son that he wouldn't leave a horrific mess at home for others to grieve over. Here, he could erase the pain for all of them without heaping more grief on survivors where it wasn't deserved.

The whiskey always dredged up agonizing memories Rupert desperately wanted to forget. Vietnam, where he'd been exposed to toxic chemicals. Something called R1 that had ruined their lives, he said over and over again.

The way his children had been born deformed from their father's exposure, even while his youngest was unaffected. Which was why Rupert talked to the boy. Because he needed to understand Rupert's intentions. He only wanted the best for his youngest son.

Rupert often wondered aloud how his mistakes as a young man could possibly be visited on his children. The guilt was overwhelming. He simply couldn't shoulder it any longer.

Audra begged him for a divorce. The once beautiful young woman now broken by years of living with a shadow of the man she'd married. Her precious children deserved better, she'd said.

Rupert had told Dax all about it. How he'd joined up to fight after his big brother was taken prisoner. How he'd served two tours trying to avenge his brother's death when his body couldn't be found. How he'd been sprayed many times with the toxic chemicals that had hurt his children before they were ever born.

Dax was Rupert's only hope. He was perfectly, beautifully formed. He was smart as anything. He was outgoing and athletic. He could shoot the beak off a bird at twenty yards.

Dax deserved a good life. A life without being dragged down by caring for his siblings. They would always need care. Never thrive. Rupert didn't want that life for himself or his wife, and he certainly didn't want Dax to live that way.

Rupert sent Dax to spend the weekend with his friend at camp so Dax wouldn't actually see the carnage.

He hadn't considered that Dax might also need an alibi.

Rupert had delayed long enough. It was time.

He drained the last of the whiskey, took a deep breath and pushed up to steady himself on his feet. He grabbed the pistol from the table, holding it in his right hand.

Crying softly, he stumbled toward the small bedroom where the children slept piled into bunk beds like a litter of puppies.

He stood by their beds and raised the pistol and tried to shoot them. His hand trembled and his tears intensified. He raised the pistol again.

But he simply couldn't bring himself to do it.

He dropped the gun on the rug and returned to the kitchen, crying at the table until he passed out.

Through the entire performance, Dax had been hiding in the closet, watching. He'd slipped away from his friend's cabin and snuck over here to see the show. He didn't know exactly what his dad had planned, but he knew he wanted to see it.

At this point, Dax was disgusted. He spat on the floor and shook his head. His father had failed again. No surprise. Rupert was a failure long before Dax was born; and he'd be a failure forever unless someone put him out of his misery.

Which was exactly what Dax decided to do.

He slipped on a pair of canvas gardening gloves and picked up the gun.

His dad had taught him to shoot when he was barely big enough to lift a pistol. Even then he was damned good at shooting. Better than Rupert or his brother, Carl. Better than his uncle Ryan or his grandad. He had a gift.

Rupert had fitted the gun with a suppressor, but it made the gun heavier, and it hadn't been necessary. He'd drugged the family to be sure they wouldn't wake up when the gunshots exploded and there was no one else close enough to hear.

Dax took a deep breath did the job that had to be done.

He padded softly into the kitchen and shot Rupert first. One shot, one kill.

It was the smart thing to do.

Dax thought the rest of Rupert's plan was solid, too, so he followed that as well.

He strode into the small bedroom where his siblings were snoring gently in drug-induced oblivion.

Dax aimed and fired, dispatching them swiftly, one after another. His older brother and two older sisters. Not one uttered so much as a whimper.

He examined their faces with curiosity as their chests stopped rising and falling with their breathing. They looked peaceful, as if they were still sleeping. Which was annoying and a little boring, honestly. He'd expected a more exciting reaction.

Leaving their bloody bodies in the cabin beds, Dax crept to the master bedroom door and looked into the dimly lit room.

His mother's snoring greeted him. The drugs Rupert had secretly given her at dinner now rendered her oblivious as well.

Dax moved to her bedside with purpose, raising the pistol one last time.

His mother's eyes fluttered open with confusion.

"Dax?" she murmured. "What are you doing?"

Dax stared but said nothing. He raised the pistol to aim one last time.

Her eyes went wide with sudden fear. She opened her mouth to scream, but it was too late.

Dax pulled the trigger without hesitation, ending her life in an instant.

As he'd done with the others, he watched to be certain she was no longer breathing before he placed the pistol carefully into his father's hand and let it drop to the floor and hurried outside into the cool night air.

The tranquil lake shimmered in reflected moonlight as Dax made his way to the rental canoe he'd stolen from the lodge across the lake.

He jumped into the water to shed himself of any evidence that might have spattered onto his body.

Then he climbed into the canoe and paddled swiftly until he reached the spot where more canoes were stacked for the campers to use in the morning. He placed his on the rack with the others.

Dax would have a normal future now, finally free from the pain his weak father could not bear any longer. Dax's desire to break free of his dysfunctional family, always whining about the unfairness of their lives, had been overwhelming and frustrating and infuriating.

He'd always thought his new life would begin in a moment of rebirth. He'd been right.

He chose the precise moment when he'd shot his mother right between the eyes as his chosen birth date.

And it felt glorious.

When he opened his eyes again, the driver had already turned onto the backroads leading to the cabin on the edge of the lake. The temperatures were colder in June than that August so long ago. But the excitement forming in the shooter's body warmed him through and through.

CHAPTER 11

Saturday, June 18
Key West, Florida

THE NOISE OF GUNSHOTS was absorbed by the raucous volume of nighttime Key West. If Kim and Curry hadn't been staring directly at the group, the whole thing would have gone unnoticed until the morning.

"Let's go," Curry said, weapon drawn, heading toward the men with Kim close behind.

As they approached, one of the men spotted them. Shouting a warning, he brandished his gun, but Kim was faster. She drew her weapon and fired a controlled shot. He dropped his gun as chaos erupted.

The men scrambled, some pulled out their guns and others fled deeper into the alley's shadows.

Kim and Curry split up. She moved forward, using the narrow walls for cover. More gunshots rang out, echoing against the old buildings.

Curry, from the forward position, took down one of the fleeing suspects with a shot to his leg. The man dropped his gun and screamed like a banshee as he fell into the filthy alley, squirming on the ground.

Kim used the distraction to confront the leader who was still holding the heavy briefcase in his left hand. The burly man with a wicked scar running down his cheek aimed at her, but Kim was quicker. She shot the briefcase, tearing it from his hand. He dropped his gun to flee, but Kim kicked the gun aside and delivered a swift punch to his knee, sending him to the ground.

She handcuffed him swiftly. "Stay down. Try to get up and I'll shoot. I can't possibly miss from this short distance."

Sirens wailed in the distance, growing louder.

Curry approached, surveying the scene. The briefcase was open on the ground where the burly man had dropped it, revealing an assortment of firearms.

"We need to clear out before the cops arrive," Curry said, looking around warily. "We're not exactly on the invitation list for this party."

"Yeah." Kim's gaze lingered on the two men down. The sirens were a few short blocks away now. "We've done what we could. Let's go."

They slipped away just as the police cars turned into the alley, blocking both ends to keep the revelers away.

Kim and Curry slipped out, blending into the crowd on Duval Street. Kim hurried along, searching for an empty bike taxi.

"What do you think that was about?" Curry asked. "Drugs? Gun running?"

"Hard to say. Could be anything. Look, I've got a plane to catch, and I'll be lucky to make it," she said apologetically.

Curry looked at her briefly with a mix of admiration and concern. "You're something else, Otto. But one of these days, your luck might run out."

Kim gave him a look reflecting the resolve that had always driven her. "Not tonight, Curry."

He shook his head and offered no reply. The deafening music, the noise of the crowd, and the unrelenting traffic drowned out the opportunity for whatever quick comeback he'd been planning.

Kim said, "You get any blowback on this, let me know. Uncle Sam will take care of you."

"It'll all be fine." Curry shrugged and smiled. "Hell, they'll probably give me a medal. I took down that arms deal all by myself. For an old dude, guess I've still got it."

Kim flashed a grin in return half a moment before a bike taxi driver stopped and yelled, "Lady! Hop in! Quickly! Let's go!"

She did exactly that and the guy began to pedal like crazy toward the airport.

Curry watched her go.

Kim figured she hadn't seen the last of him.

Guys like Curry never listened to reason.

The Key West heat was a tangible presence, wrapping around Kim as she navigated the modest airport terminal with efficient haste. Her mind was still back on Duval Street replaying the calculated violence that had almost danced in the streets. Curry seemed competent enough, but she couldn't shake her concern for leaving him behind with Marilyn.

She hustled to the locker where her bags waited and turned the key with a satisfying click. She slung her laptop bag over her shoulder, feeling the familiar weight of it against her back and grabbed the handle of her travel bag, rolling it toward the gate.

There was no time to shake off the residue of adrenaline. At the security checkpoint, Cooper had paved the way and her credentials preempted further questions about her rush to board.

Once through security, she quickened her pace to the designated gate, her boarding pass on her phone scanned by the attendant as she passed through the final barrier. The plane was boarding its last few passengers, and Otto slipped into her first-class seat with a silent sigh of relief.

She glanced outside into the twilight, her window framing the last views of Key West she'd have for a while and maybe forever. She hadn't really given the place a chance. Maybe she'd come back on a real vacation one day.

No sooner had she buckled in than her phone pinged with a message from Cooper. She opened it to find a secure link to the classified files.

Cooper's message was terse: "Review before meeting. Urgent."

She connected to the secure satellite while the plane was still on the ground and downloaded the files from her server.

She watched as the information, locked behind layers of encryption, cascaded onto her laptop. The flight attendant offered coffee, which Kim accepted with a request for a second cup. She needed the caffeine.

Kim's fingers danced across her laptop to confirm she'd received all the files. The screen illuminated her determined expression as she delved into them.

A quick skim of the file names caused her eyes to widen with surprise. Why did Cooper send files on Congresswoman Sheryl Tardelli's death? Marilyn Stone had mentioned the name to Kim only a short time ago. Cooper had been watching. Of course he had.

And who was the second subject? Judge Matt Gunston. Kim had never heard of him.

After takeoff, the flight attendant replenished Kim's coffee as she absorbed the images and reports on Tardelli and Gunston. Her brain cataloged details, making connections where there seemed to be none.

The congresswoman's stance on chemical legislation, the judge's recent controversial ruling. Background pieces of a larger puzzle she would be tasked to solve.

The flight attendants dimmed the cabin lights as the plane reached cruising altitude. Soon the constant hum of the engines provided the backdrop for her concentrated review. Passengers around her settled into their own routines, as oblivious to Kim as she was to them.

She worked methodically, sifting through reams of data, while filtering out the noise. Every so often, her eyes would flick to the window, where the world was nothing but clouds and the setting sun in contrast to the darkness unraveling in Cooper's files.

Kim made notes, cross-referenced data, anticipating the conversation with Cooper. He was a man of few words, but each one counted, and she would need to be ready to discuss the intricacies of the cases.

So far, though, she'd found no connection between the two victims, and she wondered why they'd been tethered together.

Too soon, the flight began its descent and the seatbelt signs flicked on. Kim stowed her laptop and prepared for landing, gripping both armrests as if her life depended on them. Which, she knew, it did.

The plane touched down with a gentle jolt and rolled toward the gate. Kim relaxed her grip, collected her thoughts along with her bags, and stepped off the plane. Reagan National Airport enveloped her with its usual chaos of a totally different kind than Duval Street. It was like landing on another planet.

Five minutes later, her phone pinged again, but she didn't stop to check it. She was late already. She exited the terminal and merged with the flow of the city in the spring evening's bracing welcome chill.

Cooper had a lot of explaining to do this time. She wondered whether he'd tell her what the hell was going on.

That would be a first.

CHAPTER 12

Saturday, June 18
Washington, DC

THE DRIVE TO COOPER'S office at FBI headquarters was a blur of familiar streetlights and shadows. Kim had moved from Washington, DC long ago, but the city memories were indelibly stamped in her brain.

Visceral awareness of the smells and the noise rushed over her even inside the taxi. The sign pointing to Georgetown, where she'd been a law student and a young bride, made her shudder.

That trusting, vulnerable Kim Otto no longer existed, thank God. These days, her motto was strictly "be skeptical and triple verify," especially while hunting Reacher.

The taxi dropped her near the front of the J. Edgar Hoover Building on Pennsylvania Avenue. She stepped into the cool spring air and grabbed her bags from the trunk. The driver rolled away as she hurried toward the entrance.

She passed through the familiar dance of protocol and necessity at the security checkpoint. The elevator ride to Cooper's office was a quick vertical trek into the beating heart of FBI bureaucracy.

The building was one of the most secure places in the world.

Which was a whole different thing from totally safe.

The brass plaque on his office door read simply, *Charles Cooper*. She knocked twice and entered without waiting for permission.

Cooper stood behind his desk watching the well-lit city. "Sit," he ordered without turning around.

Kim took the chair opposite, her posture relaxed, expression neutral. "You wanted to see me."

He turned and lowered himself into his throne, fingers steepled, leaning slightly back in the oversized chair. "Key West, Otto. Explain."

She recounted the events leading up to the present moment in chronological order, succinctly with clinical precision. He listened without comment until she said, "Curry and I discovered an arms deal in progress in Old Town. We intervened—"

Cooper's hand slammed down on the desk, the sound like a gunshot in the quiet. He scowled and barked like the Army general he once was.

"You took a civilian into a firefight? Are you out of your mind?"

Kim didn't back down. She'd learned the hard way that he respected only strength. Show him a slight crack in her armor and he'd destroy her without a moment's hesitation. She'd seen him do it to others and she didn't imagine he would treat her any better.

"I was there. You weren't. I made a call. Heat of the moment," she said flatly. "It was the right thing to do. I'd do it again."

His scowl deepened and his voice was a whip. "And Marilyn Stone?"

Kim paused before she admitted what she figured he already knew anyway. "I was lucky to stumble over her. She's a solid lead in the Reacher case."

Cooper's jaw clenched with a tremor of anger. "Stone is off-limits. You should have known that."

The rebuke was a jolt. Her instincts flared in a silent warning that she ignored. "Stone knows Reacher and she was willing to talk to me. Why on earth would she be off-limits?"

He cut her off by slicing his hand through the air. "My call. Not yours. You have more important things to worry about."

Was he worried about Reacher committing premeditated murder? Somehow, she didn't think that inconvenient truth would bother Cooper in the least.

She'd have pursued the matter, but he didn't give her a chance. He shifted the conversation, a tactical maneuver that left her questions hanging.

"Tardelli and Gunston," he said, his tone a shade cooler. "Two high-profile murders. Everybody's all over both cases. There's a team working on this already. But you've reviewed the files. Are they related?"

"To what? To each other?" She leaned forward. "There's nothing concrete linking them. Unless you have something more that isn't in those files you sent."

Cooper's eyes narrowed. "Call it a hunch."

A hunch? What a load of crap.

She said, "You don't operate on hunches."

The corner of his mouth twitched sardonically. "Okay. Call it years of experience distilled to the kind of instincts that have kept us both alive long past our expiration dates."

She cocked her head as if the wheels were actually turning in her mind. "You think there's a connection. Not only between Tardelli and Gunston, but to Reacher and Stone as well."

"The killer thinks there's a connection between the two victims." He nodded slightly, a subtle concession. "And possibly others."

"Others?"

"Our intel suggests there are others on the killer's list. We need to find the connection between the victims and stop this madness. Quickly. Permanently. Before the FBI gets a request to form a task force and the situation gets out of control."

By which he meant out of *his* control.

"Why?"

He said nothing. Possibly waiting for her to figure it out. Maybe betting she wouldn't.

"Whatever the connection is between the victims, you think Reacher could get into the fight," Kim said as the realities unfolded in her mind. "Which sounds good to me. Because if he does get involved, we'll be able to find him. Why is that a problem? We've been hunting Reacher for more than eight months now. Locating him is exactly what you wanted, isn't it?"

"Not quite," Cooper said slowly, as if he were weighing his words. "We want Reacher for a classified assignment. Which means he needs to stay off the grid. We can't use him if he gets his mug plastered across every broadcast in the country."

"I see," she said.

And she did see. Clearly.

Cooper wanted Reacher to serve as some sort of secret weapon. Which meant the assignment Cooper wanted Reacher to handle would be not only classified but covert as well.

Possibly illegal as hell.

Could even be treasonous.

But what could she do about it?

Not one damned thing.

She didn't even know what the mission was.

And she certainly wouldn't accuse Cooper of crimes against his own government.

Not without a hell of a lot more than a hunch or intuition and guesswork.

She needed hard evidence. The airtight kind. And lots of it.

She gave him a sharp nod to indicate understanding and acceptance of the challenge.

"I'll need a partner. Can't do this one alone. Reggie Smithers," Kim said. "I've worked with him before. He's good at the job. And he'll supply the muscle we need to get this done."

It was Cooper's turn to pause. She could tell he wanted to refuse. The gleam in his eye was a dead giveaway.

But she'd made up her mind. She was through being the target for every miscreant Reacher had pissed off in the past fifteen years.

Pairing up with Smithers would at least give her a fighting chance.

Reggie Smithers was an excellent FBI agent. Not the least bit bent. Cooper could neither control him nor sacrifice him.

Kim had worked with Smithers twice before. In both cases, he'd been both competent and reliable. Beyond that, she could trust him.

Which was exactly why Kim wanted Smithers. She could count on him to do the right thing. She knew it as well as she knew anything. Smithers was as good as she could get on short notice, since Gaspar was not up to the physical demands of the job.

Finally, Cooper relented and gave her a solid nod. "I'll make the call."

"Do it now. We'll start with forensics. Smithers can meet me there."

The meeting was over, though it felt like nothing had been resolved. Kim stood and waited until Cooper pulled a burner cell phone from the drawer to call Smithers.

Before she walked out, she said, "I knew Tardelli. Dedicated to service, devoted to military veterans. She was one of the good ones."

"Yeah. Gunston was one of the good ones, too, if it matters." Cooper's eyes followed her to the door. "Don't make me regret giving you free rein on this. And keep away from Marilyn Stone. I'll deal with her myself when the time comes."

Without reply, Kim left the room.

The door closed behind her with a quiet click punctuating Cooper's final words.

She had not promised to stay away from Marilyn Stone.

Kim needed to know what Stone knew about Reacher and why Cooper wanted to keep Stone to himself.

Beyond that, they were way too far down the road for her to submit to Cooper's orders without question.

She'd crossed that line months ago.

CHAPTER 13

Sunday, June 19
Rural Vermont

NORA RAMSEY KNEADED THE muscles in her shoulders. She was bone weary, in body and spirit. Tardelli's death two weeks ago was both a tragedy and a disaster for Ramsey Chemical's plans.

Simply put, with Tardelli gone, Ramsey couldn't see any way forward.

She'd been alone in her office at the Ramsey Chemical plant. Despite hours of effort aimed at finding a replacement for Sheryl Tardelli, she'd found no viable prospects.

The proposal was a political hot potato, sure. But Tardelli had seen the merit, the potential. Tardelli had vision.

No one else Ramsey had approached so far was willing to touch it. They lacked Tardelli's strength of purpose and willingness to fight the uphill battle.

Tardelli had believed in the R2 project and its goals. She seemed to be the only politician brave enough to do the right thing. The others were cowards.

After consuming three pots of coffee, the caffeine was no longer keeping Ramsey's mind sharp enough to avoid mistakes in her work. The kind of mistakes it would take her hours to fix later.

She'd wanted to find something positive to keep her hopes alive, but she was spinning her wheels here. It was foolish to keep going.

Everyone else had left hours ago. She glanced at the clock. Well after midnight.

"Time to go home, make the phone call, and get some sleep. You can start again tomorrow," she said aloud to the empty room.

Ramsey shrugged off her lab coat, stowed her work securely into her personal safe, and locked the doors behind her as she trudged toward the exit. She reset the alarms using the biometric keypad and walked through to the empty parking garage.

Cool night breezes enveloped her as she stepped into her SUV, started the engine, and exited the garage.

As she drove down the narrow, tree-lined road leading away from the plant, Ramsey was preoccupied with the phone call she had to make. It was late spring in rural Vermont. The trees were leafing out, but they did not yet present a solid wall of darkness. The new moon did that all on its own.

All of which was why, lost in thought, she barely registered the black SUV that slipped out of the fire trail between the trees and onto the road behind her. Traveling with its lights off, the black SUV blended into the darkness.

When the vehicle roared to life and began closing the gap between them with alarming speed, Ramsey glanced into the rearview mirror. The SUV's lights came on, bright and strong and menacing like a leaping tiger.

Ramsey pressed her foot down on the accelerator, urging her smaller SUV forward away from the predator.

The black SUV followed, persistently matching her speed, leaving only a two-foot gap between them.

Ramsey tightened her grip on the steering wheel and pushed the pedal to the floor.

Her SUV jumped ahead as if it had taken on a life of its own.

Ramsey had lived in these woods her entire life. She knew every bend and branch. But the big SUV was faster and more powerful. In a crash, the black SUV would win. No question.

Up ahead was a two-lane dirt road. She kept her speed until she was close and then swerved into a hard right turn. Her headlights cut a path through the semi-leafed trees, and she slowed as much as she dared, but kept going.

The black SUV missed the turn.

Ramsey was able to put some distance between them.

But too quickly, the black vehicle growled relentlessly behind her again, rapidly closing the gap.

Ramsey sped up, but the dirt road wasn't meant for speed. The big SUV slammed into her rear bumper and shoved her forward. Her body jerked against her seatbelt now locked in place.

The force of impact had thrust her forward and the safety restraint slammed her back into the seat.

"Come on," Ramsey muttered under her breath as she gave her vehicle as much speed as she dared along the bumpy winding road.

The big SUV matched her every turn, surprisingly agile for close to a ton of hurtling weight.

The road ahead was a treacherous path in the pitch-black night. Ramsey navigated each turn at high speed, struggling to keep the wheels on the ground.

Her experience on the road's twists and turns should have given her an advantage, but she couldn't shake the SUV off her tail. Every time she thought she'd lost him he came roaring back.

A big bend in the road came up faster than she'd expected. She took the curve too fast. When she rounded the bend, she caught her breath as a deer leapt across the road.

Ramsey's breath caught as she gasped and swerved sharply to avoid the doe's back legs. Sharp hooves landed on the hood of her SUV and pushed off.

The doe scampered deeper into the trees.

Ramsey's vehicle skidded, gravel flying, as she fought to regain control.

The big SUV used the moment to gain ground, kicking up dirt and gravel and closing in fast.

Ramsey struggled to straighten her wheels in the ruts. Just as she stopped swerving, the black SUV rammed into the back of her vehicle again.

The jarring impact at speed, metal grinding against metal, terrified her. But she couldn't stop.

Ramsey's vehicle lurched forward violently, the force of the collision pushing her to one side of the narrow road and nearly causing her to lose control.

Despite the damage to her vehicle, Ramsey managed to steer it back onto the road. The engine was struggling now, groaning under the strain.

The black SUV rushed forward again, unrelenting, headlights blindingly bright in her mirrors, and slammed into her vehicle a third time.

How much more could the smaller SUV take?

"Crap!"

She couldn't outrun them. She swiveled her head quickly, looking for an alternative.

She saw it up ahead.

Her only chance was to get there first.

Ramsey pressed the accelerator. She rushed ahead.

Half a moment later, she took a desperate turn onto a narrow path. A hiking and snowshoeing shortcut she knew through the woods.

But she'd never tried to run any kind of vehicle through here before.

Branches scratched against her SUV. The eerie sounds added to the tension of the chase.

The path was barely visible in the near total darkness.

The big SUV had reversed to the path and hesitated at the turn.

Which gave her a moment's breathing room.

But then he barreled after her.

The bulky SUV simply wasn't suited for the narrow confines of the path.

Tree branches and trunks gouged the big SUV, slowing it down, and destroying the paint. A huge branch yanked one of the big side mirrors completely off the door.

Ramsey's heart pounded as she navigated the perilous path as quickly as she could.

Every twist and turn was a potential disaster.

She kept the accelerator as close to wide open as she could manage while the uneven surface of the path bounced her around inside the vehicle. She didn't stop to consider the bruises she'd have on her body tomorrow from the incessant pounding.

The black SUV kept coming, crashing through the underbrush, in unstoppable pursuit.

Soon, the path would return to the main road.

The big SUV would have the advantage again.

What would she do when that happened?

Disaster struck.

Ramsey's vehicle, traveling too fast, landed in a huge hole in the ground, slamming down on its springs to the chassis.

The jolt was immense.

A shockwave traveled through the vehicle, jerking her hands off the steering wheel.

She struggled to maintain control, but the effort was futile.

The vehicle spun wildly.

She tried to right it again and again.

She failed.

Her SUV plowed head-on into a large granite boulder with a deafening crash.

Dazed, Ramsey tried to gather her senses. Her vehicle was wrecked. Steam hissed from beneath the crumpled hood. She reached for her phone to call for help. Before she could dial, the SUV pulled up behind her, blocking all escape routes.

Two doors slammed. Heavy footsteps approached.

Her door was yanked open. and a dark figure loomed over her, outlined against the faint light from the SUV's headlights.

"Ms. Ramsey," he said, his accented voice cold and unyielding. "You can't run forever."

Fear and defiance mingled in her chest.

The man reached out. But before he could grab her, a blinding light flooded the area, accompanied by a wail like a siren.

The man hesitated for a brief moment looking over his shoulder.

Ramsey seized her chance. She pushed past him and scrambled out of the wrecked vehicle and bolted into the woods.

Behind her, voices shouted as a chaos of sounds filled the night.

She ran blindly, underbrush tearing her clothes, breath ragged.

Then, quickly, the bright light vanished. Ramsey was once again engulfed by the darkness.

She stopped, panting, her heart pounding like a thousand drums.

She was alone in the dark woods now. Every sound seemed amplified, every rustling leaf a potential threat. She crouched, trying to steady her breath and make sense of the situation.

Which was when she realized where she was. Less than a mile from home.

Suddenly, she heard a rustling sound behind her.

Ramsey froze. Her heart skipped a beat. She strained her eyes attempting to see through the darkness.

A man emerged from the shadows, moving toward her.

Ramsey had to make a decision. Confront the unknown threat or keep going.

She hesitated one moment more before she turned and ran.

CHAPTER 14

Sunday, June 19
Rural Vermont

NORA RAMSEY COULDN'T STOP shaking. June weather was unpredictable in Vermont under the best of circumstances and her home office was always cold, even with the heat on and a fire burning in the fireplace.

At the moment, the cold wasn't her most pressing problem.

Her body was scratched and bleeding, but fear had carried her all the way home and kept her alive.

For now.

The only light in the starkly minimalist room spilled from a sleek, modern desk lamp, casting deep shadows across her face. Her pistol rested on the side table. A rifle was close at hand. Both were loaded and ready.

She had showered and wrapped a gray cardigan around her. For warmth. And to keep her hands steady.

She sipped more hot rum to steady her nerves and dialed the number.

After a long pause, the phone finally rang twice.

"Iniko Makinde," he said, with a blend of authority and weariness in his deep, heavily accented voice.

"Nora Ramsey," she replied as evenly as possible. "We need to discuss recent developments."

Makinde paused, a moment of silence that stretched too long for Ramsey's comfort. Was he actually surprised to hear from her? Had Makinde sent those men to harm her tonight?

She shook the idea out of her head. Makinde was ruthless, but he had no motive to kill her. Just the opposite.

Which meant he had something else in mind.

"I've heard about Tardelli," he finally said, perhaps betraying a hint of concern. "A setback."

"*A setback?*" Ramsey echoed sharply. She wanted to surrender to hysteria, but that would serve no one. She took a steadying breath and tried again. "It's a disaster. Without her, our push for US approval is barely hanging on. Momentum has slowed to a complete halt."

"That's unfortunate. For you." Makinde's sigh was audible. "But this means nothing for us. For our project here."

Ramsey leaned back in her chair, her gaze fixed on the darkness outside the wall of windows on the north side of her home. "It means we need to be more careful. Until we get US approval."

"More careful? Impossible. We've been more than careful all along." Ramsey felt the hard shift in Makinde's response from the other side of the world. "We've finally been successful. The tests show this most recent batch of R2 works. Malaria rates are down. We've saved thousands of lives. Children's lives. You can't back out now."

"I'm not backing out," Ramsey replied firmly. "But we need to be realistic about the situation. Without US government support, we have nothing. There are eyes on us now. Eyes that weren't there before."

She didn't mention she'd been attacked tonight. She knew the attack had to be related to R2. What else could it be?

Was Makinde involved, though? She hoped not. The point of this call was to find out.

"And whose fault is that?" Makinde demanded. "You promised me this would be smooth sailing. Weeks ago, you said that US support was a mere formality. We're all in with you now. We have no alternatives."

"What would you have me do?" Ramsey's fist clenched as if she held her calm by force. "Tardelli's death is a big problem. Out of my control. Not one damned thing I can do about it. We're seeking an alternative, but it will take some time."

Makinde spoke again, his tone colder and harder. "Here's what is and has been totally within your control. Your operations here. They haven't exactly been... legal."

Ramsey's breath caught in her throat. "What are you implying?"

"I'm not implying anything," Makinde said bluntly. "I'm stating a fact. Testing a chemical defoliant with a tainted history. Inside my country. Without proper authorization or disclosure of the risks. There have been casualties. What do you think would happen if the wrong people found out about all that?"

Ramsey's pulse pounded in her ears. "Exactly how would that happen? How would the wrong people find out? And what is it you think they would do?"

Makinde's silence filled the empty air like a shrug of indifference. "You come here with your promises and your

American influence, and we give you more than you deserve. Now you talk about being 'realistic.' Well, let's be realistic."

He paused to be sure he had her full attention, and then continued, "You need me. You need Nigeria. Without us, R2 is just another of your failed experiments. Should that happen, Ramsey Chemical will be totally destroyed. You will go to prison, along with all Ramsey Chemical executives. I will make it so."

Ramsey's reply was barely above a whisper. "Blackmail? Is that what this is?"

"It's business," Makinde countered. "You of all people should understand that. With Tardelli gone, you need all the support you can get. And we can be very supportive... for the right price."

Ramsey's clenched fist pounded quietly on her thigh.

The ungrateful bastard.

She'd risked everything to prove that R2 could save thousands, maybe millions of lives. Now that she'd proved R2's worth, she couldn't just walk away without the vindication she'd worked for all her life.

Coldly, she said, "What do you want, Iniko?"

Makinde's reply was smooth, confident. "R2 distribution to Nigeria continues. Uninterrupted. Indefinitely. And as compensation for taking 100 percent of the risks, Nigeria gets a bigger cut of the gross revenue after the US approves the product. Fifty percent seems fair to me."

"This is a humanitarian aid project. Not some get-rich-quick scheme." Ramsey's jaw clenched. "That's not possible. The margins are tight as it is. We don't have money like that to throw around. We're not price gouging anybody on R2. Absolutely not."

"These are not my problems. Find a way to make it possible," Makinde shot back. "Because if you don't, the world will know exactly what Ramsey Chemical has been up to in Nigeria. And trust me, the world will not be kind."

Ramsey went silent. Makinde's demands were impossible. This wasn't about money or business.

It was about survival.

Human lives.

Her father's legacy.

Her company's future.

Her life's work.

She'd put everything on the line.

Which was why she knew that Makinde was right. She had no viable alternative.

"Fine. I'll find a way. But I need your assurances, too."

"As long as you keep yours." Makinde said with too much satisfaction for Ramsey's comfort. "I must go. Don't forget what I said. Uninterrupted delivery of R2. No excuses."

He didn't actually remind her that they knew where she lived. But the threat was more than implied.

The line went dead, leaving Ramsey alone in her quiet office, wondering what the hell she was going to do.

Then, slowly, she reached for her phone again, dialing another number.

The line clicked as the second call connected and a gruff voice answered. "Hello?"

"I need your help, John."

John wasn't his real name. Ramsey had no idea what his real name was. She liked it that way.

But John was the most common name in the English language. A name easily adaptable to every other language on the planet. He'd been using it a good long while and it served both their purposes.

There was a pause, and then came John's cautious reply. "What kind of help?"

"I've hit a snag with the R2 project. I need someone with... your unique set of skills."

He chuckled dryly. "What's the situation?"

She took a deep breath. "Nigeria. Blackmail."

"That's a dangerous game. Who's the player?"

"Iniko Makinde. He's threatening to destroy our operation unless I agree to his terms."

"Makinde. Nasty fellow. Well connected, though. You want him eliminated? Should be doable."

"No. I need him alive."

"Then why call me? I'm not a kidnapper. Too much work."

"Good to know." Ramsey grinned for half a second before she said, "I need you to find something I can use to level the playing field."

"Okay. With a guy like Makinde, shouldn't be hard to find. He's got plenty of enemies," John replied. "It'll cost you, though. Bribery is pricey in Nigeria."

"I'll pay whatever it takes," Ramsey replied staring at the deep gouges on her legs scraped by heavy branches during her flight through the woods. "I'm too close to success. I won't let him defeat me."

"Alright," John said after a moment's pause. "Give me a few days. I'll dig around and see what I can find."

"I'll be waiting for your call like a teenager expecting an invitation to the prom." Ramsey said flatly and disconnected while he was still chuckling.

She took her drink and her guns and went into the master suite to draw a hot bath. As she lowered her body into the steamy water, the cuts and scratches stinging everywhere, she considered how her evening had unfolded.

Makinde had tried to frighten her. First by the chase in the woods. Then, with threats and blackmail. She knew it had to be him. Felt it in her bones.

She'd made a deal with the devil. Now she had to figure out how to escape with her life and her life's work still intact.

But she needed proof to keep Makinde in line. Her intuition was not enough.

CHAPTER 15

Sunday, June 19
Washington, DC

KIM WAS ALREADY AT the airport waiting for her flight when Smithers called. "Otto here."

He said, "Looks like Cooper's called in the A-Team, eh? What are we up to this time? I got the files but haven't had a chance to read them yet."

"Looking forward to working with you again, too," she replied with a grin. "There's a regular FBI team on this. We're supplemental. Reporting solely to Cooper. And there are two bodies, so far."

"That we know of," Smithers pointed out reasonably.

"Yeah. The Tardelli and Gunston murders were evaluated separately because they occurred in separate jurisdictions. But once the crimes were flagged by the FBI, all forensics were delivered to Dr. Kyla Debrew at Quantico. We're meeting her there in a couple of hours," Kim explained.

"Can you push it back? I'm in Boston. More than four hundred miles away. An FBI helo can get me there, but not that quickly," Smithers replied. "Hang on. Let me see what I can do."

Kim heard him clacking keys on his computer as he checked commercial flights.

"Looks like I can meet you there by four o'clock. If I leave right this minute. Best case," Smithers said.

Which is how she came to be waiting for Smithers at the airport at four-thirty. She saw him exit the terminal and hustle to the big black SUV Cooper had provided.

Kim moved to the passenger seat because she was number one on the case and Gaspar had made it plain that the number two agent always did the driving. Simple as that. She liked the symbolism of it, too.

Smithers tossed his bag in the cargo hold and slipped into the driver's seat as if he'd been fitted for it. Which was saying something, given his huge size.

Kim's confidence in Smithers never wavered. He was everything she'd want in a partner since Gaspar was no longer available.

"Hey, Otto," Smithers said, extending a big paw in his friendly, boisterous way. "What's shakin'?"

"Good to see you, Smithers," she replied, her tone a mix of professional focus and genuine warmth. She grinned and shook his hand, which fully engulfed hers. "Glad you could make it. We've got a lot to unpack here."

"No problem. We'll figure it out." He adjusted the seat and the mirrors and fastened his seatbelt with easy, practiced moves. Less than a minute later, they were rolling into traffic.

Kim glanced over at Smithers's reassuring presence. He could handle himself. She knew that much from prior experience. Kim could take care of herself. Which was one reason her partnership with Gaspar had worked well enough. She'd never needed him to rescue her. But having a partner who could hold up his end on the physical defense side was a bonus with Smithers.

He caught her looking. "I read the files during the flight. Tardelli's case... that's some sophisticated and twisted stuff. And Gunston, a sniper-hit in his own front yard on the way to his kid's soccer game? Do we have a cartel here? This feels like we're dealing with totally different killers, doesn't it?"

Kim watched the scenery blur past as they headed toward the FBI's forensic headquarters at Quantico, Virginia. "I can't shake off the feeling that there's a link we're missing. Both victims were high-profile in different ways. Both murders executed with a level of expertise and forensic awareness that's... unnerving."

Smithers maneuvered the SUV onto the highway, his large hands steady on the wheel. "Yeah, feels like we're dealing with pros. The type who don't leave any kind of trail."

Kim's gaze moved to Smithers. "Exactly. Dr. Debrew is the best we've got on the payroll. Either to link these cases or understand the motives behind them. With luck, she'll supply us something to go on."

Smithers gave a brief nod. "We'll crack it, Otto. We always do."

His tone was lighthearted, but Kim heard the steely determination, too.

"How's my buddy, Gaspar, doin'?" Smithers asked after a bit. "Still soakin' up rays in Miami?"

Kim smiled. "Pretty much. He's got a sweet job with Scarlett Investigations now."

"Nice outfit." Smithers whistled. "Pays well, too. Tell him to put in a good word for me if they need to add more agents."

"I'll do that," Kim replied.

She didn't mention Michael Flint. After Gaspar, Flint was Scarlett's best operative. Hell, in some ways, Flint was better than Gaspar. Flint had provided backup for Kim more than once and she'd been well pleased with his skills. No question, Gaspar had jumped out of the FBI into a great job. Smithers would be lucky to join that team, too.

The FBI's Quantico lab facility was straight through the gates. Kim had called ahead, and Dr. Kyla Debrew was waiting when they arrived. After brief introductions, she led them to a conference room where she had assembled the evidence they'd come to discuss.

Dr. Debrew pointed to the coffee and then jumped directly into the cases while they helped themselves to java. "We're all familiar with the facts surrounding these murders. So let's start with the toxin used to kill Congresswoman Tardelli."

"Were you able to identify it?" Kim asked.

Debrew shook her head. "We collected samples from her clothes and her body and ran them through our systems. I can say with certainty that we haven't seen this one before."

"That's hard to believe," Smithers said.

"Damned straight it is. Every chemical on the market must be registered. New chemicals are usually patented, which means they'd be in our databases."

"But not this one?" Kim said. "How can that be?"

Debrew shrugged. "It's probably experimental. Nothing has been filed on it yet."

"Is that unusual?" Kim asked.

"Not necessarily. Companies spend millions of dollars developing new products. They want to keep the formulas secret until they're ready to let competitors know about them," Debrew replied. "What's unusual is that somehow, this one escaped the laboratory environment and was used as a murder weapon."

"How would that happen?" Smithers wanted to know.

"Industrial espionage, most likely. New chemicals can become extremely lucrative and profitable, depending on what they're used for. With slight modifications, this one might be worth more than enough to justify murder," Debrew said.

"What's this one meant to be used for? Because there are too many cheap and effective chemical weapons already on the market. We don't really need another one, do we?" Kim asked.

Debrew shrugged. "That's not a question I can answer. But I can tell you that this might not be a weapon. Not in the sense you're talking about, anyway."

"What do you mean?" Smithers asked.

"Well, the chemical composition is very similar to products that were on the market a few decades ago. Defoliants. They were used to kill plants. You know, like weed killers."

Smithers's eyes widened. "Weed killers?"

Debrew nodded. "The most infamous one was R1. You've probably heard of it."

"Yes, of course," Kim replied. "My father was in the Vietnam War. My mother was a war bride. R1 was liberally used back then to clear out the jungle plants that provided enemy cover. Made the enemy easier to see."

"The chemical that killed Tardelli was R1?" Smithers asked as if he were still trying to wrap his head around the idea.

Debrew frowned. "Not exactly. But the two have certain commonalities. In layman's terms, the Tardelli weapon was a stronger, lethal form of R1. One more likely to kill humans."

"The old version didn't kill humans?" Smithers asked, obviously still confused.

Debrew leaned against the stainless-steel table and rested her hands in her pockets. "There's some debate about that. Many scientists say there's no definitive connection between the old R1 and any deleterious health effects at all."

"But other scientists disagree," Kim pointed out. "We studied those cases in law school. There were experts who tied R1 to various diseases and birth defects in the children of soldiers who were exposed back then."

"Yes, that's right," Debrew replied. "But we know R1 didn't kill Tardelli, partly because it hasn't been manufactured since the 1970s."

"Then what killed her?" Smithers asked.

Debrew said, "The main chemical believed to place humans at risk after exposure to R1 was dioxin. You may have heard of dioxin poisoning, too."

"But you're saying the chemical that killed Tardelli wasn't dioxin," Kim stated flatly.

"Definitely not. But similar enough."

"So if dioxin doesn't kill, why did Tardelli die?" Smithers wanted to know.

"Two things. First, because she wasn't simply exposed to this toxin. She consumed it. She inhaled it. It was in her eyes, her nose, her mouth. And it was both thick and sticky," Dr. Debrew explained, displaying a postmortem photo on the screen where they could all see clearly. "Here's her body on the ground at the cemetery. She's covered in the stuff. It's all over her."

"So cause of death was a combination of the chemical itself and the exposure dose?" Kim said, nodding as she looked again at the photo. She shuddered. "What a horrible way to die."

"Yes," Dr. Debrew said. "Someone must have really hated her to kill her like that."

"That's hard to imagine," Kim said. "I knew Sheryl Tardelli. She was one of the most genuinely kind people I've ever met. Who would hate her that much?"

Smithers swiped a palm across his face. "Yeah, well, not everybody felt the same way you did about her, obviously."

Dr. Debrew said, "But the toxicity that killed Tardelli was significantly enhanced by the added cyanide."

"Cyanide?" Smithers asked, eyes wide.

"The actual cause of death was cardiac arrest caused by acute cyanide poisoning," Dr. Debrew replied. "From the amount of cyanide we found on her body and her clothing, I'd say whoever poisoned her wanted to be damned sure she didn't survive."

CHAPTER 16

Sunday, June 19
New Slope, New York

FROM HALF A MILE away as the van approached, the shooter watched Harold Zabrinski move like a man with a purpose that belied his age. His hands were steady and strong as he lifted a box of asparagus from the back of a pickup truck parked outside the New Slope Community Center.

The late afternoon sun was not too hot to interfere with his labor. Delivering vegetables he hadn't sold at the farmer's market the day before was his regular Sunday ritual. Feeding his neighbors had always been his life's work, the shooter had overheard him say more than once.

According to the description on the town website, New Slope, usually bustling with activity, was quieter on Sundays. People around here still went to church and then spent afternoons with their families.

The shops were closed, and the pool hall didn't open until later. It was a quiet town where everyone knew their neighbors and tried to help out when they needed a hand.

The shooter shook his head. He didn't understand men like Harold Zabrinski. Born in a Podunk town like New Slope, he'd lived here most of his life.

The only time he'd been away was when he was in the Army. And that was long ago. He'd served his country and come straight back home, apparently content to bloom in the middle of nowhere, where he'd been firmly planted. How much more wasted could a full life possibly be?

More specifically, Zabrinski inherited his family farm and spent the decades following his father's death in Vietnam growing vegetables, like his grandfather before him. The farm was more than a hundred years old now.

Zabrinski glanced up to see the white panel van turn the corner, moving cautiously, down the street. It was the kind of vehicle one might see and forget seconds later. There were dozens of them in towns across America.

The shooter could read Zabrinski's mind. Nothing to worry about, he must have concluded.

"You're a fool, Zabrinski," the shooter muttered snidely.

Inside the van, the air was tense, thick with anticipation. Eyes hiding behind dark sunglasses, the shooter rode shotgun. He was hunched slightly, stroking the high-powered sniper rifle on his lap like a lover.

The driver kept his eyes fixed on the road, hands gripping the wheel steadily despite the adrenaline rushing through his body like electricity.

As they approached the soup kitchen, the driver's gaze flickered to Zabrinski standing outside.

"That's him," he muttered, as if the target might hear him.

The shooter nodded once.

"Pull up here," the shooter said.

The driver obeyed, easing the van to a stop a discreet distance away. Out of Zabrinski's line of sight, but close enough for the job at hand.

Zabrinski set a box down on the dolly with a grunt and wiped his brow with the back of his hand. He turned once again to the truck, ready to grab another box, unaware of the driver's watching eyes.

In the van, the younger man carefully assembled the rifle with practiced and efficient movements. He pushed the passenger seat all the way back, creating a makeshift sniper's nest. Then he positioned the rifle on a rested bipod.

The driver watched for interference that might happen on the street and kept track of Zabrinski.

The driver and the shooter worked like a well synchronized team now, anticipating and performing the practiced choreography.

The shooter peered through his scope, adjusting the focus. Zabrinski was now in the crosshairs, seemingly unaware of the imminent danger.

The crosshair settled on Zabrinski's chest, clearly marking his heart.

"Ready," the shooter whispered, finger resting lightly.

The driver nodded.

They both knew the plan, knew what was about to happen. It was too late to stop, to drive away and forget this ever happened.

Even if they'd wanted to stop.

Which they didn't.

Stick to the plan.

The shooter steadied his breathing, watching through the scope.

Zabrinski reached for another box. His movements were slow and methodical. Which made him an easy target. Much too easy, really. There was no challenge to this one. None at all.

Zabrinski paused. A slight frown creased his forehead as if he sensed something amiss. He turned slightly, looking down the street.

His gaze passed over the white van without a flicker of recognition or concern.

The shooter wondered how this guy had survived for forty-eight years when better men had died. He seemed as oblivious to his surroundings as a tree stump.

The shooter hesitated. A flicker. No more.

But it was enough. The perfect moment passed.

"Wait," the driver reached out and gripped the shooter's arm.

The younger man turned—his eyes cold, dangerous.

"What are you doing?" he hissed angrily.

"Look," the driver said, pointing toward the sidewalk near the back of the truck. "A kid."

A beat of silence followed, stretched taut with tension.

The kid, maybe twelve years old, emerged from the community center to chat with Zabrinski. A cursory glance was all it took to see they came from the same gene pool.

Zabrinski's kid stood directly in the line of fire.

Which meant the shooter lost his perfect shot.

Or he could hit them both.

Easy enough. He'd made double taps before. Spiced things up a bit.

Yes. That would work. Stop the Zabrinski gene pool right here and now. Do the world a favor.

The shooter prepared to squeeze the trigger.

Without warning, the driver grabbed his arm again and yanked him away from the window.

"Stick to the plan," he snarled.

The shooter's rage boiled over. He abandoned the rifle and lunged at the driver.

His hands reached for the driver's throat. The van's old springs rocked with the sudden violence, but the sounds of struggle were muffled by the closed windows.

"What the hell is wrong with you?" the shooter whispered angrily, giving the driver a hard elbow to the ribs.

All the air expelled from the driver's lungs, leaving him doubled over in his seat and unable to reply. He gasped in pain as the shooter turned toward the window again to reposition and set up his shot.

Outside, Zabrinski's head turned toward the van. He squinted, trying to make sense of the shapes he couldn't see through the tinted windows.

The shooter watched carefully through the scope. Zabrinski must have imagined that something was wrong. Like he could feel it in his bones, or some damned Army crap.

"Come closer, you old fool," the shooter whispered under his breath as Zabrinski took a step toward the van.

Zabrinski reached into his pocket, his fingers fisted around a small object. Probably that stupid can of pepper spray he often carried. Like a can of damned pepper spray could defend against the rifle.

"Moron," the shooter muttered.

The kid was still standing near the truck. Still in the line of fire.

"Come on, Zabrinski," the shooter said under his breath. "Just a few more steps."

The driver had regained his ability to speak through his bruised vocal cords. "Don't hit the kid. I mean it. You hit the kid and I'm done."

"Shut the hell up," the shooter snarled, slowly moving his finger into position.

The driver pushed his arm just as the shooter squeezed the trigger.

A single, deafening shot exploded in the confined space.

The bullet tore through the van's thin metal wall like paper.

Outside, Zabrinski, who had only taken that first step toward the van, felt what must have been a searing pain explode in his shoulder.

He staggered back, his eyes wide with shock, as a warm rush of blood soaked through his shirt.

The pepper spray fell from his hand, clattering to the pavement.

In the van, the shot brought a momentary halt to the argument.

Both men froze, the reality of what had happened dawning on them.

The driver, eyes wide with horror, stared at the shooter.

The shooter froze in place.

The older man recovered first. He lifted his foot off the brake pedal and rolled the van away from the scene, using an eighteen-wheeler passing on the opposite side to block Zabrinski's view.

The shooter held the rifle ready just in case he needed a second shot.

As the van pulled away, he saw Zabrinski, clutching his wounded shoulder, climb off the pavement and stumble forward, leaving a trail of blood behind him.

When he reached the young boy's body, blood oozing from a head wound, dead eyes wide open, Zabrinski crumpled onto the pavement next to the boy.

Back in the van, the driver pushed the shooter toward the back of the van. "Get in the back. Get that rifle down. Now!"

The van took the first turn off the main drag. The side street headed south.

He kept the accelerator steady, traveling just below the speed limit. The last thing they needed was to be stopped for speeding.

A dead child and a wounded man outside and the police undoubtedly on their way. The driver shook his head and steadied his grip on the steering wheel.

A siren wailed in the distance, growing louder with each passing second. The shooter, peering out through the van's back windows, saw flashing lights approaching fast.

The driver cursed under his breath.

When they reached the next intersection, he jerked the steering wheel left, headed east, away from the scene.

"Hold on," he said, both hands gripping the wheel tighter. He floored the accelerator and the van lurched forward, tires screeching against the pavement.

When they reached the county road south of town, he turned again heading away from the community center as fast as he dared to go. The turn was too sharp and too fast.

The shooter fell off his feet and rolled over on the floor in the back of the van. When he hit the side panel he began to laugh maniacally.

The driver scowled but ignored the commotion and kept his focus firmly on the road.

CHAPTER 17

Sunday, June 19
Quantico, Virginia

"LET'S TURN TO THE Gunston murder now," Dr. Debrew said, gesturing Kim and Smithers to positions on either side of the screen to allow them an unobstructed view. She began with a slideshow of images reflecting the Gunston murder scene. Each view was closer to the victim.

"This is Gunston's neighborhood. You can see the position of his home amid the usual grid pattern of the best houses on the outskirts of small American towns." Debrew's laser pointer circled Gunston's colonial style building.

The painted two-story structure was centered on a one-acre parcel surrounded by other big dwellings of similar style on similarly large lots. The homes were far enough apart for seclusion and privacy.

Set back more than fifty feet from the sidewalk, surrounded by generous green lawns and well-designed flowerbeds on all sides, the Gunston home was picture perfect. *Better Homes and Gardens* might have featured the place on some sort of annual list.

The wide, paved driveway was on the south side of the lot, leading to a garage behind the house. A late model black Mercedes sedan resembling a hearse was parked there. The car's passenger door stood wide open.

"That's Gunston's sedan. He'd just returned home from work. The daughter was waiting inside the car when her father was gunned down," Kim said, repeating what she'd read in the file. "She didn't witness the hit."

Debrew's next slide was a drone's-eye view of the body, showing its position in relationship to the house and the car. Her laser pointer demonstrated as she explained the crime scene.

"The daughter came outside through the front door first. Judge Gunston followed moments behind her. He hurried across the porch and down the steps. He avoided the flowerbed and strode across the lawn toward the car where she was waiting."

Smithers said quietly, staring as the next slide moved into place. "Easy target in that pink shirt, too."

Debrew further described the scene specifically, including measurements and distances. The gist of it was that Gunston had been felled by a single precise gunshot to the head.

"Not an easy thing to accomplish, even for me," Kim said, with no false modesty. She was one of the best shooters in the FBI and had the medals to prove it. She was justifiably proud of the accomplishment.

At just under five feet tall and slightly less than one hundred pounds, the only way she could do the job was to be better than her opponents expected. She'd spent much of her career developing and honing the skills that made her formidable and kept her alive.

She made no excuses for her extreme expertise. But she knew what was required to achieve it.

Hours of practice with that specific rifle and those bullets, under similar weather conditions, allowed this shooter to take one shot resulting in a kill that looked effortless but was not.

His ability to take Gunston out like that meant the shooter was a pro.

Where did he get the necessary training and practice? Finding the answers might lead to the killer.

"Do we have ballistics yet?" Smithers asked.

"Not much, so far." The next slide was a close shot to demonstrate Debrew's answer. "They recovered this bullet embedded in the porch. It's a .223 caliber fired from a rifle. Possibly a Bushmaster, which is common for hunters in the area."

"What about the velocity of the bullet?" Kim asked.

"Good question." Debrew gave her an appreciative glance. "The exit wound suggests the bullet's speed places the shooter one- to two-hundred yards away from the target. Depending on the weapon."

"Reasonably close, then. And the angle of entry and exit?" Kim prompted. "What can we tell about that?"

"Gunston was six feet, two inches tall," Debrew said, shooting a red laser beam into the wound on the screen to show the angle of entry and exit. "The shooter would have aimed from a prone, seated, or kneeling position."

"Which means the shooter was elevated," Kim replied, rubbing the tension gathering at the back of her neck.

She visualized the imagined location, the shooter's position, the weight of the rifle, the slow squeeze of the trigger. In her mind's eye, she saw the bullet hit the target and watched the victim fall.

"Right. Positioned himself on a hill or on top of a stand of some sort. Something that gave him a clear vantage point, but allowed him to leave quickly without being noticed," Debrew nodded as if Kim were a particularly apt pupil.

"Gunston looks like he just crumpled to the ground, mid-stride," Smithers observed. "Poor bastard never saw it coming."

"Definitely a calculated hit. The shooter knew Gunston's routine. Knew when and where to strike. Knew where he could set up to get precisely the correct conditions," Kim said, searching the images on the screen as if something in the photos would give her more intel.

"Anybody figure out the location of the sniper's nest?" Smithers asked.

Debrew shook her head. "They're looking, but nothing yet. Not as far as I know."

"Okay. Anything else we should know for now?" Kim asked, squeezing her eyes closed briefly to clear her vision.

"Yeah. One more thing," Debrew said, shutting down the slideshow. "The bullet is not standard manufacture. It matches nothing in our databases."

"Meaning what?" Smithers asked.

"Meaning our shooter is sophisticated, organized, and well trained," Kim said, giving Smithers a steady look.

"So you're thinking he was armed forces or law enforcement," Smithers replied flatly.

Kim reached into her pocket for an antacid to calm her thrashing stomach and said nothing.

"It's possible the bullet was custom-made either for the shooter specifically or for a specialty shop where he bought it," Debrew said, handing Kim a sheet of paper. "Here's a specific description and a list of possible manufacturers who could have created a bullet like that. You might get lucky."

Kim's phone vibrated in her pocket. She glanced at the screen and walked away to a quiet corner to pick up the call. "Otto."

Cooper said, "They've got a possible witness to the Gunston shooting. They're holding her at the sheriff's office. How soon can you head up there?"

"We're done here. But it's a ten-hour drive, at least. We can get there tomorrow morning if we sleep in the car. Unless you can get us on a jet sooner," she replied. "But Bristol isn't exactly a hot spot. I'm guessing commercial flights are limited."

"Stand by. I'll call you back," he said and disconnected the call.

Kim handed her business card to Dr. Debrew. "Call us if you come up with anything else that might help. They've located a witness. We've got to go."

"I've given you everything we are likely to know for the next couple of days. We couldn't pull anything from the bullet itself. No DNA or prints or anything else. The bullet was too damaged," Debrew said, shaking hands as they passed her on the way through the door. "We'll finish and finalize the autopsy, but in this instance, tests on the body aren't likely to give us more than we already know."

Smithers walked on Kim's left as they headed through the lobby to the exit. "So that was Cooper on the phone?"

"Yeah. He wants us to go to Bristol. They might have a witness. The shooter is long gone," Kim said as she pushed through the glass door into the warm afternoon springtime.

"Maybe we can locate the sniper's nest. Forensics might be able to find something there," Smithers suggested reasonably as he stepped out behind her.

"Like what?" Kim asked.

"Tire tracks, shell casings, trash. Something we can lift DNA from."

Kim gave him a side-eye. She liked Smithers and he was no dummy. But they both knew this killer wasn't likely to leave trace evidence. He was way too sophisticated for mistakes like that.

Smithers was simply hoping to avoid the likely outcome. They'd go all the way to Bristol and find more of nothing.

"We need to get ahead of this guy instead of following behind him," Kim said.

"Agreed. How do you suggest we do that?" Smithers asked as they climbed into the SUV, and he started the engine.

Kim put her alligator clamp on the seatbelt retractor and settled in for the ride. "Cooper thinks Reacher is involved in this somehow. Or has a connection to the victims. Or the killer."

"That so?" Smithers widened his eyes in mock surprise and his eyebrows crawled up his forehead like two comic black caterpillars.

"What makes you say it like that?" Kim asked.

Smithers big laugh filled the cabin like a pounding drumbeat. "Come on, Otto. Give me some credit. Why would you be on this case if Reacher weren't connected here somehow?"

He had a point. And he was her partner. At least for now. And she liked him. No reason to keep secrets that he already knew anyway.

"Okay, yeah. That's the situation," Kim replied.

"You don't say," Smithers said sarcastically. "Back to my question. Tell me something I don't know. Is Reacher connected to the victims? Or the killer? Or both?"

Kim shrugged. "At this point, could go either way."

CHAPTER 18

Sunday, June 19
Bristol, New Hampshire

AT THE AIRPORT IN DC, they rushed through security and boarded a small jet to Manchester, New Hampshire.

The flight was uneventful, and they landed in Manchester, New Hampshire, in one piece. Cooper had arranged another black SUV. They located the vehicle and got on the road.

"The light is fading fast," Smithers said. "We won't see much."

"Yeah, we'll be here overnight. Hopefully, there's a couple of beds of some sort in the town," Kim replied. She pushed buttons on the navigation system to pull up local hotels. "Not much showing up on here. Which probably means the local places aren't paying for national advertising. Maybe the sheriff can help us. We'll ask him when we get there."

"Who is this guy? Got any intel on him?" Smithers asked.

"The sheriff? Or the witness?" Kim replied. "The answer is no to both. Unless Cooper sent something while we were in the air."

She pulled her satellite phone from her laptop and fired it up. There was a message and two files from Cooper. She read the message and then opened the laptop.

"You're gonna just keep me hanging here?" Smithers asked, relaxed in the driver's seat with one hand on the wheel.

"Sorry. Cooper sent two files. One is a quick bio on Sheriff Bernie Franklin. Elected to the position unopposed. For the past twenty years," Kim read the bio quickly and summarized the high points. "Previously army military police. Served in Germany, UK. No combat deployments, apparently. Went in for training, got it, left."

Smithers nodded. "Okay. What about the witness."

"Even less intel on her. All we have is her basic statistics. Julia Haverson. Forty-two years old. Single mother. Works at a local insurance office as a secretary," Kim summarized. "Lives with her elderly father a few doors down from the Gunston residence."

"What did she witness, exactly?"

"Cooper doesn't say," Kim replied. "That's how this usually works. He rarely gives me more information than he wants me to have. Claims he wants fresh eyes on the situation and doesn't want to prejudice my views."

"Uh, huh," Smithers replied skeptically. "Sheriff's office first?"

They were coming into the outskirts of town, headed along Main Street. The driveway to the Sheriff's office was on a side street. The turn was north at the end of the next block.

"Let's drive through and see the Gunston house first. It's not too dark yet to get a feel for the place. I'd like to get a first look, at least, before we talk to the witness."

"Your wish is my command," Smithers said with a grin. He rolled the SUV through town below the speed limit so they could get a look at the shops along the way.

The town was old. Established in the 1700s, according to the files Cooper sent. Red brick buildings, mostly. But the paint was fresh enough and the sidewalks were in good repair.

Angled parking spots on both sides of the streets were mostly vacant late on Sunday night. But there were a couple of bars in town and a few patrons must have been inside.

In short, nothing out of the ordinary about the town that Kim could see.

The sun had set a while ago, but the summer solstice was only two days away. The longest day of the year. About fifteen hours of daylight, this far north. Kim figured it would stay light enough until ten or eleven o'clock.

When she was a kid in Michigan, she and her siblings had loved the long spring and summer evenings. Bristol, too, seemed like the kind of place where people would take advantage of any chance for outdoor activity, even when the temperatures were still cooler.

"This is it," Smithers said as he parked the SUV along the curb on the quiet, tree-lined street. The Gunston's colonial-style house with its white clapboard siding and neatly trimmed hedges seemed well tended and prosperous. Lights were on inside the house.

There was no crime scene tape or other obvious signs that a murder had been committed there. The black Mercedes was still parked in the driveway.

"Two days," Smithers muttered as he looked at the house. "It's been two days since the judge was killed. The place looks unchanged."

"But for his family, nothing will ever be the same," Kim said her expression tight. "And there's not a damned thing we can do about that, either."

The house felt somber, and a sense of unease hung in the air.

Mrs. Peggy Gunston, a woman in her mid-forties, opened the door. She wore a pained expression, her eyes bearing the weight of recent tragedy.

"Agents," she said with a tremor in her voice, inviting them inside.

The interior of the house was a blend of classic and contemporary, with colonial-style furniture juxtaposed against modern accents. Kim and Smithers followed Mrs. Gunston to the kitchen, where a wooden table with a vase of fresh flowers stood at the center.

Smithers spoke gently, breaking the silence that had settled over them. "Mrs. Gunston, we're here to find out what happened on the morning of your husband's death."

Peggy Gunston nodded, her eyes filling with tears. "It happened so fast," she began, her voice quivering. "Matt came home early because of Melody's soccer game. He's one of her coaches. He was here just a few minutes to change and then they went out to the car. She was excited for the game and hurried ahead to wait for him. I was in the kitchen when they left, preparing dinner."

Kim leaned forward, her gaze compassionate. "Can you tell us if you noticed anything unusual in the days leading up to the shooting?"

Peggy took a moment to collect her thoughts. "Well, there was this man who came to the house. We don't get many strangers here. He said he was friends with Matt from Boston. He wanted to schedule a time when Matt would be home to come over. But he wanted it to be a surprise."

"What did you tell him?" Kim asked.

She widened her eyes and shook her head, looking bewildered. "He was asking about Matt's daily routine. You know, when did he leave for work, and when did he come home, and did he work weekends. Things like that."

Smithers talked as if he were gentling a wild pony. "Did this man leave a name or any contact information?"

Peggy shook her head. "No, he didn't. He seemed perfectly normal. Do you think he had something to do with what happened?"

Kim exchanged a look with Smithers. "What did he look like?"

She scrunched her brow and pressed her lips to think. "Young. I'm not good with ages. Maybe in his twenties? Brown hair. Normal looking. No tattoos or piercings or anything like that."

"What was he wearing?" Kim asked.

Peggy did the squinting thing again. "Jeans, I think. A hoodie. Sneakers. You know, the kind of things young people wear. A baseball cap. That's all I can think of."

Smithers nodded and continued the conversation. "Mrs. Gunston, can you tell us what happened on the morning of the shooting?"

Peggy wiped away a tear and began recounting the events as if she'd already told the story too many times. "Like I said, Matt was walking toward his black Mercedes, and Melody was already in the car. I was watching from the doorway when... when I heard the gunshot."

"You're sure it was a gunshot?" Smithers asked. "Only one?"

Peggy nodded, twisting her fingers together in her lap. "There are a lot of hunters around here. I hunt myself from time to time. Matt, too. I know what gunshots sound like. Yes. Only one."

Kim leaned forward, her voice gentle. "Did you see anyone? Or notice anything unusual before you heard the shot?"

Peggy's gaze turned distant as she struggled with the effort to recall. "Earlier in the day, I saw a van across the street, in the woods. It was parked there, hidden away. But I didn't think much of it at the time."

Smithers pressed for more details. "Can you describe the van, Mrs. Gunston? Anything you remember, no matter how small, could be helpful."

"It was white," Peggy replied, her brows furrowing as she strained to remember. "I couldn't see the license plate or the driver. It was almost hidden by the trees. Later in the summer, when the trees were leafed out more, I wouldn't have seen it at all."

Smithers gave Kim a quick glance. Two other witnesses had reported seeing a white van speeding away from the scene after the murder. Peggy was the third.

"Do you know who owned the van? Had you ever seen it before?" Smithers asked.

Peggy shook her head, tears leaking from her eyes.

Kim shifted the focus. "After you heard the shot, what did you do?"

Peggy's voice trembled as she continued. "Nothing really. Like I said, there are a lot of hunters around here. The shot sounded like it came from a distance. I-I didn't know Matt had been hit."

"When did you realize your husband was down?"

"M-Melody came running in, shouting that her daddy had been shot." Peggy squeezed more tears from her eyes. "I ran out to check on Matt, but he was a-already gone. I tried to shield Melody. She became hysterical. Kicking, screaming. I could barely hold onto her."

Peggy's voice faded and she cleared her throat before she continued. "The police arrived, and an ambulance came. But there was nothing they could do. It was too late. Not with a shot like that. Matt was gone before he hit the ground."

Kim leaned back, absorbing the information and sifting through what she'd learned before she arrived, trying to put the pieces together.

Smithers nodded and placed a reassuring hand on Peggy's arm before he asked, "Did your husband mention any recent threats or concerns that might help us figure out what happened here?"

Peggy shook her head, tears glistening in her eyes. "No, nothing. Matt was a good judge. He took the work seriously. People liked him. He was re-elected twice. Some of his cases were hard, but he was just doing his job. He never mentioned any particular problems. He didn't like to bring his work home with him."

Kim stood, pulling a business card from her pocket. She handed the card to Mrs. Gunston. "Thank you for helping us. We're sorry to intrude. Please call me if you think of anything else that might be useful."

Peggy took the card and nodded woefully, and more tears ran silently down her cheeks.

"No way that guy was a friend of Gunston's," Kim said when they were outside again. "Let's see if Sheriff Franklin is still at the station."

"Okay," Smithers replied, using the remote to open the SUV's front doors.

CHAPTER 19

Sunday, June 19
Bristol, New Hampshire

AFTER THE SHORT DRIVE to the police station, they convened in the cozy, dimly lit office at the Bristol sheriff's department.

Sheriff Franklin, a stocky man with salt-and-pepper hair, sat behind a cluttered desk piled high with files and coffee-stained mugs. His weathered face displayed a mix of emotions that Kim figured were equal parts frustration and determination.

Kim began the conversation by handing him her card. He took it without reading it and tossed it aside.

"I've got enough FBI cards to organize a poker game already," he said. "Why do I need two more?"

Bristol was a small town. Judges worked closely with law enforcement in places like this. She figured Franklin and Gunston must have been at least friendly neighbors, if not close friends.

Her tone was professional yet empathetic. "Sheriff Franklin, thanks for inviting us into the Gunston case. We're here to assist with the investigation team and help you bring those responsible to justice."

Franklin sighed, his gaze fixed on the wall of commendations behind Kim and Smithers. "It's a real tragedy. Matt Gunston was a pillar of this community. Everybody knew him. Liked him. Voted for him. We'll do everything we can to get to the bottom of this as quickly as possible."

Smithers nodded. "We understand the gravity of the situation. Can you tell us what your team has uncovered so far?"

"Not much, I'm afraid. And I've already shared it with the other agents." Franklin leaned forward, his expression tense. "Briefly, we've been canvassing the neighborhood, house to house, questioning witnesses. We found a few people who heard the gunshot, but no one saw the shooter. No time, really."

Kim continued, "We spoke with Mrs. Gunston. She mentioned a stranger who came to the house and asked about her husband's routines. Have you looked into that?"

The sheriff scratched his chin thoughtfully. "Yeah, we have. Guy went to Gunston's house, but he also asked around at local businesses. We've been trying to track him down, but so far, no luck. No one seems to know who he is or where he came from or even what he really wanted. All we know for sure is that he's no longer in Bristol."

Smithers paused a moment before he asked, "What about the white van near the scene of the shooting? Three witnesses, including Mrs. Gunston, reported seeing the van in the woods across the street. Did your team find anything useful at that location?"

Franklin leaned back in his chair, running splayed fingers through his hair in frustration. "We did find tire tracks leading to an elevated spot in the woods across from the Gunston house. It looks like that could be where the shooter was positioned. But we found no hard evidence left at the site. The shooter appears to have stayed contained inside the van. After they killed Gunston, they seem to have simply vanished."

"They?" Kim exchanged a glance with Smithers. "So the shooter had an accomplice. Someone driving the van."

"Why do you say that?"

"Because the van got out of here so quickly. One man acting alone would have been slower," Kim said, thinking about the logistics. "Means the shooter was both skilled and cautious. And he's not alone."

Smithers asked, "How many witnesses reported seeing the van leaving the area? Anybody get even a partial plate number? Can they tell us which direction it took? Have you checked the traffic cams?"

"A couple of folks mentioned hearing the van's engine as it sped away, but it's a dead end from there." The sheriff's words were terse. Like this was eating him alive. "We couldn't get a clear description of the vehicle or the direction it went. There're no traffic cams on our backroads. And most folks don't have cameras on their homes and businesses like people who live in a city. We all know each other here. Crime rate is virtually zero."

"Right," Kim agreed because there was nothing to be gained by pointing out that crime happens everywhere, not just in heavily populated areas. "So where else can we look?"

Franklin said, "We might be able to find the van on video from the cams once it hit the interstate, but we haven't contacted anyone about that yet. We've been trying to keep this low-key as long as possible. Last thing Peggy Gunston needs is to have Melody hounded by media every minute."

Kim made a mental note to get the traffic cam search going before she took a deep breath and nodded. "Sheriff, we'd like to examine the sniper's nest in the woods. It's pretty dark out there by now. Do you have flood lights set up?"

"Yeah. We do. But you won't see much tonight. Tomorrow would be better," Sheriff Franklin suggested. Kim didn't agree and he caught the vibe. "I'll have one of my deputies accompany you to the site if you want to go out there now. You won't be able to find it by yourself."

"We'd appreciate that," Kim said.

Franklin sighed. "Okay. Maybe you'll spot something we missed. But you'll probably need to wait for daylight."

Kim didn't argue, but she didn't back down, either. Franklin gave in gracefully. He called in a deputy and told him what to do.

With the deputy in the driver's seat, they arrived at the wooded area where the shooter was believed to have been located. The thick trees cast long shadows in the darkness as they left the vehicle and ventured deliberately into the dense underbrush.

Deputy Daniels led the way with his flashlight beam cutting through the gloom. They followed the tracks that had been discovered earlier, which led them to a small clearing atop a slight hill.

In the clearing, they found a secluded spot that provided an unobstructed view of Judge Gunston's front yard.

"We think they waited here," Daniels said. "Based on the tire tracks we found."

Kim pulled out the flashlight on her phone and scanned for signs that the shooter or his van had been there.

"This could be the spot," she murmured, pointing to Gunston's porch light in the distance. "There's a clear sight line from here to the point where Gunston was hit."

Smithers nodded and turned to Daniels. "Did your team collect any evidence here?"

Daniels shook his head. "We looked. Found nothing much. No shell casings, fingerprints, broken branches, footprints, trash. Nothing."

Kim crouched down to examine the ground. She brushed over fallen leaves and twigs, moving the flashlight around as she looked. "Had to be professionals. It's not easy to set up and kill like that while leaving no trace behind."

Smithers leaned against a nearby tree facing the Gunston house. "Sheriff Franklin mentioned that there were no witnesses to the incident itself, only those who noticed things before and after the fatal shot."

"That's right. We've done interviews of everyone in town." Daniels nodded. "Three people reported hearing a single gunshot, in addition to Mrs. Gunston. One saw the judge fall. But no one saw the shooter or made out any details about the van, either before or after."

"Did you interview the daughter? Melody Gunston?" Kim asked.

"Yeah. She was a mess. She didn't see anything until her dad was already down. Blames herself for not being more observant," Daniels said. "But she's just a kid. She was excited to get to her soccer game. No way should she have been looking for snipers in the trees."

"Right." Kim glanced around the clearing once more, her analytical mind at work. "This was very bold. Broad daylight. Spring afternoon. People out and about. They pull in here bold as brass, shoot the guy and leave. No one sees anything."

"Balls of steel," Daniels said quietly. "Like Franklin said."

"Before the shot, people wouldn't have been looking for them. But afterward? Everyone should have been looking. Worried they might shoot again if nothing else," Kim said. "We need to figure out how these two managed to disappear so quickly."

"They weren't invisible. Just fast. And smart." Smithers paused before he added, "And the van *was* seen speeding away from the scene, but no one realized there were two people inside. Or that the shooter was one of them."

Daniels chimed in, "It's like we're chasing ghosts now. Nothing."

Smithers said, "This team knew exactly what they were doing. This isn't the work of an amateur or a pair of first timers."

"They're well trained, sure," Kim nodded, her expression tense. "They've done this before. Probably more than once."

Daniels chimed in, "And they disappeared without anyone getting a good look at them or the van. It's like they knew exactly when to strike and how to vanish."

"Which means recon, at a minimum. Some kind of surveillance, too." Kim felt the knot of tension tighten in her belly. "Whoever they are, they're determined. And they'll strike again."

"Because they got away with it," Daniels said dully.

Smithers said, "We need to find out who this shooter is, what their motive is, and why Judge Gunston was targeted. When we have those answers, we'll be able to stop them."

"We'll come back in daylight for a better look." Kim stood and dusted her hands off. "I just wanted to get a feel for things tonight. Let's find a hotel and get some dinner."

Daniels said, "Tucker's Diner is good. The Tucker Inn is next door. That's about the best we've got here in Bristol."

"Thanks. That'll work great," Kim replied. "Do we need to call ahead?"

"Nope. They'll have rooms. Sheriff Franklin told them you'd be coming," Daniels said as he slipped behind the wheel and drove carefully along the trail to the street.

Daniels dropped them off at their SUV with directions to The Tucker Inn. After they checked in and washed up, Smithers and Kim walked next door to Tucker's Diner.

CHAPTER 20

Sunday, June 19
Bristol, New Hampshire

TUCKER'S DINER HAD A warm, cozy vibe. Neon signs cast a warm glow through the large windows. Even at this late hour, the aroma of sizzling bacon and freshly brewed coffee filled the air. People were too hyped up to go home and lie awake.

They were greeted by a buzz of conversation as a dozen locals huddled in small groups, sipping coffee and sharing stories. The atmosphere was filled with a mixture of curiosity and apprehension, as the seriousness of the case had begun to soak into the townspeople.

The sign at the hostess stand said, "Please seat yourself."

As they walked toward and settled into a corner booth, a dozen conversations hushed to near total silence.

"Looks like the whole town is in here," Kim said, offering a nod of greeting to a couple of diners who looked up and met her steady gaze. People wanting to reassure themselves that their town and their neighbors would eventually be okay again.

Smithers leaned in, keeping his voice low. "We need to gather as much information as we can. They might have seen or heard something without realizing it."

"Okay. I'll take the left side of the room." Kim nodded in agreement as she approached a group of elderly men at a round table playing poker.

They looked like locals who'd probably lived in Bristol for decades. Four men who had the appearances of grizzled veterans. She guessed they could easily have served in Vietnam. They were the right age, anyway.

If she could break the silence with them, the others might be more forthcoming.

Kim initiated the conversation by introducing herself and showing her ID. They offered wary nods in return. The sounds of frying food and clanging plates carried from the kitchen in the back through the silence.

Kim said, "Sheriff Franklin asked us to assist his investigation of the murder of Judge Gunston, and we could use your help. Did you know Matt Gunston?"

One of the men snorted. "Course we knew him. Knew his dad, too. Fine man. Served with him."

"Army?" Kim asked and four gray heads nodded knowingly. "Have any of you heard about a stranger asking questions about the judge recently?"

One of the men folded his cards and spoke up. "I did hear about that. Folks were talkin' 'bout a fella they didn't recognize askin' about Matt's routines and such. I didn't see him myself, though."

Kim pressed for more details. "Do you know who this stranger might be or if anyone got a good look at him?"

Another man piped up. "Young. Maybe twenty-five or so, give or take. Respectful, people said. Like maybe he'd been taught some manners."

Kim exhausted their limited knowledge of the crime and moved on to the next table. Smithers was making the rounds on the other side of the diner. After about twenty minutes, they'd covered everyone.

When Kim returned to their table, Smithers was already there. The waitress brought coffee and took their orders, giving them a few moments to discuss what they'd learned.

"Like most small towns," Smithers said, "everybody seems to know everything, and it's all the same. Place like this, they know all the characters, and all see the same film."

Kim grinned. She grew up in a town like this, too. She knew exactly what Smithers meant. "A neighbor was watering his flowers. He mentioned hearing the single gunshot and then seeing Judge Gunston fall."

"Yeah, a few told me they hadn't witnessed the shooting, but they gave me the same story about what the neighbor saw."

Kim replied, "I got the same sort of stuff. One of their neighbors recalled seeing the unfamiliar white van parked in the woods a few hours before the murder, but no one I spoke to actually saw it themselves. Same with the stranger who had been asking about the judge. All hearsay. No firsthand knowledge."

"Yeah, a teenager mentioned to his parents that he had noticed the same stranger at a gas station and a local diner a few days prior to the murder," Smithers said. "He had overheard the stranger's inquiries and found them peculiar."

"Of course, no one in the diner right now is the neighbor or the teenager," Kim said, wagging her head.

"Right," Smithers replied. "But it confirms what we've been told and shortens our work for tomorrow. Did you get anything else?"

"The owner of a convenience store mentioned receiving a strange phone call before the murder," Kim said after a big gulp of coffee. "The caller claimed to be a friend of Judge Gunston. Said he was running late. Wanted to know what time Gunston got home from work."

"Why ask the convenience store guy about that?" Smithers cocked his head and frowned.

"Confirmation, I suspect," Kim shrugged. "The caller knew they were golfing buddies. The store owner said the guy sounded all friendly, like he knew Gunston, too, and wanted to meet up with him."

Smithers's frown deepened. "At least three people claim to have heard or seen the van speeding away after the shot was fired. It left the woods and headed south, they said. No one recognized it or got a plate."

"Or saw the driver or passenger, I guess," Kim said, swiping a palm over her face.

The waitress delivered their burgers and refilled the coffee, barely interrupting the conversation. When she left, they ate in silence, thinking things through.

"Okay. Let's get some sleep. I'll report to Cooper. Maybe he's found something else we can work with. We'll reconnect in the morning and interview Franklin's witness," Kim said as Smithers tossed a couple of twenties on the table and they made their way outside.

They walked silently toward the inn until Kim said, "The shooter wasn't taking any chances. He had studied Gunston's movements. Confirmed his information at least twice with at least three witnesses, and maybe more."

"Absolutely. There was no element of luck involved in this murder. None at all. One sure shot. One and done," Smithers said. "Gunston walked right into it, poor bastard."

"Balls of steel," Kim echoed the deputy's words while she opened the door and walked inside the inn, where they split up. "Breakfast at oh eight hundred."

"See you there," Smithers said as he headed down the corridor to his room.

Kim watched him go inside and then slipped into her room while she fished Cooper's phone out of her pocket and pressed the redial.

"Where are you?" Cooper asked without any sort of civilized greeting.

"Where you sent me. Bristol, New Hampshire. Why?" Kim asked as she plopped down on the bed and kicked her shoes off.

"We've got another victim," Cooper said. "Hit by a sniper who shot from a white van and then took off."

"At least the method is similar enough that it suggests the same killer as Gunston. Where did it happen?" Kim closed her eyes and kneaded the tension headache coming on with a vengeance.

"This afternoon. New Slope, New York."

"I don't suppose you've got any good news," Kim said sourly.

"Sure I do. Good news is the intended target, Harold Zabrinski, didn't die. He'll be out of surgery and awake soon. You need to reach him before they try again," Cooper said. "I'm sending you the files now. Best way to get there is to drive. Take you about five hours. Leave now, and you'll be there before dawn."

"We're not done here. We haven't even examined the crime scene in daylight. Or talked to the witnesses. And we need to sleep," Kim objected, but Cooper had already disconnected the call.

Wearily, she dry-chewed a couple of Tylenol while setting up her secure hot spot and firing up her laptop. She connected to her private server and downloaded Cooper's files on Zabrinski.

He'd also included a list of victims, which now had four names on it.

One survivor, and three dead.

The youngest death was a twelve-year-old kid also named Zabrinski. Harold, Jr.

Kim shook her head. She'd seen too many children shot and killed since she'd joined the FBI. Most were gang-related murders. A few were mass shootings. Others were domestic violence or, even more sadly, suicides.

What could this boy have done to make him a target? Or was he in the wrong place at the wrong time?

Cooper had also listed two witnesses who saw a white van speeding away from the scene of the Zabrinski shooting.

The common thread for the Gunston and Zabrinski murders was the sniper's white van and shooting precision. It meant at least the last two deaths were probably executed by the same shooter.

Which was the first solid evidence that a serial killer was in play.

But nothing connected these two murders to Sheryl Tardelli.

Or to Reacher.

Kim closed her eyes and asked aloud, as if hearing the questions would trigger the answers. "Why does Cooper think Reacher is involved in all of this? What does Cooper know that he's not telling me here?"

She flipped through the pages of her meticulous reports, hoping to find a detail she'd ignored before. Nothing caught her attention.

She paused when Marilyn Stone's photo popped onto the screen. She was an attractive woman, but definitely not Reacher's usual type.

Marilyn Stone was older, for one thing. More mature. She didn't work in law enforcement, and she wasn't a cop or a veteran.

What was her connection to Reacher? And why was she off-limits to Kim?

Cooper had told her to stay away from Stone in no uncertain terms.

Which meant Stone knew something Cooper didn't want Kim to get out of her.

Without violating Cooper's direct order, Kim couldn't simply ask Stone what she knew.

Which wasn't the problem. She didn't worry much about staying on Cooper's good side these days.

No, the problem was that Cooper would be watching Stone's every move now that he was aware of her meddling.

If Kim approached Stone now, Cooper would know. Instantly.

Which meant he'd put the smackdown on whatever she tried to accomplish before she even had a chance to do anything. He might even move Stone to keep her away from Kim if he thought it necessary.

So Kim would get only one chance to follow up with Marilyn Stone. She wanted to keep her powder dry until she knew for sure she could make effective use of the intel.

She stood to stretch the kinks out of her muscles, considering all the angles she could reasonably assume. No flashes of brilliance occurred to her tired brain.

How could she find out what Stone knew without approaching the woman?

She grinned when she remembered Curry. "There's always a way."

In this case, the easy way back to Marilyn Stone was through the investigator. Curry had been looking for Reacher before he settled on the idea of contacting Kim. Of course Marilyn would have told him whatever she knew about Reacher that might help to locate him.

Kim's assumption was simple. What Marilyn Stone knew, Curry knew, too. At least, whatever Stone knew about Reacher.

And Curry might have observed other things about Reacher that Marilyn Stone wouldn't have noticed. He was a cop. He'd worked twenty-five years for NYPD. He had skills, including observation and investigation skills Kim could exploit.

"No time like the present," she mumbled as she found a new burner phone in her bag and ripped it out of the plastic bubble.

She plugged the phone into the outlet to charge while she dug through her pockets for Curry's business card.

CHAPTER 21

Sunday, June 19
Rural Vermont

THE CLOCK CHIMED MIDNIGHT in Nora Ramsey's office, which felt like a punctuation mark to her solitude. She raised her head to stretch and take a sip of warm whiskey.

Which was when she heard the heavy boots crunch on the gravel outside her open window. She wasn't expecting visitors.

She reached into the drawer for her pistol. The grip felt cool against her skin.

She stood and walked silently toward the securely locked exit door.

The doorknob turned, but the door didn't budge. She raised the gun and aimed. If he came through, she would shoot to kill.

A light rap of knuckles against the heavy wood sounded next. Automatic flood lights shot through the darkness as bright as an intense carbon klieg spotlight.

He'd be blinded for a few seconds. Now was her chance.

Nora moved swiftly to the door. She called out. "Who's there?"

"It's John," he said, stepping to the right to allow her to see him through the door's sidelight. His voice was even, his blue eyes steady behind the shield of a palm as big as a grizzly's paw. "We need to talk about Makinde."

She lowered her gun, unlocked the door, and stood aside. "What's happened?"

He stepped across the threshold and closed the door behind him, flipping the lock on again.

He didn't waste time trying to explain. Instead, he slid a cell phone from his pocket and tapped the screen to life. "Let me show you. It's faster."

On the screen, a dark, grainy video played. The image was jerky, and the colors washed out.

It showed a man gagged and bound, lying on the dirt floor of a dimly lit shack. She'd seen places like this before. It was the kind of hut found in the outskirts of Nigeria where the jungle began to reclaim the land.

The shaky camera panned to capture a window, bars silhouetted against the scant light, the sounds of the wilderness seeping through.

"He was on recon, just starting to dig into Makinde's operations for you at my request. They took him from his hotel room." John's jaw clenched as he recounted the details. "Drugged him, beat him up, dragged him to wherever that is. Tossed him on that filthy floor."

The video played, showing the man bound and helpless, moaning in pain.

A voice, distorted, delivered the ultimatum. "You have twelve hours. Otherwise, he dies."

The video ran a few seconds longer and then stopped.

"Makinde's made his move," John said. "He wants to send you a message through me."

"You think he was after me and when he failed, he went for your operative instead?"

"Don't you?"

Nora controlled her racing heart with sheer will and her voice remained cool. "And the message?"

"That he's in charge now. He's calling the shots. Not you." John pocketed the phone while holding her gaze. "You'd do well to take his message to heart. Double up on your security until I get this handled."

She placed her gun on the desk and picked up the whiskey with a shaking hand. She swigged the last of it and poured more. She offered the bottle to John, but he declined with a quick shake of his head.

"You're going to walk right into his hands?"

He met her gaze. His blue eyes like chips of ice. "He should be careful what he asks for."

Nora folded her arms. "And what is that?"

"Me as the target," John replied. "What he won't expect is what comes after."

"What did your man find out? He learned something, didn't he? Otherwise Makinde wouldn't bother with him. Or with you," Nora said.

"If they kill him, we'll never know."

"You're going to Nigeria then?"

"Makinde's not there and it's Makinde I want," he said, shaking his head. "I sent a team. If they fail, then I'll go."

A shiver ran through her. "You think Makinde is here, then. In the US."

"He's here in Vermont. Confirmed," John said. "I came here to let you know why you won't be able to reach me for a while. I'll be offline and off comms."

"And you think you can just walk into Makinde's trap with no consequences?" she asked with sharp incredulity.

"Of course not. There will be consequences. Which is why I'm letting you know. A courtesy." John's eyes were hard as he met her stare. "I don't have a choice. I can't let them kill my team. You think Makinde will stop with one man, if I let him get away with this?"

She shook her head. "You're walking into a death trap."

"I can do two things at once." John's gaze didn't waver. "We'll get my man out. Take him home. And I'll find out what Makinde's got going on that's worth baiting me for."

Nora's fingers brushed the cool surface of her desk. "You have backup?"

"Always," he said, though the line of his mouth suggested he'd do this alone.

She exhaled, a decision forming like steel in her spine. "I'll arrange support. I've got operations in Nigeria. My contacts can be trusted."

"Appreciated." He gave a nod, the barest dip of his head, and moved toward the door. "But tell them to stay out of our way."

"John." She said his name to anchor him, to pull him back from the ledge he was ready to walk off. "I need Makinde alive. I've been working on this for years. If we lose Makinde, I don't have the wherewithal to start over. He knows that. Which is his leverage."

John paused, a statue in the doorway. "When I find Makinde, I'll make sure he understands that he'll be cooperating with you indefinitely."

She allowed herself another moment's indecision and then made her choice. "Makinde has a place in Manhattan. If he or his men were the ones who tried to capture me, they're probably staying there."

"Do you have an address?"

She jotted it down and handed it to him. He gave the note a quick glance and tossed it into the fire.

"I'll keep you posted," he promised as the door shut behind him, leaving Nora alone again with the pale blue glow of her computer screen.

She reached for the phone. Her slim network of allies in Nigeria was a lifeline she was about to pull tight.

She dialed and waited. When he picked up, she gave orders to assist John's team clearly and concisely.

"Copy that," was the terse reply.

She'd had her SUV towed to a specialist. She wanted to know what the vehicle's black box had recorded of her harrowing escape in the woods last night. There could be video of the vehicle chasing her.

The expert had not called. She'd wait until morning. No longer.

CHAPTER 22

Monday, June 20
Bristol, New Hampshire

KIM PACED THE FLOOR and waited a dozen rings before the private investigator picked up her call.

"Yeah." Curry sounded distant but fully awake instead of roused from sleep. Which, given the hour, could have gone either way.

She heard no background noises and wondered where he might be at the moment.

She didn't immediately recognize his voice. "Curry?"

"Yeah."

"Kim Otto here. Got a minute?"

"Yeah."

Kim smiled. "If I didn't know better, I'd think your vocabulary was severely limited."

"Bad timing," he said, preoccupied. "I'm in the middle of something here. What's up?"

"I've changed my mind."

"About what?"

"Are you still in Key West?"

"No. We left soon after you did. Why?"

"You and Costello were colleagues. Worked together at NYPD."

"Yeah, so?"

"Costello was able to find Reacher…" she let her voice trail off suggestively.

"You trying to mess with me, Otto?"

"Just the opposite. I'm saying that Costello did a great job. I'm assuming he wasn't a better NYPD detective than you," she replied.

"Damned straight he wasn't," he replied laughing. "You trying to flatter me into helping you out after you left me with nothing in Key West?"

"I'm asking if you've found Costello's files and whether there's anything in there that might help us locate Reacher."

A long silence filled the space between them until he finally said, "I was actually wondering how long it would take you to ask me about that."

"So you have Costello's files," Kim confirmed. "I'd like to see them. Can you encrypt the files and send them to me?"

"No. We'll need to meet up for that. Costello was old school." Curry was still distracted, only half paying attention.

"What do you mean?"

"He liked hard copies. Didn't believe in digitizing and sending stuff off. Said once things went out of his hands, they'd land in places he didn't want them to go," Curry explained half-heartedly. "He used to say that 'internet privacy' had to be the biggest oxymoron on the planet."

"He wasn't wrong," Kim agreed, rubbing a palm over her weary eyes.

She considered another cup of coffee, but sleep was probably a smarter option. She'd turn in when she finished this phone call. Catch a few hours of rest and then get going again.

"I figured that's what got him killed," Curry said quietly. "Somebody came looking. Found things they never would have found. Stuff Costello would never have told them voluntarily."

"Like what?"

His response was another long pause which seemed to last all the way into next week before he finally spoke again. "The FBI leaks like a sieve. You know that, right?"

Kim kneaded the tension headache sending a spike between her eyes. "You want me to disrespect my own agency?"

"I want you to admit you're aware that not everybody at the FBI is a hero in a white hat," Curry said. "No organization is that good. There're always bad apples. They're not easy to spot. And you never see the bull gator that bites you in the ass when your back's turned."

She held back a long sigh. "Let's say we can agree on that. In theory. So what?"

"Same for NYPD."

Kim replied, "Where are you going with this?"

"Like I said, Costello was old school. Like us, he'd been burned trusting the wrong people. More than once." Curry stopped as if he were still making up his mind. Reluctantly, he said, "I found a file Costello had kept when he was looking for Reacher. It's got a name. A woman. Linked to an old case Reacher was sniffing around back then. I followed up. Found some more names."

"What's the woman's name?"

Curry ignored the question.

"What does Marilyn Stone say about all that?"

"The woman can't be found. Marilyn is looking, using her contacts, but so far, nothing."

Kim waited. Curry was a talker. He wouldn't accept silence as a deterrent.

"Got me to thinking, though. Led me to another guy. Dead now. He was a Vietnam vet. The only survivor of a helo crash over there. He was a nasty piece of work," Curry said with a wry chuckle. "Too mean to die, or something, I guess."

"So Marilyn Stone met the missing woman and the guy?"

"Yeah. I met them both, too."

Kim's pulse quickened. "You can't find the woman, and you won't name her, but can we interview the guy?"

"Not unless you can talk to ghosts. He's dead. Reacher killed him. Self-defense," Curry said flatly.

Kim's heartbeat quickened. "Costello's files say that?"

"Nah. Costello was dead by then," Curry said. "But we don't need him to know the guy. I saw it all happen."

Kim heard what sounded like a turn indicator blinking in the background.

"Where are you right now? We need to talk about this. I have resources you don't. Let me get people started on it," she said.

"Before the guy died, I remembered hearing a list of names straight from Reacher's mouth," Curry said with a little oomph, as if he were moving awkwardly while he talked. "One of them was Tardelli. See where I'm going with this?"

"Are you driving?" she asked.

"Yeah. In my piece of junk POV. Cheap and ancient little sedan. Not meant for clandestine work, for damned sure."

"What clandestine work are you doing?"

"New Yorkers don't drive, so we don't need a new car every five minutes like you Detroiters. When I was NYPD, they gave me a car," he said, distracted by something not quite right inside the vehicle. "Anyway, I'm headed upstate. To a place called New Slope. Barely a crossroads on the map."

She heard the navigation system offering directions in the background. Hearing the name of the town again so soon after Cooper mentioned it raised the little hairs on the back of her neck.

"Why are you going to New Slope?"

"Looking for a guy named Zabrinski. Somebody tried to kill him yesterday. He's alive right now," Curry said. "Gotta talk to him while I still can. Just in case he doesn't make it."

Kim didn't share Cooper's theories. "And Zabrinski was on Reacher's list of names you mentioned?"

Curry paused as if he were trying to figure something out. Driving directions, probably. Then he said distractedly, "Couldn't have been Harold Zabrinski. Guy's too young. But he had an older brother. Martin Zabrinski. Might have been the one Reacher mentioned."

"Who else was on this list, Curry?" Kim asked to bring his attention back to the call.

"It's black as pitch out here. Crazy wild animals just dart into the road all over the place. Barely missed a possum couple miles back."

Kim barely held onto her patience. "Who else was on that list?"

"The GPS is useless and whoever is responsible for road signs in this berg should be fired," Curry said with exasperation. "Hang on a minute while I figure this out."

Which was when total chaos erupted.

"What the hell is that?" Curry's shocked voice yelled just before the moment his words were cut off by the tumultuous roar.

A heavy, shuddering thud resonated through the phone, so deep and violent that Kim felt the impact in her bones.

Metal crushed and the world seemed to spin through the audio in a disorienting whirl of motion conveyed like the soundtrack to a pulse-pounding disaster film.

Screeching tires caused by Curry's full weight on the brake pedal created a desperate symphony where the rubber met the road as his car careened out of control, followed by a long stream of curses.

Then, a second sickeningly loud crash cut through the commotion.

Next came instant and total silence.

Kim's heart stuttered when the instant quiet left only a hollow echo in its wake.

In the breathless pause that followed, the call dropped, leaving Kim clutching nothing but air.

Her mind raced, piecing together the auditory puzzle into a harrowing image of Curry's old sedan spinning, the shifting weight of whatever hit the sedan altering its course, sending it into a wild, uncontrolled dance that ended with the unforgiving slab of a huge and solid tree.

Out there in the countryside, no other vehicles on the road at this hour, she imagined the sequence was set in motion when he'd collided with one of the animals he'd mentioned. A buck? A bear? A moose?

"Curry?" she repeated into the phone just in case he still had contact. "Curry? Can you hear me?"

No response.

She hit the redial, each ring echoing her heartbeats.

When Curry didn't pick up, she dialed emergency services and reported what little she knew. The dispatcher took her report and promised to send first responders.

Kim hung up and called Smithers.

"Get dressed. Cooper called. There are two more victims. We've got to go."

"Meet you downstairs in ten," he said, asking no questions.

Kim rummaged until she found the burner that connected her directly to Gaspar. She hit the redial while she tossed everything into her travel bag.

Gaspar picked up on the second ring. "What's up, Suzy Wong?"

"I need you to research something for me. All I have for sure are two names. But I think we can add a third," she said as she zipped the travel bag and slipped on her jacket. "Tardelli and Zabrinski for sure. Gunston is my solid guess for number three."

"Okay. Where should I start?" Gaspar asked.

"Army, I think. Vietnam era, possibly," she said as she left her room and headed toward the SUV. "I don't have much to go on. All I know is that Reacher is connected to these people somehow. There might have been a helo crash involved."

"And let me guess. Cooper knows the connection and isn't saying," Gaspar said snidely.

"Possibly. I don't know. Add two more names to the list. William Curry and Marilyn Stone. They're not in the same group as the others, but there could be a connection to Reacher," Kim said, hurrying toward Smithers and the SUV. "I'll call you from the road."

"Where are you, anyway?" Gaspar said before she rang off.

"New Hampshire. But I'm headed south to New Slope, New York. Call me back if you find anything," she said as she hung up and slipped her phone into her pocket.

She stowed her bag in the cargo hold and climbed into the passenger seat half a moment before Smithers slid the transmission into drive and the SUV began to roll.

CHAPTER 23

Monday, June 20
Upstate Vermont

WITH HEADLIGHTS ALREADY OFF and windows lowered to hear threatening noises, the driver squelched the ignition and rolled the white van silently into the gravel driveway. The damp morning air wafted inside the van carrying the mixed scents of the surrounding forest.

The home was secluded in rural Northern Vermont.

"Are you sure this is the right house?" the driver asked for the tenth time. "We could be approaching innocent civilians. We need to be certain."

The shooter refused to listen to any more nonsense. "Aborting the mission is not an option. Pressing forward is the only way. We've been over this."

"Civilian casualties will bring never-ending heat down on us, you know that," the driver said, adrenaline roughening his voice like heavy grit sandpaper.

"All we need to do is get into the house without alarming any local residents who might be out birdwatching or whatever these yokels do up here," the shooter insisted, patience wearing thin.

"Stop talking. She'll hear you."

They had attached stolen magnetic signs to the van's steel side panels impersonating Green Mountain Electric. That detail had also been the shooter's plan. He was devious. And clever. Which had served them well so far.

The driver rolled to a stop and moved the transmission into park as quietly as possible.

"Ready?" the shooter asked, slipping the counterfeit Green Mountain Electric cap onto his head.

The caps matched the green overalls and green paper booties they'd donned to cover their clothes and shoes.

Both were the shooter's idea. The costumes suggested authenticity and would reduce the risk of forensic evidence they might inadvertently leave inside the house.

Better to be too careful than too sloppy.

"Yeah." The driver pulled his cap on and gave a quick nod in response.

The shooter, younger and leaner, placed his feet carefully and firmly on the gravel. Ready to go.

The driver stepped out of the van slowly, experience evident in his steady, assessing gaze. He scanned the perimeter silently. He signaled that he noticed nothing amiss.

They made their way to the door, porch wood creaking under their weight.

The driver raised one gloved hand to ring the doorbell. The chime sounded loudly inside and echoed through the still morning air.

Nora Ramsey, a striking woman in her late forties, opened the door. She was dressed for the day already. Which meant she could have been watching as the van approached.

Her gaze was sharp and alert as she studied them with frank curiosity.

"Can I help you?" she inquired, her voice clear, poised.

She held her right arm slightly behind her, hand out of sight. She could have been holding a pistol.

A woman living alone in the woods was likely to know how to defend herself. Which was a contingency they'd planned for. But they needed to get inside the house first.

"Good morning, ma'am." The driver offered a friendly but apologetic smile as he touched the bill of his cap politely. "We're from Green Mountain Electric. There's been a report of faulty wiring in the area. We need to check your house."

Ramsey's brow furrowed. "I didn't call for an electrician."

"Safety precaution, ma'am," the driver replied, his voice tinged with concern. "Faulty wiring can be quite dangerous. Could start a fire. Better to be safe than sorry."

After a brief pause, Ramsey pushed the door to close them outside. "I'll have my own people check it out."

The shooter moved quickly.

He stepped forward and shouldered his way into the house, thrusting her aside and off-balance.

She stumbled left while raising the weapon in her right hand.

In one continuous motion, the shooter shoved her hard and she landed on her ass on the floor.

As she fell, he grabbed her gun.

His maneuver bent her wrist backward and she yelped with pain.

He wrenched her fingers from the pistol with a sharp twist and gave her a solid kick in the right side with his heavy boot at the same time.

Ramsey groaned, fell sideways, and her head hit the hardwood floor knocking her unconscious.

Her body slumped like a boneless rag.

He gave her a firm nudge with his boot, but she didn't stir.

"Stick to the plan," the driver said, laying a calming hand on the shooter's shoulder. "It's too soon. We have more to do first."

The shooter seemed to hear the older man's warning through his rage.

He stared at Ramsey's inert body, as if fighting to suppress his need to kick her again and again.

When she didn't move after a full second, he managed to control himself. He turned away and the driver released his breath.

The shooter sniffed the aroma of coffee blending with a subtle hint of something else. Wood smoke from a fireplace. Which explained why the interior of the house was so warm.

"Split up," the shooter said, tilting his head toward the attic.

The driver quickly ascended the stairs and the shooter lingered on the main floor before heading to the basement. Each carried a tool bag that held more than just tools.

In the attic, the driver must have quickly found the secondary power controls. He cut the power, plunging the house into darkness.

The shooter had located his flashlight and moved toward the natural gas boiler on the far end of the basement. He set the tool bag down and went to work.

He'd been engrossed in the task for a while when he heard noises on the main floor above. How long had they been going at it? He stopped his work to listen.

"What's happening?" Ramsey's voice, mixed with confusion and alarm, traveled through the quiet house.

Damn. Should have kicked her harder.

He heard Ramsey moving across the floor above. What was she searching for in the dark? Flashlights? A cell phone?

The shooter grabbed his gun and his night vision goggles from the tool bag and climbed the stairs as silently as possible. Concealed by shadows, he returned to the kitchen.

He watched her, knowing she couldn't see him.

It would be so easy to kill her now. But the driver was right. It was too soon.

He moved to intercept her instead.

On his third step, a floorboard groaned under his foot.

Ramsey spun around when she heard the noise. In a flash, she dashed toward the back door, fueled by adrenaline.

CHAPTER 24

Monday, June 20
Upstate Vermont

THE SHOOTER LUNGED AFTER her, but she was surprisingly quick. The back door swung open with a crash as loud as a cannon in the morning stillness before he could stop her.

Ramsey burst into the weak daylight, her cries for help slicing through the air.

She ran away from the house along a pathway leading north, continuing to shout "Help!" and a dozen variations of distress.

Who did she think would hear her?

The nearest house was a mile away. Even if the neighbors were awake, they wouldn't hear her from that distance.

Was someone living in one of her outbuildings?

The shooter's research hadn't identified any on-site security personnel. But that didn't mean anything.

Now that he'd thought of it, clandestine security staff was the kind of thing Ramsey would absolutely employ. It made total sense.

"Dammit! Why didn't I think of that before?"

The shooter ran back into the house and down to the basement. He collected his tool bag and dashed up the stairs. When he reached the main floor, the driver was already waiting in the van.

Which meant he'd completed his tasks upstairs.

The shooter retreated quickly to the van and tossed his bag into the back as he closed his door.

The driver reversed out of the driveway as the shooter settled into the passenger seat. At the road, the driver executed a perfect turn and headed south, away from the Ramsey house and in the opposite direction from Ramsey's meandering escape path.

He glanced in the rearview mirror, searching for her. The shooter watched in the side mirror. She must have been watching the van from the woods.

Ramsey returned to stand outside on the driveway, her breathing heavy, her eyes wide with a mixture of fear and determination. She was scanning her surroundings, searching for any sign of her assailants.

The shooter grinned, rocking forward in the passenger seat until the first bend in the road when he could no longer see the Ramsey place or its owner.

"What's so funny," the driver said angrily. "She almost killed us."

"She's spunky. Not a boring science nerd after all," the shooter said, laughing now. "She's going to be a lot more fun than I thought."

"Coming back here is not an option." The driver scowled. "Did you finish? Or were you too busy playing cat and mouse with Ramsey?"

The comment was more than enough to light his already short fuse. The shooter moved fast. He delivered a swift gut punch with plenty of weight behind it.

The blow pushed all the air from the driver's belly in one big whoosh.

He gasped for air, unable to inhale, while struggling to keep the van between the ditches.

"You're not in charge here. You should remember that," the shooter growled angrily.

The driver continued sucking air into his lungs one small, swift gasp at a time.

The shooter ignored his distress and pointed to a dirt two-track on the right. "Pull in there."

The driver didn't have enough wind to protest. He turned the wheel onto the fire trail and kept going.

The trail backtracked a bit as it wound into the trees and upward at a slight incline. When they'd traveled about two miles, the shooter figured they were in the right place.

He said, "Turn right again."

Between painful breaths the driver did as he was told, lacking the will and the air to speak.

The shooter scanned the area as the van moved slowly through the trees for another mile or so. Then he held up his hand like a traffic cop.

"Stop here."

When the driver parked the van, the shooter opened the passenger door and stepped out onto the composted leaves atop sandy soil.

He walked forward a few dozen steps to a small clearing he'd identified a few days ago. He'd judged the distance and direction perfectly.

He grinned as he confirmed the position. Secluded by trees on the incline that overlooked the Ramsey house, he had a clear sight line directly to Nora Ramsey.

She stood in the front garden, hands on hips, peering toward the road. As if she were waiting for someone.

Police, probably. Sure. That made total sense.

A woman like Ramsey would call the police. It was the sort of thing a normal citizen did when victimized by a home invasion.

How long would it take first responders to arrive?

Too long. He was certain because he'd calculated all of it before they arrived. They had more than enough time.

He mimed his usual sniper's position and pretended to squeeze the trigger.

One perfect shot to reach the target with a fatal hit.

He imagined he felt the ground bounce as the weight of her body fell to the earth.

The fantasy was enough to satisfy him. For the moment.

"Soon, Ramsey. Very soon," he said aloud before he returned to the van.

Quickly, he stripped off the Green Mountain Electric coveralls, cap, gloves, and booties and tossed them into the cargo section. Then he pulled the magnetic signs off both sides of the van and dumped them inside, too.

"Ready?" the driver asked, holding his sore stomach. He had also stripped off his disguise while the shooter was busy gloating.

"Been ready for years," the shooter snarled, giving him an angry stare across the cabin.

He had one foot inside the van when he heard the unmistakable sound of a helicopter approaching.

The canopy of trees was too dense to see the bird, but the noise grew louder by the moment.

"Bitch called a helo?" Angrily, the shooter spat on the ground as he hurried into his seat and slammed the door. "She's probably got CCTV, too. We'll have to dump the van now. Damn her! Go! Go!"

The driver pressed his lips into a hard line and said nothing. He gripped the steering wheel tighter as he pushed the accelerator as close to the floor as he dared, and the van leapt into motion like a heavy cat.

Cursing angrily, the shooter pulled out a paper map of the county searching for a suitable place to dump the van as they bounced over the ruts and potholes in the dirt trail for another mile before they found a paved road.

CHAPTER 25

Monday, June 20
New Slope, New York

SMITHERS PULLED INTO A drive-thru for coffee and then returned to travel the back roads as fast as he dared while Kim brought him up to speed on the facts as far as she knew them.

"Cooper says Harold Zabrinski is another victim of the shooter. But the killers got sloppy. Killed Zabrinski's kid instead of the father."

Smithers asked, "So now we've got four victims, three dead. Tardelli, Gunston, and two Zabrinskis. But there should have been only three total?"

"That's the working theory," Kim said, scalding her tongue on the hot coffee. "Probably because there's less reason to kill a kid. If there's any reason to believe the fourth victim was a mistake, I haven't heard it yet."

Smithers kept both hands on the wheel and slowed to avoid overdriving his headlights. "Why does Cooper think these are the same killers?"

Kim shrugged. The perfect all-purpose gesture. Could mean anything.

"Okay. Then why does he think Reacher's involved?"

"Another good question," Kim replied as she pulled her laptop from its bag and opened it. She scanned the incident reports from all three crime scenes again.

"Are these victims connected somehow? This case is starting to feel like that old Beltway Sniper situation," Smithers said. "Two dudes in a vehicle shooting at random victims. Mostly hit their targets, but there were a few misses."

"Geez, I hope not. Last thing we need is a copycat." Kim punched a few keys on the laptop to bring up the news reports on the old case. She scanned the text, mentioning the relevant facts aloud. "Two perpetrators, one driver and one shooter. Seemingly random victims. Killed over a twenty-two-day period."

"Yeah, we thought the crimes were random at the time, but turned out a few of the victims were related to the suspects, if I recall correctly. So it was a mixed bag," Smithers said, slowing for a bend in the road. "Man, it's dark out here."

"That's what Curry said just before he crashed," Kim replied.

"Let's not do a repeat performance, if it's all the same to you," Smithers teased. "On the Beltway Sniper thing, seems like I remember they eventually connected earlier murders, in different locations, right?"

"Yeah," Kim said, still scanning the text. "Looks like the whole crime spree lasted about six months. Total was seventeen dead and ten injured."

"Cooper thinks we've got a copycat going on here?" Smithers asked.

Kim finished reading the FBI reports on the case. "Sounds like he's worried about things getting out of hand and going in that direction."

"Why?"

"I don't know."

"Why does he think Reacher's involved in all of this? I mean, Reacher's an excellent sniper. Cooper thinks Reacher would kill civilians like that?" Smithers asked.

"I don't know what Cooper thinks. But no. Reacher wouldn't do that," Kim said. "Not without a damned good reason, anyway."

"So the question is, does he have a damned good reason to kill these three targets?" Smithers murmured.

"What the hell would that even be?" Kim snapped. "I knew Sheryl Tardelli. She was one of the finest women. She didn't deserve to die. Reacher wouldn't kill her."

"Okay," Smithers said, as if he were placating a mental patient.

"And even if Reacher had a damned good reason to kill her, he wouldn't have done it by soaking her in toxic chemicals," Kim insisted. "Why would anyone do that?"

"Off the top of my head? Poetic justice. Revenge. Insanity. Rage. Money. All of the above." Smithers said, listing a few options. "It's worth remembering that Cooper knows Reacher and you don't."

Kim said nothing more because Smithers was right. Cooper knew Reacher and she didn't. Cooper also knew a lot of things she didn't know. Mostly because he wouldn't tell her.

But she didn't believe for a minute that Reacher doused Tardelli with poison. She didn't think Cooper believed that, either.

On the other hand, she was sure that Cooper was worried, although she wasn't sure exactly what he was worried about. Or why.

They arrived at New Slope General Hospital in just under five hours. The parking lot was almost empty. Smithers easily found a place to park, and they hoofed through the chill toward the entrance.

The ER was a beehive of activity, even at this early hour. Smithers approached the desk, showed his credentials, and then gestured her through the security door into the patient care area.

"Zabrinski is in one of the ICU rooms. This is a shortcut. They didn't want to move him to the floor. Easier to keep him safe there," Smithers explained as they moved along the corridor.

Patients on rolling beds lined the walls and hospital personnel wearing colorful scrubs hurried from one to the next. Threading through the chaos wasn't easy.

Halfway down the first corridor, Kim saw Curry on a gurney propped up with his nose bandaged and two black eyes forming. He was groggy, lost in a haze of pain and morphine. His eyes fluttered open at the sound of Kim's voice.

"Curry. It's me, Kim Otto," she said, touching his arm.

He opened his eyes briefly and then closed them again.

"Can you talk?" Kim asked, her tone soft but urgent.

"Yeah," Curry slurred, struggling to focus. "Didn't see it coming. Damned thing ran right into me. More than two hundred pounds of him. Then the tree."

"You okay, though?"

His replies were mumbled and garbled, but Kim could make out most of it. "Car versus tree. Damned lucky. Bruises. Except for the nose. It's been broken before. Won't kill me."

"What were you doing out there, anyway?" Kim asked.

"Following a lead. Like I told you."

"What lead?" Smithers interjected, leaning in closer.

Curry blinked slowly, trying to gather his thoughts. "Tardelli and Zabrinski... recognized the names."

Kim and Smithers exchanged a quick, puzzled glance.

"They were Army," Curry continued, his words slow but clear. "Vietnam."

Kim cast a puzzled look toward Smithers. Tardelli wasn't in the Army. She was too young for Vietnam. Zabrinski was too young for Vietnam, too.

"Died. Helo crash. Long time ago," Curry slurred as if his mouth was filled with cotton.

Kim's brows furrowed in confusion. "What? Zabrinski's here, in this hospital."

"Yeah," Curry murmured, his eyelids heavy. "Doesn't make sense. That's why I was headed here. To ask him."

Reggie straightened up and gave her a quizzical look. "What's he talking about?"

Kim shook her head. "No clue."

"Doesn't make sense. But it's true," Curry murmured again, repeating himself through the haze of morphine they'd administered for pain.

Kim leaned in closer, her expression serious. "How do you know all this, Curry?"

Curry's eyes, clouded by pain and drugs, flickered with a glimmer of clarity. "Heard the names together once... Tardelli, Zabrinski. A few others. From Reacher."

Reggie's eyes narrowed. "Reacher?"

"Yeah," Curry confirmed, his voice a mere whisper. "Long time ago. Must have stuck in my head."

Kim straightened up when a nurse came to wheel him into an ER room. "Get some rest. We'll take it from here."

They made their way along the corridor to a set of double doors that led to a private elevator for hospital personnel only. They exited two floors up where a uniformed officer was posted at the security door leading to the ICU.

This time, both Smithers and Kim showed ID.

"We're here to interview Harold Zabrinski," Kim said. "Room 4C.

The officer studied their ID and handed it back to them. "He's marked no visitors. But my CO said you'd be coming and to let you through."

"Is Zabrinski able to communicate?" Kim asked, not surprised that Cooper had paved the way. He could be useful when he bothered to try.

"I'm protective detail. Haven't been allowed to talk to him. I don't know his condition." The officer pushed a set of buttons on a keypad to release the secure door lock and stepped aside with a gesture. "Room 4C is all the way across in the far corner."

Kim went in first and Smithers followed.

Unlike the busy ER, the ICU was quiet except for the various medical equipment noises hissing and beeping. No visitors wandered the halls. All of the patients were in single rooms not writhing on gurneys in the corridor.

The patient rooms were laid out along the perimeter of an open floor plan and the central nurse's station occupied the middle of the space. Each room was equipped with CCTV and a nurse monitored the video feeds at the central desk.

Zabrinski's video feed was clearly marked and visible as Kim turned the first corner. She stopped and gestured to the nurse watching Zabrinski's feed.

He pulled one of his headphones aside. "Can I help you?"

"Mr. Zabrinski have any visitors?" Kim asked, showing her ID again.

The nurse peered at the ID and then replied, "Not since I came on duty. But I've only been here an hour."

"Has he spoken to anyone?" Smithers asked.

The nurse shook his head.

"Is he awake?" Kim asked.

"Sometimes. In and out. He seems conscious, but I'm not sure how lucid he is," the orderly said. "Before they took him to surgery, he kept asking for his boy. Harry, I think his name was."

"He doesn't know his son died in the attack?" Smithers asked.

"He's been told. More than once. But it just didn't seem to sink in, you know?"

"What kind of surgery did he have?" Kim asked.

The orderly glanced through a few computer screens on the chart. "Shoulder repair. Bones and muscles and tendons were pretty messed up. Long time under anesthesia. Means he'll be a while coming out of it again."

Cooper's report said Zabrinski was shot in the shoulder with a rifle. Bullet went straight through. Exited from his back with sufficient velocity to reach and kill the boy.

The shooter would be charged for attacking both victims, even though the boy's death was a freak accident, Cooper said.

Which was probably no comfort to his father whatsoever.

CHAPTER 26

Monday, June 20
New Slope, New York

KIM THANKED THE NURSE for his help and headed for Zabrinski's room with Smithers close behind. She turned the knob and stepped inside.

Zabrinski's eyes were closed, and he was breathing oxygen through a nasal cannula. The monitors by his bed showed normal heart rhythm, pulse rate, and blood oxygen levels. But his face looked ashen. His arms were attached to IV tubes running to bags of fluid on poles on both sides of the bed.

"Mr. Zabrinski," Smithers said in his rumbling bass. "Can you hear me? FBI Agents Smithers and Otto. We need to speak with you."

Zabrinski's eyelids raised open slowly, as if they were too heavy to lift, and then fell closed again. "Can you dim the lights?"

His voice was weak and raspy, probably due to the anesthesia tube scraping his throat during surgery. But he seemed lucid enough to string a complete sentence together at least.

"Sure." Kim found the light switch and flipped it off, leaving the lights of a dozen glowing gadgets to illuminate the room. "How's that?"

He opened his eyes again and managed to keep them open this time. He reached for a paper cup with a straw protruding from the lid and took a long swallow. "Better. Thanks."

"We're sorry to bother you now," Kim said, "but we need to talk while the facts are still fresh in your mind."

Zabrinski pushed the button releasing pain medicine to flow through his veins. "My boy is dead. The facts will always be fresh in my mind."

"We're sorry for your loss, Mr. Zabrinski. I know that's of little comfort," Kim said.

Zabrinski's eyes closed and opened again as a brief acknowledgment. "What do you need from me?"

"Did you see anyone or anything unusual before you were attacked?" Kim asked.

"I was in the Army. Trained to be observant. And I've lived in New Slope all my life, so I know every inch of the place." He paused for another sip of water. "The only odd thing I noticed was a white van parked across the street. Older model. I remember thinking I hadn't seen it before."

Kim and Smithers exchanged glances. There had been a white van at the Gunston crime scene, according to witnesses. It was a tenuous connection between the crimes, as Cooper said.

"Was there anything else unusual about the van?" Smithers asked.

"Yeah, that's what caught my eye. It was kind of moving sideways on its suspension. Like there was a big dog bouncing around inside or something."

"Could you see the driver?" Kim asked.

"The side windows and the windshield were tinted. Too dark to be legal," Zabrinski replied. "I wondered how the driver could see well enough to drive. But I only took a brief glance. It wasn't so unusual that I studied it much. Wish I had."

"So you didn't see the license plate or any markings that might help us identify the van?" Kim asked. "Dents, rust, signs, anything like that?"

"Just a plain white box with dark windows bouncing like a prize fight was going on inside. That's it." Zabrinski closed his eyes and shook his head. Tears leaked from the corners of his eyes. "Next thing I knew I heard the rifle. Felt the pain in my shoulder. Cried out. Saw my boy hit the ground. No chance to push him out of the way, you know?"

Kim waited a moment for Zabrinski to regain his composure and then she took a guess. "Did you know Congresswoman Tardelli?"

"Sheryl. Yeah, sure." Zabrinski replied, his words slurred slightly. "She organized our group."

She narrowed her eyes, realizing that Curry might actually have found something. "How about Judge Matt Gunston?"

"Yeah. Known Matt for years. Why are you asking? You think the same guy shot me and my boy?" Zabrinski's anger seemed to lift him from lethargy.

"I don't know. Just trying to figure this thing out," Kim replied. "Tell me about your group. The one Sheryl Tardelli organized."

"Not much to tell. Met once a year when we went to the wall in DC. Had a meal and a few beers. That's it."

"The Vietnam War Memorial Wall?" Smithers said, shooting a quizzical glance toward Kim.

"Who else was in your group?" Kim asked.

"Sam Soper. Drew Kaplan," he said, frowning as he struggled to remember the names through the medication haze. Finally, he had it. "Nadia Bamford. Six of us. Could have been eight, but Vic Hobie was an only child. His parents didn't have any other kids, so no relatives. We tried to reach Allen's family, but they'd left Boston and Sheryl couldn't find them. So just the six of us."

"Was Reacher involved with your group?" Kim asked, making a mental note of the names.

"Reacher? He was just here." Zabrinski frowned and shrugged as if he didn't understand the question. "Has he been shot, too?"

"No, but I thought you might know him," Kim said. "What did he want?"

"Asking what happened. Seemed angry. Like maybe he knew who did this," Zabrinski replied in a drugged haze. "Never met him before."

"So how did he find you?" Kim asked. "Where did he go?"

"Dunno. Just us six. That's all," Zabrinski said, slurring his speech heavily now that the last dose of pain killers was setting in. His eyelids seemed too heavy to hold open.

"Any reason somebody would want to hurt you or your boy?" Smithers asked quietly, placing a hand on Zabrinski's shoulder.

"Harry? He was twelve years old. What could he possibly have done to anyone?" Zabrinski replied as he began to sob and then fell into snoring gently.

"Thanks for your help. We'll let you get some rest now." Kim caught Smithers's eye and they left the room.

"Shouldn't we try to find Reacher? If he was just here talking to Zabrinski, he could still be close by," Smither suggested as they walked toward the elevator.

"Zabrinski's out of it. We won't find Reacher hanging around. Believe me, I've tried chasing after him," Kim said. "But he's working this case. So we know we're on the right track."

"Cooper's got a team working these cases, too. We can circle back to Zabrinski if we need to," Smithers agreed.

"Let's find Curry. Sounds like he might be on to something after all."

They thanked the officer at the security door, took the private elevator down, and returned to the ER.

The place was busier than before. Patients seemed to be stacked up everywhere. Walking between the gurneys was like running a gauntlet.

When they found Curry's room, another woman, bloody and battered, was moaning in the bed and Curry was nowhere in sight.

Kim flagged down one of the nurses.

"We're looking for the patient who was in this room, William Curry. Do you know where he is now?"

"Probably discharged or moved to another floor. We need the beds. Big bus accident just came in. Too many patients." Before she dashed off, she said, "Go to the front desk and they'll help you locate him."

Kim led the way through the security doors to the ER lobby where the noise was overwhelming.

Desk personnel were swamped with bus crash passengers on top of the normal caseload. Local police were helping to herd and triage the injured and their families. Ambulances were lined up outside to unload victims and rush them through to emergency care.

Kim pointed toward a security guard standing near the front entrance sorting and directing pedestrian traffic.

"I'll talk to security. If Curry left, she might have noticed. Can you check the admissions desk?" she asked. "I need to call Gaspar and Cooper. If this shooter is killing the members of Zabrinski's group, there are three more names on his list. Maybe we can catch this bastard before he kills again."

CHAPTER 27

Monday, June 20
New York City

THE TWO MEN WHO broke into her home in Vermont and
tried to kill her were long gone by the time the helo arrived. Nora
Ramsey had climbed aboard and instructed her pilot to fly to
Manhattan. Ninety minutes later, she was settled inside her Central
Park West apartment where the security rivaled the Vatican.

Until this mess was sorted out, she wouldn't go back to
Vermont. She wasn't a coward, but she didn't have a death wish,
either.

Waiting for the helo and the flight had given her room to
breathe and time to think.

She'd never been targeted before Tardelli died. Her death had
been widely reported as accidental, but Nora didn't believe it.

Tardelli had been a friend to Ramsey Chemical, which made
her a target for the opposition's true believers. She'd received
threats and been subjected to vandalism, Nora knew.

Tardelli's death, regardless of the manner, had put a complete halt to Ramsey Chemical's efforts to legitimize R2. The House Veterans' Affairs Committee had postponed the final approval hearings indefinitely. Without Tardelli's support, R2's fate was uncertain at best.

Which was a catastrophe for Ramsey Chemical and for Nora personally. But an even bigger catastrophe for Iniko Makinde.

Makinde had been pressuring Nora to continue manufacturing R2 for use in Nigeria, mainly because Makinde was making a corrupt fortune off the Nigerian government.

Which meant it was a reasonable assumption that Makinde was behind the two attacks on Nora last night.

At least, she hoped it was Makinde. He wanted her alive and well and pressing forward on R2.

Makinde wouldn't kill her because she was the primary source of his income. He wanted to scare her and point out her vulnerabilities, surely. Maybe he even wanted to renegotiate their deal. He had no reason to kill her and every reason not to.

But there were crazies everywhere these days. People who would kill for no logical reason at all.

Nora aimed to keep herself safe and alive. Job one was to identify the source of these attacks and stop them before they succeeded.

After she'd showered, dressed, and made fresh coffee, she opened her laptop and downloaded CCTV of last night's home invasion.

The cameras had captured images of the Green Mountain Electric van arriving in her driveway. The license plates were obscured, but the make and model of the van was clear enough. An old Ford. There must be millions of white vans out there like it.

A quick internet search confirmed that Green Mountain Electric was totally fictitious. No such company existed within a two-hundred-mile radius of Vermont. Which meant these two were especially resourceful or they were minions for a resourceful boss.

The two men were well concealed in their protective coveralls that resembled hazmat suits. All she could see were their eyes. One was shorter, bulkier. The other was clearly the boss, which was the only surprise. He gave the orders, and the shorter one did as he was told.

Nora copied the video footage and sent it off to her head of security with instructions to submit to a forensic examiner for analysis.

She didn't expect to find the van or the two men, but she hoped the video would confirm their identity and actions after they'd been located by other means.

The specialist had sent the video footage from her SUV's black box. She'd reviewed it quickly before her shower. The images were dark and blurry. One shot captured the front grille of the big black SUV chasing her, which confirmed the make and model but not the specific vehicle or the driver.

All of which meant she had exactly nothing more to use as leverage with Makinde.

Nora stood and stretched her achy muscles and checked the time. Twelve hours since John left her home. She couldn't give him any more time.

From the thirtieth floor, she gazed down at the ant-sized people and vehicles scurrying below. She'd made this space her fortress, with its state-of-the-art security system and a view from which she could almost feel the city's pulse.

She could hunker down and wait for John. She would be safe from Makinde here.

But safety wasn't what she needed now.

Nora picked up her phone to check again. Still no word from John. For a few moments, her thumb hovered over the contact labeled *Makinde - Private*.

With a decisive tap, she initiated the call.

It rang once. Twice.

"Nora Ramsey," Makinde answered. His voice was too smooth. He wasn't the least bit worried. "To what do I owe the pleasure?"

"Cut the crap, Makinde." Nora's voice ironclad, words clipped. "We need to meet. I'm in the city. Name the place."

Makinde's edge returned in response to her demands. "Bethesda Terrace. One hour. Come alone."

He hung up. Nora's gaze moved to the clock. One hour to prepare, one hour to change the game.

She called John again. Still no answer. She left him a message with the time and place for the meeting with Makinde.

John should have called back, but he didn't.

When she could wait no longer, she settled her pistol in its holster beneath her arm and grabbed her coat, slipping it on as she left her apartment.

The door clicked firmly shut, echoing her resolve.

Makinde wasn't a foolish man. He would realize her plan made sense and he would agree. He had no real options otherwise. He couldn't manufacture the R2 himself. And even if he could, he had no distribution network or capital for inventory.

They'd been working together a long time. She could make Makinde see that they were on the cusp of success.

Tardelli's death was a setback, but not fatal to the R2 project. This was the time to be smart, not foolhardy.

The elevator ride down was fast and brief.

Outside, she walked briskly, heels clicking against the pavement toward the meeting point Makinde selected.

Bethesda Terrace was a curious choice if Makinde meant to harm her. In the heart of Central Park, it was a popular destination for tourists and locals alike. The iconic brick plaza included two levels, an arcade and a fountain.

It was rarely unoccupied. Which Nora took as an indication that Makinde wanted to work things out between them.

She saw Makinde leaning against the railing with the nonchalance of a man who believed he held all the cards. The kernel of worry embedded in her belly expanded and her step faltered.

"Ramsey, ever the punctual one," Makinde said with a scowl as she approached.

Nora straightened her spine and took a hard line. "What were you thinking? The last thing we need is more trouble. Release the agent, and we can talk terms."

His smile faded a fraction. "And if I don't?"

Nora stepped closer her gaze locked onto his. "Then I'll go to the FBI with more than enough to bury you. Your life as you know it will be over."

She produced a flash drive from her pocket, holding it up between them.

Makinde's gaze flickered to the drive, doubt crossing his features. "You're bluffing."

She tossed the drive to him. "Check for yourself."

He caught the small object, his eyes never leaving hers. "Why give me this?"

"It's only a copy. I still have the originals," Nora said flatly. "Release the agent."

"Of course. No problem." Makinde nodded to someone behind her. "As a gesture of good will, I have already released him. You had only to ask. I'm surprised you don't know that."

Nora gave him a steady stare. Makinde was a lot of things, but easygoing wasn't one of his character traits.

"You're not the only one who keeps good records, Ramsey," Makinde said with a malevolent glare. "And you have a lot of agents. If I let this one go, I can easily take another."

"You're not that foolish. Which is why you didn't actually kill me," Nora's gaze stayed firmly fixed in a hard stare.

Makinde's eyes widened and his eyebrows shot up in mock surprise. "Why, Dr. Ramsey, surely not. If I'd tried to kill you, you'd be dead. Make no mistake."

"You're saying you didn't try to kill me twice on Sunday night," she demanded flatly.

"I assure you, I did not." He shook his head. "Why would I? You are worth nothing to me if you're dead."

"You didn't send thugs to chase me down? You didn't send intruders into my home?"

Makinde shrugged. "You should be more careful. Increase your security."

Nora didn't believe him. But she didn't disbelieve him, either. "Just know the content of that flash drive holds the power to unravel your empire."

"So releasing this information is the nuclear option. It will result in mutual assured destruction." Makinde smirked, looking at the small drive resting in his large palm. "Let's see if what you have here is worth my generosity."

The drive clicked as he inserted it into a portable device and previewed the contents. Makinde's expression shifted, his confidence waning.

Nora knew she had him.

But before she could continue, a sharp sound shattered the moment.

A cry rang out from across the brick plaza, disrupting their standoff.

They turned toward the noise.

A man wearing a dark hoodie grabbed an old woman's bag and shoved her to the ground. She refused to release her bag and he kicked her in the head. People in the area came to her rescue, but the thief left the bag and sprinted off.

The moment the thief got away Nora realized the crime had been a setup. A distraction. She turned swiftly back to Makinde.

He knocked her aside and moved to blend into the gathering crowd. He hurried away from the plaza.

A shadow detached itself from the cover of the trees.

John.

He barreled into Makinde. The two men crashed into the railing, the impact echoing across the plaza.

Makinde's men had been mingling with the crowd and sprang into action.

One man aimed a kick at John's ribs, but John twisted, catching the leg and using the goon's momentum to send him sprawling.

The second man was bigger. He moved toward John, throwing punches like sledgehammers.

John, ducking and weaving with perfect timing, avoided contact.

A small crowd had gathered to watch the fight. Some onlookers were horrified, and others cheered, hoping for a blood bath.

Makinde tried to scramble away while John was occupied.

But John was on him instantly. He delivered a hard jab that sent Makinde reeling back.

The second man repositioned himself while John was occupied with Makinde.

John turned just in time to block a heavy blow with his forearm. Then his elbow came up in a sharp arc to slam the attacker's jaw. The big man staggered back, palm to his face, eyes like thunder.

Spectators applauded while encouraging the bigger man to reengage. The first man joined the melee.

John's movements were measured, his attacks strategic. He never turned his back on either opponent for more than a fraction of a second.

Both of Makinde's men were skilled brawlers. Two against one, they pummeled John with solid shots whenever they had a brief opening.

The fight seemed to last forever, but three minutes into it, Nora turned when she heard hoofbeats. NYPD's equestrian team were trotting as fast as the crowds permitted.

"John!" she called out, to be sure he heard the approaching horses.

Makinde's men lost focus.

John delivered a final, decisive blow to the larger man. He crumpled to the ground, unconscious.

The second man, bloodied and bruised, pushed himself up on his hands, his eyes wild. But John was already there, his foot planted firmly on his chest, keeping him down.

The fight had left John's breath ragged, but his stance was unyielding.

"Enough," John said, his voice no louder than a whisper but carrying all the command of a general. "It's over."

Makinde glared at John across his defeated men still on the ground.

John pulled the smaller one to his feet, restraining him with a practiced grip and pushed him toward Makinde. "What do you want to do with him?"

Nora glanced at the battered man. "Let him go."

Makinde reluctantly nodded agreement. The bigger man pushed himself up and staggered into the crowd.

John released the second man. His seething gaze promised vengeance.

Makinde frowned. "I expect to hear from you soon, Ramsey. Two days. No more."

Nora watched Makinde blend into the crowd as they dispersed, and he was soon gone from view.

John and Nora stood in the aftermath, the sounds of the city slowly creeping back into awareness. The horses had slowed amid the throng of pedestrians.

"We should move," Nora said, heading toward the terrace exit. "I don't want to get stuck talking to the police. Come with me."

John, bloodied but not defeated, fell into step beside her. "Makinde's in trouble. He's promised friends and enemies more than he can deliver. If R2 doesn't get the funding you're expecting, he won't survive."

"I was afraid it was something like that," Nora replied. "I wish I could say he's got nothing to worry about. But we all know that's not true."

"Will you get this thing back on track in time to keep Makinde alive?" John asked, stepping around a bag of trash on the sidewalk.

Nora shrugged. "We've got another problem at the moment. Makinde swears he isn't trying to kill me. He says he wasn't behind the two attacks on my life last night."

"You believe him?" John opened the lobby door to her building and allowed her to enter first.

"I believe it would be monumentally stupid for Makinde to take me out before we get the R2 approved and production flowing. And he's not a stupid man," Nora replied as the elevator began its ascent to the thirtieth floor.

"Agreed," John said. "So if Makinde isn't trying to kill you, then who is?"

CHAPTER 28

Monday, June 20
New Slope, New York

KIM THREADED THROUGH THE injured patients and their families toward the security guard standing just outside the double entry doors. She was overwhelmed by the crowd, unable to keep up with people needing attention.

Kim fished her phone out of her pocket and flipped through the photos until she found one of Curry. She approached the guard with the photo ready.

"I can see you're swamped out here. Any chance you might have seen this man? He was an ER patient," Kim said, keeping the conversation to a minimum.

The guard glanced quickly at the photo. "To be honest, I don't know if he came through here or not. I don't remember him. Check at the admissions desk or the ER desk inside."

Which was all she had time to say before she was corralled by another person injured in the bus crash.

The security guard was a long shot, anyway, so Kim gave up the effort and walked farther away from the throng to make her phone calls.

She dialed Gaspar first. After the fourth ring, she disconnected. She'd try again after she talked to Cooper. She used the satellite phone to make that call, but he didn't answer, either.

Kim dropped both phones into her pocket. She looked south along the sidewalk to the hospital's main entrance. Smithers came through the doors, walking toward her wearing a grim expression.

"Curry's dead," he said without preamble. "Talked to the doctor. He threw a blood clot, they said. Died instantly."

Kim stared like Smithers had three heads. "We were just talking to him. He had bruises and a busted nose."

"Doc said it happens. No way to predict it." Smithers nodded. "Can't see him until after the coroner does, which won't happen for a few hours yet. They won't let us see his belongings, although they said he didn't have anything with him except his wallet when the ambulance brought him in."

The initial shock was wearing off and Kim began to think like an agent again. "What about his vehicle?"

"The doctor said it should have been towed to the impound lot. I've got the address," Smithers said.

"Let's go take a look before everything Curry had in there sprouts legs and walks away." Kim stepped off the curb moving toward the SUV in the parking lot. Smithers followed.

Inside the SUV with the engine running, Kim put the address for the impound lot into the navigation system. It was twenty miles from the hospital.

Smithers followed directions while Kim located Gaspar's cell phone and placed another call.

"Any luck with those names I gave you?" Kim asked when he picked up.

"Not yet."

"I've got Smithers here with me. I'm putting you on speaker," Kim said.

"Hey, Gaspar," Smithers said by way of greeting. "Good to be working with you again."

Gaspar warned, "Don't let Cooper hear you say that. He's not happy to have me involved these days."

Smithers shot a quick glance across the cabin toward Kim. She shrugged. Smithers said, "Understood."

"Chico? Zabrinski says Reacher was here. See if you can hack into the CCTV in the hospital to confirm, will you?" Kim said.

"That's just great," Gaspar replied sourly. "How do you know Reacher isn't behind all of this?"

"You think that's likely?" Smithers asked with genuine surprise.

"No. Gaspar's not a Reacher fan. It colors his judgment. Let's add more names to the list. Soper and Kaplan," Kim continued as if there had been no interruption. "Zabrinski says the six of them were in some kind of group. Tardelli, Gunston, Zabrinski, Soper, and Kaplan. He also said Hobie and Allen should have been part of the group but weren't."

Kim could hear him typing the names on a keyboard.

"What sort of group and why were two of them not involved?" Gaspar asked.

"He said Hobie didn't have any siblings or kids. Tardelli told them Allen's family couldn't be found," Kim replied. "Which suggests we might be dealing with a second generation."

"Doesn't make sense that Allen's family couldn't be found, does it? I'll chase that down. As for the rest, we're thinking something happened to the original eight in Vietnam and these six are their survivors?" Gaspar said.

"Yeah," Kim replied, hearing more keyboard work in the background. "The original eight were probably all men. At least one of the second generation was female, Sheryl Tardelli. I'm not sure about Soper, Kaplan, and Bamford."

"How does Reacher fit into all of this? He's not old enough to have served in Vietnam," Smithers said.

"Solid question," Gaspar replied. "Have anything to do with you, Suzie Wong? Your parents? Is this why Cooper wanted you to hunt down Reacher and not someone else? Should I add your father to the list?"

Kim felt her stomach churning. She reached into her pocket for an antacid and slipped it into her mouth.

Smithers cast another glance across the cabin. He must have noticed her distress because he responded to Gaspar. "Let's put all the names into the hopper. See what shakes out."

"Roger that," Gaspar said. "I'd better get to work. Anything else for the moment?"

"We'll let you know," Smithers replied, and Gaspar disconnected the call while Kim was still green around the gills.

They rode a while in silence, following the spoken directions from the navigation system. Smithers spied a fast-food joint ahead and turned into the drive-thru lane. When he pulled up to the speaker to place his order, he said, "Two large black coffees."

Kim said nothing.

At the window, Smithers paid for the coffee and accepted the cups. He handed one to Kim and she took it.

When they were back on the road, she said, "Cooper knows what's going on here."

"Most likely," Smithers replied, turning into the impound lot. "He usually does. You didn't think otherwise, did you?"

"Not really." Kim took a swig of the coffee and placed it in the cup holder.

She wasn't in the mood to speculate about the names on Zabrinski's list. Gaspar would find the connection. Until then, she had plenty to do. "Let's go take a look at Curry's car. Follow my lead."

Smithers didn't object. He parked the SUV and shut the engine down. Kim was already out of the vehicle when he joined her on the way to the office.

Kim walked past a tow truck to the front entrance. The door was stenciled with the name of the place. *New Slope Towing*. She pushed the door inward and heard a bell ringing in the back to signal there were customers out front.

A man dressed in greasy overalls and wearing a ball cap came through the service door. The name embroidered on the left breast pocket was *Evan*. "How can I help you folks?"

Kim pulled her ID and showed him her badge. "FBI Special Agents Otto and Smithers. We're here to examine a vehicle you towed in early this morning belonging to William Curry."

"Yeah, sure. No problem," Evan said, wiping grease from his hands with a shop rag. "It's out back. Pretty messed up. Couple of big dents on the roof. Looks like deer hooves. Then head-on into a tree. We had a heck of a time getting the two separated. Follow me."

Kim slipped her ID into her pocket and followed Evan through the service door, with Smithers close behind. The back room was a large garage with three service bays. Two vehicles were on the hoists and the third was perched over the pit.

Evan walked along the side to a back door and opened it onto a big yard. Chain link fence surrounded the perimeter ten feet high. Vehicles of all sorts were parked in vague rows loosely organized, perhaps by the amount of damage they'd suffered.

"The sedan you're looking for is a silver Camry. Third row on the left. Keys are in it, but it's not drivable. Insurance adjuster will total it out when he gets here," Evan said, gesturing in that direction.

"You called the adjuster?" Kim asked.

"Nah. Sheriff will take care of that," Evan replied as he turned. "I'll be inside when you're done."

CHAPTER 29

Monday, June 20
New Slope, New York

EVAN WALKED BACK TO the garage leaving Kim and Smithers to the task at hand. Kim strode to the sedan and pulled her phone out to take photos. She shot the Camry from all sides.

Smithers fished a latex glove from his pocket, reached inside and pulled the keys from the ignition to open the trunk. "There are a lot of keys on here. Leave the ignition key and take the rest with us?"

"Drop them into an evidence bag. If we have the keys, maybe thieves won't use them to break into his home or his office, at least." Kim gloved up, opened the front door, and searched the interior.

She found Curry's phone, the one he'd been talking to her on when he slammed into the tree. She also found his wallet and a briefcase on the passenger seat.

Broken glass was strewn everywhere, and she saw blood around the driver's seat and the steering wheel. Whether it was Curry's blood or the deer's was not immediately obvious.

She documented the scene with photos and then dropped the phone into an evidence bag. Then she did the same for the briefcase.

The backseat was littered with empty paper bags from various fast-food places. A couple of sweatshirts and a gym bag completed the mess of contents. She documented those with photos, too.

Then she joined Smithers at the back of the vehicle where he was still working on the contents of the trunk.

"Find anything helpful?" she asked as she approached.

"Hard to say. I mean, it's not a crime scene. It's just Curry's personal vehicle. And man, was he sloppy. DNA techs would have to work a week to collect all the samples. You? Find anything inside the car?" Smithers said, taking photos of the contents of Curry's trunk.

"A phone and a briefcase. Could be helpful. We'll take them along," Kim said. "Far as I know, Curry wasn't married. Maybe Marilyn Stone will know what to do with the car and whatever else he left behind."

"You see anything that suggests foul play?" Smithers asked.

"It's all consistent with Curry's account of the accident," Kim shook her head. "Looks exactly like what I'd expect to see. But Cooper will want to know for sure. He'll send a team."

"Okay." Smithers closed the trunk. "Let's go before Evan decides to call his local sheriff. We don't want to be stuck here answering a bunch of questions that will cause Cooper a heart attack."

"That might be fun, actually," Kim said dryly. "But yeah, we should go. Whatever Curry was looking for, we won't find it here in what's left of his car."

They returned to the garage and located Evan in the pit under a van.

"You guys all done back there?" he asked.

"We'll be sending a team to go over the car more carefully," Kim said. "So leave it as is until we release it. But we're done for now."

"Sure. We've got room. County pays us a per diem to store the wrecks 'til they're picked up, so we're happy to keep it forever," Evan grinned and gave them a jaunty salute as they left.

After they settled into the SUV and still wearing her gloves, Kim removed Curry's beat up leather briefcase from the evidence bag.

It was a brown attaché model. An old fashioned rectangular hard-sided leather box with a padded handle.

This one sported a combination lock and two brass latches. The latches required a key. Kim examined Curry's keys through the evidence bag. None of them was the right size and shape to open the briefcase latches.

Smithers cast a look. "That thing looks like he received it as a high school graduation gift and kicked it around plenty in the decades since."

"Curry was like that. His clothes were old-fashioned, too. Everything about him suggested a man twenty years older," Kim replied as she struggled with the latches.

They weren't locked, but they were bent and busted like they'd been sprung and forced open plenty of times before.

"Good thing you're not trying to make a bundle picking locks for a living," Smithers grinned.

Kim gave him a side-eye as she removed Curry's keys from the evidence bag. She found a heavy brass door key and wielded it to pry the right lock until the latch finally popped up. After that, the left one popped of its own accord.

She flashed a victorious glance toward Smithers.

He laughed and said, "Don't quit the day job."

She lifted the lid and looked inside.

The interior of Curry's briefcase was as messy as his car. A blue marker had leaked all over a yellow legal pad covered with what she assumed was Curry's scrawled handwriting. The blue ink had soaked through the pages and dried, causing the pages to stick together.

Under the legal pad were three manila folders. Each was labeled with names in Curry's neat block printing.

Marilyn Stone

Kim Otto

Jack Reacher/Victor Hobie

Kim opened the folders one at a time.

Marilyn Stone's folder contained a standard one-page employment contract. Curry agreed to work for her as a private investigator on an as needed basis for a nice hourly rate. Certainly more than he'd made working for NYPD.

The Kim Otto file contained a standard one-page Michigan Secretary of State DMV report that looked like it had been printed on some old ink jet he picked up at a garage sale. It reflected her home address, her driving record, and her driver's license photo.

The third file was thicker. Inside were a dozen sheets of paper.

The first pages had come from Reacher's Army personnel file. Cooper provided the same pages when Kim first received the Reacher assignment back in November.

Curry probably called in a few favors to get these few pages. The Reacher file itself was fifteen years old. There was nothing remotely useful there.

Beneath the Reacher pages was a single sheet containing a list of eight scrawled names. The same eight names she'd given to Gaspar with brief notations: Hobie (deceased), Allen (deceased),

Tardelli (deceased), Gunston (deceased), Zabrinski, Soper, Kaplan, Bamford.

Curry's block printing was sloppy, as if he'd taken the names down in a hurry. Possibly during a phone call.

After the names he'd listed two dates. Forty-one and thirteen years ago.

Kim stared at Curry's notes, quickly doing the math in her head. Like a pinball game, noises seemed to chime in Kim's head as she followed the sequence.

Reacher was discharged from the Army fifteen years ago. Six months later, he was in Margrave, Georgia.

Thirteen years ago, Reacher was digging swimming pools by hand in Key West. He'd held the job for three months. Until his mentor died.

Reacher quit the Key West job to attend General Leon Garber's funeral in Garrison, New York.

Curry had said that Costello's old files had contained a name. A woman's name that tied to a case Reacher was working on back then.

Kim cocked her head. Reacher might have reconnected with the woman at General Garber's funeral.

Could it have been Jodie Garber Jacob? The general's daughter. As close as any woman ever came to being the one that got away for Reacher.

Kim had met Jodie Jacob a few months back. Jacob had disappeared and Cooper hadn't been able to find her again. Or so he claimed. Were Jacob and Reacher together right now?

"You okay over there, Otto?" Smithers's voice came through the fog. "You look like you've seen a ghost. Your blood sugar too low or something?"

Kim cleared her throat. "Not exactly. Just a little epiphany."

"Something in Curry's notes trigger it?"

"Possibly."

"Curry connected this whole thing to Reacher?"

"Seems like it." Kim nodded. "Curry told me he'd met Reacher. He said Marilyn Stone had met him, too. He also said he'd heard Reacher mention these same eight names. Looks like Curry knew they were all tied together, and he was looking to prove it to me."

"Why?"

"Curry wanted us to work together to find Reacher. I blew him off. So he decided to do it on his own," Kim said, kneading the tension headache that seemed to come from nowhere.

Smithers threw her a scowl. "He died of pulmonary thrombosis, Otto. How could that possibly have been your fault?"

"If I'd agreed to help him, he'd never have been driving last night or hit that tree. He'd be alive now," Kim said plainly.

"On the plus side, you're closer to finding out why Cooper thinks the Tardelli, Gunston, and Zabrinski murders are connected to each other and to Reacher," Smithers said. "Hell, that's probably why he made Marilyn Stone off-limits, too. Curry worked for her, right? She probably knows whatever it was he found out."

"There's eight names here. But Zabrinski said their group had six members. Let's locate the other three members of the group. Sam Soper, Drew Kaplan, and Nadia Bamford," Kim said, unwilling to argue about Cooper's motives. "See if we can figure out why they're being targeted."

"Before the killer gets them first, you mean," Smithers said flatly. "And assuming the killer isn't Reacher."

"Why would you say that?" Kim demanded, eyes flashing. "There's zero evidence that Reacher is killing these people. And we've found no reason whatsoever that he would."

"Okay. Okay," Smithers said, backing off with both palms out. "But you know that's what Cooper is worried about. And if Cooper is worried about Reacher, others will be, too."

Cooper *was* worried about Reacher, and he wouldn't say exactly why. Which meant Smithers's guess was as good as any.

But Cooper's worries were not Kim's immediate concern. Cooper could handle his own issues.

Locating Reacher was her priority.

"So where can we find these people?" Smithers asked. "Soper, Kaplan, and Bamford, right?"

"Curry has their names written down, but that's all. No photos or addresses," Kim said, searching her pockets for the burner phone. "We'll never find them without more intel."

"We know who can get that intel for us," Smithers said pointedly.

Kim gave him an impatient glance as she hit the redial and willed Gaspar to pick up.

CHAPTER 30

Monday, June 20
New York City, New York

NORA RAMSEY STOOD TO stretch the tension from her long limbs. She wandered to the kitchen for a cold drink.

She'd spent the past few hours on the phone with Sheryl Tardelli's colleagues who were members of the Veterans' Affairs Committee. She needed to get R2 back on track. Soon.

Before she ran out of time and money.

More importantly, before thousands more of Makinde's people died of malaria.

She'd hit a dozen brick walls, mostly because the R1 controversy had destroyed too many for too long. The congressional committee was terrified to touch Tardelli's proposed legislation to revive the product and the outrage surrounding it, which had begun to calm down.

The spectacular discovery, rise, and collapse of R1 had all but killed Nora's father and destroyed the Ramsey family business. After years of work, Nora was so very close to reviving the product and Ramsey Chemical.

She couldn't give up now. Couldn't let R2 suffer the same fate as R1. Certainly not before she'd exhausted every possible option.

One of Tardelli's allies, Albert Nelson, had supported R2 while Tardelli was alive. Now, the political winds had changed. She'd already called the others. Nelson was the last member of the committee who might be persuaded to help.

She dialed his number and waited on hold for what seemed an eternity before he finally took her call.

Nelson heard her out before he replied. "Dr. Ramsey, you must know what a hot potato this is. If anything goes wrong, veterans' groups and environmentalists will have our heads. Rightfully so."

"R2 is perfectly safe and effective. You've seen the evidence, Nelson. You know how well R2 is controlling the habitat of malaria causing mosquitos in Nigeria." Nora was pleading with the man while attempting to appeal to his humanitarian nature. "The R2 research we're funding there is saving lives. Thousands of lives. Mostly children. How can that be a bad thing?"

"We thought R1 and other defoliants were good products at the time. Your father and others assured us they were totally safe and wouldn't harm people or the environment. Look how that turned out," Nelson replied, preoccupied and unpersuaded. "We've had hundreds of thousands of claims. We're in the third generation of birth defects now. People say the environment will never recover. *After fifty years.*"

Nora balled her fist and adjusted her approach. "Sheryl Tardelli had more empathy for veterans and their families than everyone else on your committee combined. She had a personal stake, too. Her uncle died in Vietnam and her father was never the same after R1 exposure. Yet, she wanted R2 approved."

"What's your point?" Nelson demanded while telling someone else that he'd be off the phone in a moment. "Sheryl Tardelli won't be at the hearings to plead your case. She's gone. It's up to me to push this now and I'm simply not convinced. I've told you before. If you want approval for R2 and you want the US government to subsidize your project, get me the proof we need to do that."

Nora ran a frustrated hand through her hair. "We've already submitted that proof. You've already analyzed all of it. You know what R2 can do."

"And clean up your team, too. Find a decent Nigerian to support you. Corrupt Nigerians are not helping your cause."

Nora was stunned to silence.

"My schedule is crammed as full as it can possibly be. I'm sorry." Nelson added with finality before he hung up, "And make an appointment if you want to talk to me again."

When he disconnected, Nora threw the phone hard across the room where it landed on a sofa and bounced twice.

Her frustration lingered like a bad aftertaste as she stared at the phone on the sofa. She needed a fresh angle, something to sway the committee's rigid stance.

Which seemed impossible.

She'd already submitted every piece of evidence she'd collected. If what she'd done so far wasn't enough, what more could she offer?

Her thoughts were interrupted by the buzzing phone bouncing on the sofa cushion. A familiar name flashed on the screen.

Calvin Mercer.

She'd met him at several fundraisers for Sheryl Tardelli, who had warned her never to trust the man.

Not that Nora needed a warning.

Mercer's name was synonymous with wealth and power and ruthless business tactics. The best way to deal with him was to stay as far away from his orbit as possible.

Why the hell was he calling her, anyway?

Nora crossed the room and stared at the phone as it continued to vibrate and bounce on the sofa cushion.

Eventually, she inhaled deeply and accepted the call because Mercer wasn't the type to give up or give in. He'd pursue her relentlessly until she capitulated. Just as he'd done to so many others.

"Dr. Nora Ramsey," she said formally.

"Calvin Mercer. I'll get straight to the point." Mercer's voice was smooth, like silk laced with steel. "I was in Nelson's office just now when he shot down your proposal. I've been following your progress with R2. I see potential here and I'm willing to fund your trials."

"You persuaded Nelson to reject my proposal," Nora said flatly, heat rising from her pounding heart to her face. "Why would you do that?"

"Because you don't want or need to be on the government's payroll. They'll bury R2. The product will never reach its potential or save all those Nigerian lives you're so concerned about," Mercer said. "And neither you nor Ramsey Chemical will succeed on your own. Public opinion is against you. Nelson and I did you a favor."

"That's very generous of you, Mr. Mercer," Nora said because it was both appalling and true.

Working with the government was far from ideal. She'd done it before. Too many times.

Living with government rules and regulations was like wearing a straitjacket while weighted down at the deep end of the pool. Drowning was all too common. Bouncing back to the top for air was way less likely than sinking to the bottom.

But the government also had the diplomatic wherewithal to spread R2 around the world where it could serve the greatest number of people and do the greatest good. Once the results on R2 were released, public opinion would change. The world would be clamoring for R2.

Whether Nelson and his committee would allow that to happen was the big question. As of five minutes ago, it seemed the answer was not only no, but hell no.

Mercer's funding could avoid all of the pitfalls and solve many of her problems.

But getting involved with Mercer would create more trouble than she wanted.

He was one of the most controversial people on the planet. The last thing she needed were more protests and objections and crazies to deal with.

He also took total control over the companies he invested in. Ramsey Chemical would not survive in its current form and perhaps not at all.

"We can make this happen. We can reverse the damage to your company and make your father a hero. We can do it now, not ten years from now." Mercer cut off her spiraling thoughts by flatly stating all of the benefits. "In exchange for my support, I want a 60 percent share of Ramsey Chemical. Non-negotiable."

Nora gasped.

Sixty percent.

Nora felt trapped. She needed the funding, but if she gave up 60 percent, she'd already be lost.

Surely there were other alternatives. She could seek an angel investor and a less egomaniacal one.

Nora countered, trying to buy time. "I appreciate your offer, Mr. Mercer, but that's a significant share of the company."

"Take it or leave it, Dr. Ramsey. You're broke and you're out of options. You can't keep paying off Makinde and funding these trials on your own." Mercer was persuasive and vaguely threatening. "Or, R2 could become a cash cow and Ramsey Chemical could be at the forefront of a medical revolution. Eliminating malaria will, as you say, save millions of lives."

Nora's throat dried up. She was cornered. Without new funding, R2 was effectively over, and her father's legacy would forever be nothing but the disasters of the past.

Still, with Mercer's plan, she'd lose control of the company she'd fought so hard to preserve and protect. A bitter pill, indeed. One she simply couldn't swallow.

"I... I need some time to think about it," she managed to say.

"You have sixteen hours," Calvin said curtly before ending the call.

Nora stood frozen, the phone still in her hand.

Accepting Mercer's offer felt like making a deal with the devil.

Yet, turning him down meant watching her dreams and her father's legacy disintegrate into fine green dust.

Makinde wouldn't try to harm her again. She'd made him realize that their destinies were intertwined. If she failed, he failed. She was his golden ticket. Simple as that.

Nora collected a few things and called the helo to take her home to Vermont.

She needed time to think and the best place to do that was her family home that had always been her sanctuary. On her way up to the helipad on the roof, she called John.

CHAPTER 31

Monday, June 20
New Slope, New York

THE MOMENT GASPAR PICKED up the call, Kim put the call on speaker. "We need something to work with here, Chico. What have you got?"

"Lots of intel, but I don't know how useful any of it will be." Gaspar's easygoing style meandered through the speaker and lightened the tension. "Let's start with your list of names. Samuel Soper lives in Utica, Massachusetts. He's a doctor, deep into malaria research."

"Where's Utica?" Kim said, entering the town into the SUV's navigation system while tapping her finger impatiently on her knee. "Looks like it's about a three-hour drive southeast from here. Let's head in that direction while we talk."

"What else do we know about Soper?" Smithers asked as he started the engine and left the parking lot.

The SUV's steady low hum vibrated along Kim's back, feeding the adrenaline quickening her heartbeat. The town of

Utica was a smudge on the map. The kind of place where secrets festered under the veneer of cheery smiles and welcome signs.

Gaspar replied, "Still digging, but not a lot yet."

Smithers, sitting beside her, his gaze hawk-like in the sunlight, interjected, "Malaria, huh? Nasty stuff. What's he doing, exactly?"

Gaspar said, "Soper's on a team that regularly volunteers in Nigeria."

"Nigeria?" Kim echoed. They passed open fields under an overcast sky, nothing like Nigeria. Occasional farmhouses stood like sentinels, their windows witnessing the world without participating in any of it.

"Yeah. Nigeria leads the world in malaria cases and deaths every year, apparently. You know how medical research is. The most money goes to the stuff that's likely to help the most people," Gaspar said as if he were reading from a shareholder press release.

Smithers smirked. "What you mean to say is, the stuff that's likely to make the most money for the drug makers."

"Yeah, well, that, too," Kim nodded, thumbing through Dr. Soper's public profile on her phone. "So is he involved with a group like Doctors Without Borders?"

"No. Looks like private funding," Gaspar said.

Kim asked, "Can you find out what they're working on? And who is footing the bills?"

"Possibly. Checking his travel logs," Gaspar said. "His passport shows several trips to Nigeria in the past two years. Each time, the port of entry is Lagos."

"Can you trace his travel inside Nigeria? Find out where he's working and what they're doing there?" Smithers asked.

"I can. But it'll take a while. And I'm not sure it'll be helpful."

"What about Bamford and Kaplan?" Kim asked. The navigation system interrupted with the order to take exit twenty-two on the right.

"I'm still working on those two. I could have something soon. I'll message you," Gaspar paused briefly. "But something more interesting came up during my search. I put all eight names you gave me into a database and included the Vietnam connection."

"Yeah? How did that go?"

"Several peculiarities came up. Such as, all eight soldiers were men. All Army," Gaspar said. "And here's the hinky part. They're all listed as missing in action on the same day," Gaspar said.

"Now we're getting somewhere," Smithers said. "Were they a unit? All captured together?"

"Still checking. But that's another odd thing. They weren't in the same unit. They shouldn't have been together at all."

"So why were they together, then?" Kim asked.

"Good question. And I'm sure you'll have a million more. So just let me tell you what I know," Gaspar suggested.

When neither Smithers nor Kim objected, he continued. "After they were listed as MIA, the names never show up again during or after the war. I checked every conceivable database. None of the eight were ever mentioned. Not for forty-one years."

Kim felt the hairs on the back of her neck stand up. "Curry noted two dates. Forty-one years and thirteen years."

"Thirteen years ago? I'll put that into my searches," Gaspar said just before he ended the call.

Smithers was the first to breach the silence afterward. "Nigeria. Seems strange, doesn't it? Could be a break."

"Or a wild goose chase," Kim countered, keeping her mind focused. "Bamford and Kaplan are still unaccounted for."

"Think Soper's aware he's a target?" Smithers asked, eyes on the road.

Kim pondered, her fingers tapping on her knee. "Hard to say. Does he know that three of his friends have been shot and two are dead? So far, the national media hasn't picked up the story. If he's heard about the shooter and he's smart, he's lying low."

The silence stretched, filled only by the hum of the engine.

"Gaspar will find something on Bamford and Kaplan," Smithers said to himself. "Allen's family, too, probably."

Kim was lost in thought until her phone buzzed with a message from Gaspar. "Soper is a runner. Gaspar tracked his phone. He's jogging at the high school."

She leaned over to adjust the navigation system. They'd been driving awhile. The system said they were twenty minutes out from Soper's location.

"Think the shooter knows where to find Soper?" Smithers mused aloud.

"He's found the others," Kim pointed out. "Why would Soper be different?"

"Right." Smithers pushed the SUV's speed over the speed limit on the country roads.

The SUV raced toward the high school track following the navigation guidance. Otto's phone remained silent, which felt ominous somehow.

After a while, Smithers said, "We're almost there."

"Let's hope we're not too late to keep Soper alive," Kim replied grimly.

CHAPTER 32

Monday, June 20
Rural Vermont

NORA RAMSEY PACED HER office at Ramsey Chemical, considering her options. She was running out of time. She needed to make a decision.

Her focus on R2 had been unwavering for years. She was so close now. Closer than she'd ever been.

With Sheryl Tardelli's help, Nora had put together a solid team. Each member of the team held an ownership interest in the R2 project. Six members of the team held 5 percent each. Thirty percent, total. Which could amount to millions.

Not enough ownership to make major decisions or to derail any aspect of the project. Nora held the controlling interest and always had. But they all deserved a chance to voice their opinions.

She and Kaplan had created the perfect herbicide. It targeted only malaria-causing mosquitos. The humanitarian potential was enormous.

Zabrinski had tested it on his farm. He'd proved R2 completely safe for farm crops.

Soper had documented the reduction in malaria cases after field testing in Nigeria and the number of lives saved would grow exponentially now that they'd perfected the formula.

Bamford's PR machine had worked up a blitz of promotional materials to blanket the world and turn public opinion.

Gunston's judicial decisions in local cases had laid the groundwork for appeals to set aside false claims against R1 that might otherwise have spilled over to taint R2.

Tardelli's interest had been purely altruistic. She wasn't a shareholder because she didn't want to be. She wanted to save lives and support veterans. She had been, perhaps, the best of them.

Makinde was an essential piece of the puzzle, but not a shareholder, either. He wanted to be paid in cold cash. He took his cut off the top and the system had worked well enough.

Until Tardelli died.

That was Nora's darkest hour. She had believed none of what they'd accomplished together would matter without Tardelli's legislation.

She'd been wrong, she had to admit. Calvin Mercer's money and influence was better than Tardelli's legislation. Faster, too.

But Mercer wanted 60 percent of the company. If she gave it to him, Nora would be left with only 10 percent after the others were paid.

Ten percent was a bitter pill to swallow. After years of humiliation and despair, her beloved father had killed himself because of the fiasco surrounding R1. That Nora had finally salvaged the company's name and reputation only to be relegated to a minor shareholder seemed grossly unfair.

"Nothing to worry about," John had said. "The others will agree. They want you to be the majority shareholder of Ramsey Chemical. Even Makinde wants that."

Nora held on to John's confidence like a lifeline. Now, she would know for sure.

Drew Kaplan was the first to arrive at the conference room. He grabbed a bottle of water and took his seat at the foot of the table across from Nora's usual chair. "John. Good to see you again. What's up, Nora?"

"Good news. But I want to tell everyone at the same time," she said with a reassuring smile.

"Okay. But I've got another commitment. Are the others joining soon?" Drew asked, gesturing to the oversized speaker at the center of the table.

It was a reasonable question. Drew was the only one from the group who worked at Ramsey Chemical and lived close by. The others often met by conference call.

"We're placing the calls now," she said, gesturing vaguely toward the office next door that was usually occupied by her lifelong secretary.

"Makinde's in town," Drew said after a long swig from the water bottle. "He came by my office an hour ago. Wants you to meet him later."

"Did he say why or where?" Nora asked, shooting a frown in John's direction. What did Makinde want now?

"Said he left you a voice mail. Check your phone." Drew tapped his fingers on the table impatiently. "Can we do this later? Or tomorrow? I'm already late and I really need to bug out."

"Let me just check to see how we're doing rounding up the others," she said as she lifted her phone to call her secretary.

"I'm sorry. I can't get anyone on the phone. It's late and they must be gone already. I'll keep trying, but maybe tomorrow would be better?" Marge asked helpfully.

Realizing she wouldn't have Kaplan's full attention if she kept him here anyway, Nora reluctantly agreed. "Okay. How about tomorrow morning at nine o'clock?"

"Works for me," Kaplan said with a wave on his way out the door.

Marge said, "I'll leave voice mails for the others and follow up again tonight to be sure they're all aware."

Nora found her cell phone and searched for Makinde's voice mail. She found it buried under a list of others. She listened to it twice before she fully comprehended his meaning.

She played the message on the speaker so John could hear it.

"It's my fault, Nora. When Tardelli said she couldn't find the Allens, I dug deeper. I'm sorry now. But what's done is done," Makinde said. "Bring John. We'll need him."

At the end of the message, he'd added one final teaser.

"They broke into your home. Not me. Don't go back. It's not safe. Meet me at the southside building at midnight. We can talk privately." Makinde's rumbling voice was unmistakable.

Nora grabbed her coat and followed John out to the parking lot.

CHAPTER 33

Monday, June 20
Utica, Massachusetts

THE SHOOTER'S WINDOW WAS down, and he remembered the feel of cool evening air on his skin after the unseasonably hot day when his family died. Something he didn't think about often enough. But when he did, the memory brought calm to his too often frantic nature.

The driver cruised the black sedan, an older but well-maintained model, through the streets of Utica like a man who had lived here much of his life. Which he had not.

But the family had lived near Boston when they were young boys. They'd moved to Virginia long ago.

In Massachusetts, spring was cooler and softer than Virginia.

The high school year was finished for the summer and the immediate area was all but deserted, as planned. They made the final turn onto Lincoln Avenue and parked where they knew they would have an unobstructed sight line.

"There," the driver said, indicating the deserted track where Dr. Samuel Soper jogged alone visible through the long, wavering shadows cast by the streetlights.

Soper's footsteps pounded a rhythmic steady beat that might have been timed to his pulse.

The shooter noticed that Soper's lightweight shirt clung to his lean body. White running shorts allowed unrestricted movement and a brand of running shoes that Olympic athletes favored seemed to give him an unnatural lift.

Nothing in his costume would protect him from a well placed bullet.

Soper's fluid stride had developed when he was a long-distance track star in high school and college. Witnesses said he'd competed with fierce determination back then that he channeled into his professional life these days.

In a recent interview about his charity work, Soper claimed running was his sanctuary. Each step was a meditation that cleared his mind. He said he found peace on the track, under the open sky feeling the soft, rhythmic thud of his footsteps.

It was a ritual, this nightly run, he'd said. A necessary solitude that grounded him, reminding him of who he was beyond the scrubs and medical masks.

Which was why the shooter had chosen this time and place. Soper was a creature of habit. He'd be on the track tonight, lost in the ritual that made him an easy target.

Tonight, Soper's mind would wander to his upcoming mission to Nigeria.

It was a challenging assignment, Soper had said in the interview with a determined set to his jaw.

"The children and families suffering with malaria wouldn't survive without you. But why do you do this work?" the reporter asked. "Professional satisfaction?"

"Partially," he'd admitted.

"But it's not only that," the reporter guessed. "What about making a significant difference in the lives of those impoverished children living amid chaos and suffering? It's your chance to give back, right?"

Soper, the very highly paid Boston internist, had seemed embarrassed by the sentiment. He'd nodded and lowered his gaze. "Something like that, yes."

The shooter shook his head. Even as a kid, he'd had an infallible bullshit meter. Soper was full of crap. Always had been.

The car's presence was incongruous in the evening stillness. But to Soper, absorbed in his run, it should be just another fleeting shadow in the night.

Inside, the shooter and the driver were silent, focused on the task at hand.

They had transformed the back of the sedan into a comfortable but unlikely sniper's nest.

Meticulously modified after news reports of the setup used by the infamous Beltway Sniper. The shooter had studied those crimes, practicing intently until he could recreate the process.

No way was he going to fail like the Beltway sniper did. That kid was too young. Only seventeen. The shooter had years of experience. He was older, better, steadier, deadlier.

The Beltway kid made only seventeen kills. The shooter would double that number before he stopped.

The shooter had removed the rear seats of the sedan, creating a cramped but functional space. Next, he had installed a flat platform covered with a thin, dark mat to minimize noise.

The platform served as a stable foundation base for a sniper to lie prone.

The most critical modification was to the sedan's trunk. He cut a small, rectangular section from the lid, just large enough to allow the barrel of his high-powered rifle to protrude.

The makeshift firing port was cunningly concealed. He'd inspected it from every angle, and he was certain. Undetectable to an unsuspecting eye, for sure. It could be quickly covered up if needed.

The setup offered a narrow field of vision, but for a skilled marksman like him, it was more than sufficient for a precise shot.

Inside the sedan tonight, the air was thick with tension.

The shooter had considered every detail.

The sedan's windows were darkly tinted, obscuring the interior from outside view. Soundproofing material lined the walls of the trunk.

The rifle itself was a testament to engineering, equipped with a silencer and a high-grade scope. It was a weapon designed for a singular purpose and satisfyingly effective.

The sedan was stocked with other necessities. Water, nonperishable food, and basic first aid supplies, in case prolonged stakeouts were required.

The meticulousness of the setup reflected the shooter himself. Prepared. Lethal.

The shooter checked his watch. "It's time."

The driver nodded, scanning the area. "Copy that."

The shooter maneuvered himself into position.

In the confined space, every action was precise, each motion calculated.

He settled onto the flat platform, a position he had practiced countless times, and took a moment to center himself.

In this work, mental preparation was crucial. He closed his eyes, took a deep breath, and let it out slowly, steadying his heart rate, calming the adrenaline that threatened to spike.

Opening his eyes, the shooter peered through the rifle's high-grade scope, adjusting the focus until the view was crystal clear. The scope was his narrow but critical vantage point.

He scanned the track methodically, his gaze moving in a practiced pattern until he spied Samuel Soper.

His body was intermittently lit by the streetlights as he jogged, creating a rhythmic pattern of visibility. The shooter considered donning his night vision, which would reverse but not eliminate the pattern. He decided to stay the course.

The shooter watched Soper, studying his pace, stride, the rhythm of his movements. Timing was the key to placing the shot.

He needed to predict Soper's position, to anticipate the precise moment to send his bullet to hit the moving target.

The shooter adjusted the scope to bring Soper into sharper focus.

He observed the way Soper's arms swung, the tilt of his head, the steady rise and fall of his chest with each breath.

He shifted his attention to environmental factors. The wind was a gentle breeze, barely noticeable. He adjusted his aim to compensate.

Once again, he checked his weapon with clinical detachment. Suppressor secure. Ammunition ready.

CHAPTER 34

Monday, June 20
Utica, Massachusetts

SOPER CONTINUED HIS RUN, unaware. The shooter's finger rested lightly. He waited for the moment, the perfect alignment of time, space, and motion.

In the quiet of the sedan's modified trunk, with his eye pressed to the scope and his finger poised, the world outside was reduced to a series of movements, wind speeds, and trajectories, all converging to a single, critical point in time.

The sedan's engine produced a barely audible hum and soothing vibration.

The shooter made another minor adjustment. "I've got him."

On the track, Soper was oblivious to lurking danger, lost in his own world.

Inside the car, the shooter's trigger finger hovered.

He steadied his breath, his finger resting on the trigger.

Soper ran, one long leg in front of the other, like a metronome, unaware of the crosshairs trained on him.

Just as the shooter was about to take his shot, a loud, unexpected noise shattered the silence.

A car alarm went off nearby, a blaring siren echoing through the empty streets. Followed by gunshots and squealing tires as the car thieves made their escape.

Startled, Soper stopped running, looking around in confusion. The sudden break in Soper's pattern defeated the shooter's precise aim.

"Damn it!" he said, adding a stream of curses as he pulled back.

"What happened?" the driver demanded.

Between curses, the shooter replied, "I lost my shot."

"We need to move," the driver said. "Right now."

The shooter nodded as he returned the rifle to its resting place and climbed into the front seat.

Soper, still on the track, took out his phone, perhaps calling to report the alarm and the gunshots. He glanced around wildly as they heard approaching sirens.

The driver rolled away with the sedan's lights off, blending into the night.

The shooter was silent.

"We'll come back in a couple of days," he said, his gaze lingering in the rearview mirror. "There's a cop car at the track, talking to Soper."

The shooter leaned forward, peering into the side mirror. His voice was like cold, hard steel. "We'll wait. We need to do this now."

The driver circled the block and parked in a shadowed alley, hiding the sedan from view. The shooter climbed out. Flattening his back to a brick retaining wall, he inched to the intersection and craned his neck for a better view of the track.

He caught a few words wafting in his direction but couldn't hear Soper's conversations.

More police arrived, blue lights flashing in the darkness. Soper spoke with them, probably explaining what he'd heard.

Two officers returned after a quick sweep of the area. After a brief conversation, Soper nodded and headed toward his car.

He'd parked a short distance from the track, and he kept looking over his shoulder, which made the shooter smile.

From his position in the alley, the shooter watched a few moments more until the police left the track. He returned to the sedan and climbed inside to grab the rifle.

"Now's my chance. Wait here. Be ready to go," he said.

"Got it," the driver replied.

The shooter moved stealthily to his vantage point at the entrance to the alley. He readied his shot as Soper came closer to his car.

Soper placed his hand on the door handle.

But then he stopped and turned slowly, as if his gaze were magnetically drawn to the alley where the shooter was hidden in the shadows.

A glint off the rifle's metal seemed to catch his attention. It was brief, almost imperceptible, but for Soper, it was enough.

The lucky bastard dropped to the ground just as the sound of the suppressed gunshot whispered through the air.

The bullet zinged toward Soper's position.

The shot, meant to silence the heartbeat of a man who had dedicated his life to saving others, buried itself in the hard steel of Soper's car instead.

The shooter's face was a mask of intense concentration. He cursed under his breath.

The shot had been perfect. The execution should have been flawless.

Failure.

Soper's reaction time had been almost impossibly fast.

Soper, on the ground, must have realized with chilling clarity that the shot was meant for him.

The shooter could almost feel the panic clawing at Soper's chest. Through the scope, he saw Soper's breaths coming in short, rapid bursts.

The shooter waited. Patience was a practice he'd cultivated. He could wait forever for the perfect shot. But he knew he wouldn't need to.

What would Soper do next? He would move. His instinct would be to get away into the open. Foolishly thinking the shooter wouldn't take him down if he left the shadows.

Which is exactly what he did.

"You're mine now, you bastard," the shooter murmured through the tense smile on his lips.

Rolling to his feet, Soper sprinted, hands pumping at his sides as he ran for cover.

The shooter adjusted his position.

The first shot's miss had been a deviation in his otherwise perfect record. He wouldn't allow a second.

Peering through the scope, he found Soper again. This time he was a moving target, which made the shot more interesting.

He tracked Soper's movements through the scope with icy detachment. The same way he'd put down two dozen wild hogs.

Soper, exhibiting the same survival instincts as a cornered animal, zigzagged across the parking lot.

Distant sirens were headed in the wrong direction to help Soper now.

The shooter's finger rested, his breath smooth as Soper's body entered the crosshairs.

The shooter smiled and fired.

The bullet found its mark.

Soper's run ended abruptly.

He collapsed, face first, onto the pavement.

The shooter watched through the scope for a moment longer, to be certain. Soper was dead. No question.

Satisfied, he hustled to the idling sedan and placed the rifle inside.

Lights still off, the driver rolled away and slipped into the night, leaving behind only exhaust fumes.

The shooter leaned back and closed his eyes wearing a satisfied smile. "Four down. Two more."

"We're pushing our luck," the driver said. "Isn't four enough?"

The shooter gave him an angry glare. "Stick to the plan."

"It won't be easy to finish the Ramsey woman. And then there's Reacher if the plan works," the driver said nervously. "Better to walk away and live to fight another day, isn't it?"

Coldly, he replied, "Failure is not an option. You want to bail, that's fine. I'll finish the mission without you."

The driver shook his head, took a deep breath, and returned his full attention to the road.

Which was the precise moment when the shooter made his decision. The driver was old and weak. Left to survive, he might live to be as old as his father. The shooter absolutely did not want that to happen.

The decision had been lingering for weeks, but now he knew exactly what he wanted to do.

CHAPTER 35

Monday, June 20
Utica, Massachusetts

AS THEY MADE THE last turn, Kim saw red and blue flashing lights ahead.

Smithers pulled up as far as he could and parked hastily.

"Looks like we're too late." Kim released her seatbelt, opened the door, and slid onto the pavement.

They approached the scene on foot. The EMS unit was parked with its lights flashing, but Kim didn't see paramedics operating with a sense of urgency. Which meant that emergency medical care for the injured wasn't required.

Police officers and other first responders were moving about the area methodically. The running track was cordoned off. A body was splayed out on the pavement.

Kim approached one of the officers, displayed her ID and gave her name. Then she asked, "What happened?"

The officer looked grim. "Local citizen. Dr. Samuel Soper. Looks like he was gunned down running away from the track. Shooter's long gone."

Kim's gaze scanned the scene. No white van in sight. Smithers stood beside her, his expression a mix of frustration and anger.

"Witnesses?" Kim asked.

"None we've found so far," the officer replied. "There was a vehicle theft reported before the shooting. We do have some gang violence in this area from time to time. We'll be looking into that along with everything else."

Smithers clenched his jaw and spoke for Kim's ears only. "Soper was our best lead."

"Any useful evidence so far?" Kim asked as she stepped closer to the body, still checking the vicinity for the sniper's nest.

She confirmed that the shot most likely came from a vehicle parked along the street. Surrounding buildings would have blocked the shooter's sight line.

"Still processing the scene at this point," the officer said. "But whoever did this was no novice."

"Right." Kim broadened her visual scan of the area, taking note of distances and possible trajectories. "We'd like to see the body."

"Sorry. We need to protect our crime scene," the officer replied, shaking his head. "You don't want to come back to testify or help with the paperwork, I assume."

"I'll make a call," Kim replied, gazing directly into the officer's eyes while reaching for the satellite phone that would connect her to Cooper.

The officer didn't relent. "If my boss says you can look, that's all I need."

He moved to prevent a couple of kids on bikes from riding closer to the victim.

While the officer was preoccupied, Smithers inched around to get a better view of Soper's body.

Even from her position, Kim could tell that Soper had been shot in the back. He never saw it coming.

Smithers scanned the surroundings. "Killer could've been anywhere along this street. Perfect vantage point."

The officer interjected, "We're checking nearby security cams. If we find anything, we can let you know."

Kim was still holding the satellite phone to her ear, but Cooper never answered. After two dozen rings, she disconnected the call.

"Can't reach my boss," she said. "Can we just take a quick look? We won't contaminate your scene."

The officer shook his head. "Sorry. You know the drill."

"Yeah. We get it. No worries," Smithers said as they walked toward the SUV.

Kim called Gaspar and brought him up to speed. "Soper's dead. Shot in the back with a rifle, from the looks of things. We couldn't get close enough to see much. Can you breach video cams surrounding the scene?"

"Let me find your precise location," he said, making keyboard sounds in the background. "Okay, I've got you. Yeah, there are several cams in the area. Maybe a few are easily vulnerable to hackers. The high school track should be visible. Not much of the street, though. I'll see what I can do. Call you back."

Kim slipped the phone into her pocket and Smithers said, "Looks like our theory is holding, I guess."

"Yeah. Which means we've got two more chances to catch this guy. After that, who knows where he'll strike," Kim said disgustedly.

She called Gaspar again. "Got anything on Kaplan and Bamford yet?"

"Home addresses. GPS coordinates on their personal vehicles in case they're not at home. I'll message them to both of you." Gaspar said and hung up.

When they climbed inside the SUV, Kim settled into her seat and adjusted her seatbelt. She opened Gaspar's message to see the two home addresses she'd requested.

"Let's split up. I'll take Kaplan. You go after Bamford. Let's see if we can keep them both alive."

"We'll need a second vehicle." Smithers started the SUV and rolled away from the Soper murder scene.

Kim searched for car rental companies and found one located a couple of miles away. She used the website to reserve an SUV. Smithers dropped her at the parking lot.

"Remember what we're dealing with," he said as she slid out to the pavement. "Snipers can kill from a long way off."

"Yeah. You never see the bullet that gets you." Kim checked her weapon, her movements precise. "Keep your phone close. Stay in constant contact."

Smithers echoed, "Let's hope we get to them before the shooter does."

Kim closed the SUV's door, collected her laptop case and her travel bag from the back seat, and headed for her rental through the crisp foreboding air.

A strong sense of urgency propelled her, tying her stomach in familiar knots as she stowed her bags and climbed into the driver's seat. Moments later, they were on the road, Kim in front and Smithers close behind.

Bamford was located in upstate New York. Kaplan lived and worked in rural Vermont. The two towns were a few hours apart. Which offered both an advantage and a deepening sense of danger.

As she drove, Kim's mind replayed the events leading up, and discovered nothing she'd missed before. Nothing she'd considered at the time glared brighter now, either.

When they reached a major intersection, Kim flashed her lights and turned west. Smithers flashed a quick response and headed in the opposite direction.

Kim continued alone through the unfamiliar landscape like a soldier crossing a mine field, knowing the sniper could have his scope trained on her or Smithers already.

The roads leading to Vermont were nearly empty. Few vehicles were driving in any direction. The eerie silence exacerbated her uneasy nerves. Her hands ached from the tight grasp of the steering wheel even as she tried to relax her grip.

Gaspar's burner phone rang, and she picked up the call, grateful for the virtual company.

"What's up, Chico?"

"I've found more details on the connection between the eight veterans. Got time to talk?"

"Plenty of time. Nothing but time." She might sound a bit hysterical if she kept going, so she cleared her throat and said, "Fill me in."

Gaspar didn't seem to notice her nerves, which was good. She didn't need a lecture on the perils of working dangerous cases alone. She was already too aware.

"So we know all eight soldiers were declared MIA on the same day. After more digging, it looks like their helo got shot down behind enemy lines." Gaspar paused to slurp something. Probably the excessively sweet Cuban coffee he mainlined.

"Sounds about right." Kim's internal threat meter dropped back off the red zone.

"To recap, there's nothing in the records about those eight guys for forty-one years," Gaspar continued. "Which is when it gets interesting for your purposes."

"How so?"

"Thirteen years ago, the names were added to the Vietnam War Memorial," Gaspar said. "All eight names. All at one time."

CHAPTER 36

Monday, June 20
Rural Vermont

"MIAS WERE PLACED ON the wall right from the start of the memorial project, weren't they?" Kim asked. "Why weren't the names already listed?"

"The rules for which names were included and which weren't are complicated and probably not relevant," Gaspar explained. "Again, the first important point for these purposes is that the eight names were left off for more than forty years."

"And the second important point is that all eight were added at the same time thirteen years ago?" Kim teased, which made her feel better even if Gaspar found her jibes annoying.

She stopped for a red light at a lonely intersection not too many miles from the Vermont state line. On the other side she spied a burger place where she could get coffee.

When the light changed, she drove through and pulled into the parking lot.

"Exactly." Gaspar paused to slurp again. "Could have something to do with Reacher. And Leon Garber. And possibly Garber's daughter as well."

"Because?"

"Because otherwise, Cooper wouldn't care about all of this, and you wouldn't be an easy target out there in Nowhereville."

"I sort of guessed all that," Kim said dryly. She couldn't see the scowl on his face, but she was sure it was there.

"So I made some calls. Off the record," he said, ignoring her jibes. "And finally connected up with a legendary old man named Nash Newman."

"Uh, huh," Kim said as she climbed out of the SUV and walked toward the restaurant. Her stomach was too anxious for food, but coffee would help.

"General Newman's last duty station was the Central Identification Laboratory in Hawaii," Gaspar said as if he were imparting the wisdom of the ages to a simpleton.

"Can you hang on a second?" Kim said as she made her way to the counter where a bored teenager seemed mildly pleased to have a customer.

She paid for her coffee and then stood aside while he brewed a fresh pot. "Okay. So General Newman…"

"I knew the general, briefly. Met him a few times at official functions. So I contacted him. Asked him if he'd known General Garber. Of course, he had. At those levels, most officers know each other. But, get this, turns out he knew Reacher, too," Gaspar said sounding very pleased with himself.

"Now you have my full attention," Kim said, meaning it.

"Thought so. Newman said Garber and Reacher and Jodie Garber Jacob had come to see him about these eight guys. Wait for it," Gaspar said, like a kid relating an especially great story.

"Because *seven* of the bodies had been finally recovered from the jungle inside a downed helo. *Thirteen years ago.*"

Kim's surprised gasp was genuine. Not about the timing so much as the bodies. "Seven? What happened to the eighth one?"

"The eighth dog tag belonged to Victor Hobie. He should have been on that helo, but he wasn't," Gaspar's tone suggested that he too felt a little let down. "General Garber died. And if Reacher ever figured out the end of the story, he didn't fill Newman in."

"So Hobie must have survived the helo crash?" Kim said slowly, thinking it through.

"Doesn't matter," Gaspar replied. "He'd be way too old now to go around shooting anybody fifty years later regardless."

"Right." Kim collected her coffee from the teenager and headed toward the parking lot. "So this is all academic. We still don't know who is targeting the six survivors and why."

"Zabrinski said there were six members of their group. He said Tardelli put the group together. And he said relatives for two of the original eight soldiers were excluded," Gaspar said, "Hobie and Allen."

"But remember Zabrinski told us that Hobie had no surviving relatives. And Allen's survivors couldn't be found." She started the SUV and placed the hot coffee into the cup holder.

"Yeah, and I don't buy that. Everybody in America is on some database somewhere. If Sheryl Tardelli tried to find Carl Allen's relatives, she could have found them. She was a sitting US Congresswoman, for cripes sake."

"I see your point," Kim said. "So you're thinking what? She didn't look? She didn't want to find them? She did find them and just excluded them from the group for some reason?"

"I'll keep looking for Allen's family, but for now, we've taken this as far as we can. Let's cover something else quickly," Gaspar said, switching gears. "Kaplan lives in Vermont. Tardelli lived in Vermont. Possible they knew each other before Tardelli started the group."

Kim nodded, keeping her eyes on the road again. "What else do you have on Kaplan? What kind of work does he do?"

"He's a chemist. He works for Ramsey Chemical Company. Located in…" he let his voice trail off as if he were giving a kid a clue on his homework.

"Vermont. Okay. I get your drift," she smiled. "What do we know about Ramsey Chemical Company?"

"Not a lot and most of it isn't good," Gaspar said as if he were reading the screen as he talked. Then he stopped breathing into the phone's speaker.

"What?" Kim asked.

"The founder, Norman Ramsey was the guy who invented R1, the hugely controversial herbicide used extensively during the Vietnam war," Gaspar said, still speed-reading through a bunch of pages. "Lots of fanfare announcing the herbicide initially because it was meant to clear the jungle where the enemy was hiding and give US soldiers an advantage…Then all the disastrous consequences later…Lawsuits…bankruptcy…suicide. Norman Ramsey killed himself."

The rush of intel was difficult to absorb all at once. She had a million questions. But she started with Kaplan.

"If Ramsey Chemical Company went bankrupt and the owner died, how can Kaplan be working there now?"

"Seems like the company has been resurrected somehow. Congresswoman Sheryl Tardelli was supporting a bill to rehabilitate Ramsey Chemical's reputation," Gaspar said, still speed-reading through whatever report he'd tapped into. "When Tardelli died, the bill died with her."

"What was the legislation about?" Kim asked.

"Seems like Ramsey Chemical has developed a new herbicide. It's patented. They're calling it R2. Tardelli's bill would have approved R2 for use and sale by the US government in developing nations," Gaspar said, still scanning. "Says here that Tardelli had been getting death threats over the bill, too."

"So one of those crazies made good on his threat," Kim said flatly. "But which one?"

CHAPTER 37

Monday, June 20
Upstate New York

IN THE BUSTLING PARKING lot of the strip center, the shooter saw the young mother herding her two children toward their car. She seemed preoccupied. Perhaps her mind was running through the list of errands she'd managed to complete with this late-night shopping trip.

"Mom, can we get ice cream?" her youngest piped up, tugging at her sleeve.

The woman smiled, "Maybe, if you and your brother can buckle up without any fuss."

As they approached their car, the driver rolled the dark sedan slowly past them, stopping at the end of another row. He placed the sedan out of camera range.

These all-night box stores ran on thin margins. They usually had cameras at the entrances and exits, but not all the way out at the back of the parking lot.

There weren't as many vehicles at this hour, but they were parked haphazardly, making the sight lines difficult. After a couple of tries, the driver found a solid vantage point.

"That's her, right?" the driver said, indicating the woman pushing the shopping cart and the two kids dancing around it.

"Yeah, that's Nadia Bamford. You ready?" The driver kept his eyes fixed on the rearview mirror, watching Bamford and her children.

The shooter checked his rifle, a quiet click confirming it was loaded.

"Always ready," he replied with unsettling calm.

Bamford's eldest looked curiously at the sedan. The shooter heard him say, "Mom, why's that car parked there? No one's getting out."

She followed his gaze, noting the vehicle's odd placement. "I'm not sure, honey. Stay close."

The shooter watched Bamford's movements closely. "Looks like she's getting suspicious."

"Mom, look!" her youngest exclaimed, pointing to a balloon vendor nearby.

Bamford turned to look, her back now to the sedan, shielding her children from view but not from bullets. "After we're in the car, okay?"

The shooter peered through the scope, his breath steady. "Target's turned. Waiting for a clear shot."

The older boy's attention drifted back to the sedan. "That car looks weird," he said, a note of concern in his voice.

Bamford spun around. "Get behind the car, now!" she ordered, pushing her children away.

The shooter's finger hesitated on the trigger. He didn't have a clear shot. He'd made that mistake with Zabrinski. He didn't want to hit these kids.

Bamford, perhaps sensing the danger, positioned herself between the sedan and her children, her eyes searching for the source of her son's alarm.

"What are you waiting for?" the driver's patience was wearing thin. He turned to get a better view through the rear window.

The shooter inhaled deeply, ignoring the question as he realigned the rifle.

"On it," he murmured with conviction.

The oldest boy grabbed her arm. "Mom, that man's looking at us!"

"Get down!" Bamford's command was sharp as she pushed her son to the ground and joined him there half a moment too soon.

The shot rang out, echoing across the parking lot.

"Dammit!" He'd missed. Again.

Bamford fell to the pavement, her eyes wide with shock, slapping a palm over her bleeding bicep.

"Mom!" her children screamed, scrambling to her side.

The rifle's report still ringing in his ears, the shooter said, "I hit her."

The driver shouted, aghast. "You were supposed to take her out, not wing her!"

Bamford clutched her arm, scrambling to shield her children with her body.

"Mom, we need to help you!" the boy cried, tears streaming down his face.

Patrons started to notice the commotion as they left the store. A crowd was beginning to form.

"We can't stay here," the driver said.

The shooter didn't move, his gaze locked on the scope, watching the unfolding horror.

Shoppers were now rushing to Bamford's aid. Calls for help mingled with the sounds of approaching sirens.

A big black SUV rolled up fast. The driver, a large Black man, slammed it into Park and flung the door open. He pulled a pistol from a holster and ran toward Bamford shouting, "Get down! Get down!"

"We have to go now!" The driver's hand reached for the transmission shifter.

Bamford locked eyes with the driver through the sedan's rear window. She held him steady with a hard gaze as if she were memorizing his image.

The shooter's heart hammered, but he held his position, willing the kid to move out of the crosshairs.

The boy stood protectively in front of his mother and brother, his small frame trembling.

The big armed man's long legs pounded the parking lot toward the family.

The driver snarled, "We're leaving!"

Before he had the chance to move the sedan, the shooter fired his second shot.

"Bingo," he whispered as the bullet penetrated Bamford's head, knocking her to the ground.

"We can go now," the shooter said calmly as he slid inside, closing the hole and placing the rifle carefully.

The big man turned and fired toward the sedan. Two shots hit the rear bumper as the driver slipped the transmission into drive and sped away from the grizzly scene.

The shooter returned to the passenger seat, a smile on his lips. "What a rush!"

The driver shot a scowl across the cabin. "Wild boars don't shoot back. We're not bulletproof, you know."

"Kaplan's the last target before Ramsey. We're three hours away," the shooter said, refusing to lose the euphoria of the moment.

CHAPTER 38

Tuesday, June 21
Rural Vermont

THE SHOOTER HAD CHOSEN this place with care. He watched through his scope as Makinde stepped over fallen logs and around tangled brush with the agility and stealth of a jungle cat. He moved relentlessly toward his objective. Eyes constantly scanning. Ears tuned to the slightest sound.

The crumbling facade and boarded-up windows of the abandoned chemical factory in remote Vermont was a place forgotten by time. Makinde said he had come across it during a visit to Ramsey in the winter season a few years back, when the factory's existence was revealed by bare trees and accentuating snow.

In June, nature's camouflage concealed the old building so effectively it was as close to invisible as a brick structure could be.

No one would stumble upon this place. There were no homes or businesses nearby. No nature trails or campgrounds. When the manufacture of R1 halted and all the subsequent misfortune was heaped on old man Ramsey, this was the place he'd come to kill himself.

Makinde had promised information, sensitive information that he couldn't deliver even over secure channels.

He needed absolute privacy, which was impossible to find in twenty-first century America. This old place came as close as he could get without triggering alarms he didn't want to trip, he'd said, as if he imagined he was baiting the hook.

He'd made it clear that the intel he planned to share was for Ramsey's ears only. They'd worked together for a long time, and he trusted Ramsey to know her best interests would be served by coming alone, he'd said, and she wouldn't bring backup.

Of course, the shooter knew Ramsey wouldn't show up at all. The two explosions, one at her home and one at the operating Ramsey Chemical facility, would take care of her.

Once Makinde was inside the building, the shooter adjusted his position and donned his vision equipment. Ambient light was almost nonexistent. But there was enough.

The shooter easily located Makinde standing deep in the shadows as was his habit. He wasn't expecting trouble. But bad experiences had taught him to operate with constant vigilance.

Which made him a challenging target. The shooter appreciated a challenge.

The silence was oppressive, broken only by the distant hoot of an owl. Makinde checked his watch, a subtle movement because he expected Ramsey to be there soon.

Suddenly, the air shifted. Makinde peered through the darkness and focused his attention on the gaping maw at the entrance.

The driver strode into the warehouse as if he owned the place. He was backlit. Makinde couldn't see his face clearly, but the shooter could see him through the night vision.

"Show yourself." The driver's voice was a low growl, but Makinde recognized it.

Makinde had talked to him on the phone twice before.

"That seems unwise," Makinde replied flatly, keeping his expression composed and neutral as he stepped further into the shadows.

An evil, twisted grin was the man's only response.

The driver's moves were slow and deliberate.

"What do you want?" Makinde asked evenly, but the shooter knew he was nervous. His heart must be pounding like a drum in the silence.

Makinde withdrew his weapon from his holster and held it out of sight, but the shooter noticed.

"So you were spying on me. Planning to report to Ramsey. To double cross me," the driver said, as if he knew the facts. Which he did. "You think you can save the R2 project. Keep the money flowing to you."

Makinde gasped quietly, but the shooter heard him and grinned.

The driver glanced up into the rafters briefly. Which was when Makinde realized the driver was not alone.

The shooter was like a ghost, hidden in the shadows, biding time, poised for the perfect kill.

Two against one now.

Makinde had to find a way to neutralize both threats.

He scanned the area, seeking anything that could give him an advantage.

The factory was stuffed with discarded crates, rusted machinery, and forgotten relics of the industry in its heyday. Makinde crouched and moved with purpose, keeping low, seeking an escape before Ramsey walked into an ambush that would leave them both dead.

Makinde's hand landed on a discarded length of metal pipe.

He gripped it tightly and moved with calculated stealth, keeping to the shadows.

His every breath was controlled, and his movements deliberate, closing the gap, inch by cautious inch as the shooter watched.

"We have thermal vision, Makinde," the driver said, a sadistic chuckle escaping his lips. "You're a big Black man creeping around in the dark, which gives you an advantage to the naked eye. But we see you."

Makinde ignored the warning. Maybe he believed they couldn't see him. He didn't take the bait.

He continued to slink closer to the man he could see clearly enough.

Then he would move onto the second one. It wasn't a bad plan. Simply an inadequate one.

And then, just as he was about to round a stack of crates, Makinde must have sensed the whisper of movement above him as the shooter adjusted his position to follow his moving target.

Instantly, Makinde realized he'd made a tactical mistake.

The driver had spoken the truth.

They could see Makinde.

They knew exactly where he stood.

The shooter was forced to act quickly. He took his shot.

Makinde had the instincts of a jungle cat. He dove to the side, narrowly avoiding the speeding bullet that tore through the air where he'd been standing half a moment before.

Makinde understood the language of war and offered a brief nod to acknowledge the terms of engagement.

Kill the two of them here and now, or Makinde would die. Ramsey, too.

No negotiation. No options. No mercy.

The shooter grinned with renewed determination when Makinde launched into action. Shooting at a sitting target was never as much fun as hitting a moving one.

Makinde swung the metal pipe with all his strength and let it go like a javelin, aiming for a stack of crates near the shooter's location.

The crates tumbled to the ground with a deafening crash, creating a cloud of bright green dust and confusion.

Makinde didn't waste a single second.

He sprinted toward the sniper's nest, hoping to catch him off guard. But the shooter was already on the move, agile and elusive.

As Makinde reached the nest, he found only an empty perch.

The shooter had vanished into the darkness, leaving no trace behind. Pursuing him now would be futile.

Makinde whipped around to focus on the villain he imagined he could stop.

He ignored the sweat rolling down his forehead, stinging his eyes as he stared into the darkness.

The shooter repositioned quickly and released another round. A loud crack split the silence as the gunshot echoed through the warehouse.

Makinde instinctively dropped to the ground, narrowly avoiding the second bullet. The shooter cursed softly under his breath.

Hidden in the shadows now, Makinde surely expected the shooter to ready another shot.

"Makinde, you're too good at getting yourself into trouble," the driver sneered, holding his own weapon ready.

Makinde's response was swift. He lunged forward, tackling the driver to the ground.

The two men grappled in the dim light, breath coming in ragged gasps while the shooter watched through his scope, seeking a clear shot.

Makinde was bigger and better trained.

But the driver was determined.

It was a fight for survival, a battle of strength and will.

Above them, the shooter adjusted his aim, lining up the crosshairs on Makinde's broad back.

From this distance, the shooter's bullet would kill both men. So he waited.

Makinde had to end things quickly or die.

With a surge of strength, he managed to disarm his adversary, sending his weapon clattering to the floor.

A moment later, the shooter squeezed the trigger, but Makinde's sudden movement threw off his shot. Again.

The bullet missed by the thinnest of margins, striking the ground with a deafening crack.

Makinde couldn't stay in the open any longer.

With a final push, he disentangled himself from the driver's grasp, shoving his head against the concrete floor before Makinde sprinted toward cover.

The driver's head hit the concrete with a sickening thud. He lay still. Unmoving.

The shooter shrugged. If the driver was dead, so be it. The shooter's plan had always been to live as a lone wolf. He could begin now.

Makinde took refuge behind a stack of crates. He scanned to find a way out of the warehouse.

He crouched behind the cover. The shooter imagined he could hear Makinde's heart pounding like mortar fire in the deadly silence.

Makinde must believe every second mattered. That Ramsey was on her way, and she would be walking straight into an ambush. Which was not Makinde's plan. Not at all.

Above his prey, the shooter was hidden in the shadows, biding time for the perfect shot. Makinde had to find a way to neutralize the unseen threat.

Could he do it? The shooter grinned.

Makinde scanned the area, looking for anything that could give him an advantage.

He would never be fast enough. The shooter tired of the game.

The final shot from the shooter blasted through the quiet, traveling 2,600 feet per second, more than 1,800 miles per hour, faster than the speed of sound.

Which meant that Makinde had no warning this time before the projectile ripped into his body and traveled clean through.

The bullet traveled faster than the pain and left Makinde standing for longer than seemed possible.

He remained on his feet briefly and then shuffled sideways before he fell onto the filthy concrete floor.

The pain showed up half a moment after that as his shirt front bloomed with deep crimson blood.

Makinde's hand fell aside and released its grip on his pistol. It clattered onto the floor.

The driver pushed himself upright off the concrete. Slowly, he approached, dusting himself off. He stood above Makinde, shaking his fuzzy head.

Coldly, he said, "I trusted you. That was my mistake. Yours was screwing me over. No chance you'll ever do that again, eh, Makinde?"

Makinde stared into the driver's depraved gaze, watching a thin line of blood drip from his ear, and said nothing in response.

Makinde's life seeped away as his blood continued to pulse from his wound with every beat of his heart.

The driver raised his gun, aimed at Makinde, and fired.

One shot to the groin to hit the femoral artery.

Makinde yelled with pain as the driver walked away, knowing Makinde would be dead before he reached the exit.

The shooter collected his rifle. *Follow the plan.* The driver was still useful. For the moment.

One more target now. And Kaplan was close by. He'd set out to kill them all. Every one of them.

They wanted to resurrect R1 and give it a new name and claim it was harmless. What crap. The war was bad enough. But R1 had taken every member of Dax Allen's family, one way or another. He couldn't let that slide.

Nora Ramsey was the worst. She was the one who just wouldn't let it go.

But Sheryl Tardelli was almost as bad. She gathered all of the others and persuaded them to help Ramsey.

If Tardelli had really tried to find Ryan and him and include them in her little circle of helicopter crash survivors, Dax would have had a chance to prevent this whole thing. He'd have told them not to try. Let sleeping dogs lie.

But Tardelli didn't give him that chance. Like a bird on a wire, she'd been protected as long as she stayed up there, both feet off the ground.

But when she reached out and touched the lives of all the others, she'd left the safety of her perch.

And all the others paid the price, too.

Which was when he noticed headlights outside and two people approaching the building. He'd been too focused and failed to see them before.

CHAPTER 39

Tuesday, June 21
Rural Vermont

KIM'S HEADLIGHTS ILLUMINATED THE pavement immediately ahead, and the dim dashboard inside the SUV provided some relief from the relentless dark, but monotony had lulled her into stupor. The windshield wipers' slow steady slapping made things worse.

She hadn't seen a house or another vehicle or even a streetlight for miles. Her eyelids felt like heavy grit sandpaper every time she blinked.

Staying alert was the best way to avoid the same fate Curry had suffered, if she could keep her head in the game. She flipped to the Janis Joplin classics station on satellite radio. Definitely not sleep music.

Cooper wasn't taking her calls. Which could mean anything. Or nothing. He'd told her to stay away from Marilyn Stone and as long as she followed his orders, he seemed content to leave her alone.

Kim had talked to Smithers a while ago to relay Gaspar's intel. She'd expected to hear a report from him when he reached Bamford, but he hadn't called. His radio silence had turned up her anxiety to an uncomfortable level. Which was something she could fix.

She placed the call through the SUV's Bluetooth system, keeping both hands on the wheel and her eyes on what she could see of the road ahead.

"Smithers," he said wearily when he picked up. "Sorry. I was just about to call you. It's been a madhouse here."

Her queasy stomach warned her what he would say next.

"You were right. He's picking them off one at a time. Kaplan will be next." Smithers reported without embellishment or excuse, as was his way. "Bamford's dead. Damned sniper was lying in wait for her. Took her down before I could reach her."

"You saw the sniper?" Kim said, ignoring the bad news to focus on something that might make a difference.

"Saw the car. It's an old sedan. Black Ford. No plates," Smithers said flatly. "It was across the parking lot. By the time I reached Bamford and her two kids, the sedan had peeled out. Local sheriff's on it. I told him to call in the FBI, which he's agreed to do."

"He killed more kids?" Kim said, blinking away the tears that sprang to her eyes.

"No. Just Bamford. He's a remarkable shot," Smithers said sourly. "I've been assisting the locals here, but I think they can handle things on their own now. Where are you? Find Kaplan yet?"

"Not yet. I'm about twenty miles from his home address now, which is very remote." Kim stretched the tension from her neck and shoulders, relaxing her white-knuckle grip on the steering wheel as much as she dared. "The road will take me through the town first. Place called Maron. The last sign I passed said the population is 720."

"Maron is the same town where Ramsey Chemical Company is headquartered, right?"

Kim replied, "Nobody will be working there at this time of night, I suspect."

"What do you want me to do?"

"When was Bamford hit? Any chance the sniper has reached Maron already?" Kim asked.

"Probably not. You're a four-hour drive from here," Smithers said. "They'll drive instead of flying because they need the sedan. They're using it for a sniper's nest as well as a getaway vehicle."

"That's how I figured it, too. So I'll get to Kaplan, try to keep him alive," Kim said, thinking out loud. "We could get you a helo, but if the killers hear it, they'll spook, and we might not get this close to them before they kill again."

Smithers let out a long stream of frustrated breath. "Yeah. Let's not give them any warning if we can avoid it."

"Are you on the road now? Can you get here before they do? Or should I call for backup?"

"On my way. And if they get there before me, kill the bastards," Smithers growled to cover his emotion. "They don't deserve to live another day."

"We're federal agents, Reg. We catch them. The judicial system does the rest," Kim reminded him gently. "It's not our job to execute the bad guys. That's where Reacher gets himself in trouble. We're no help to anyone if we head down that same road."

Smithers sighed. "Some days I'd be more than glad to do things the Reacher way, though." He wasn't serious. He was feeling the grief of failure.

"I know. Me, too," Kim said and changed the subject. "Call me from the road. I'll check in when I find Kaplan. And be careful out there. Remember what happened to Curry."

She disconnected the call just as she passed the sign that said Welcome to Maron, Vermont's Warmest Town.

Kim snorted. She was driving with the heat on inside the SUV's cabin because the outside temperature was forty-two degrees.

The town came up quickly, seeming to spring up out of the darkness. There were streetlights, but they weren't on tonight. The town had rolled up the sidewalks for the night.

She reduced her speed to the posted fifteen miles an hour.

Small towns across America often had traffic cameras in place to issue speeding tickets and other traffic violations even when they had no other law enforcement presence. It was a revenue raiser, pure and simple.

Passing through, Maron seemed a quaint place, established in 1754 according to the welcome sign.

Kim passed The Maron Inn, which seemed to be still in operation. The Maron Village Store and a white clapboard church were the three largest buildings.

"There must be some tourism business here, at least," she said aloud to keep herself alert. "Hiking and biking and such, probably."

Also along the main street were a few shops offering artisanal this and that, which was another sign of active tourism. Maron's visitors were particularly attracted to jams and honeys and scented soap, apparently.

Ramsey Chemical Company's address was listed in Maron, but it must have been somewhere off the main drag. Perhaps the controversy over Ramsey's Vietnam-era business meant Maron's town fathers preferred not to spotlight it.

Still, Ramsey Chemical must have been the largest employer in this miniscule town. More than half the residents probably worked there at one time or another, just like Kaplan did.

The navigation system announced the end of the fifteen-mile-per-hour speed limit. Kim glanced in the rearview mirror as she was leaving the town and found it once again invisible in the darkness.

A moment later, her destination was ten minutes ahead on the right. Her high beam headlights illuminated more than three hundred feet ahead, but only along the damp pavement's straight segments.

She'd been driving through a steady drizzle for the past hour. Now, the rain intensified. A bright lightning flash, followed by a loud thunderclap, turned the shower to torrents.

The narrow two-lane road twisted through a forest for the next few miles. The gravel shoulders were narrow and ungraded. She slowed her speed as she went around the curves just in case deer or bears or other nocturnal creatures decided to cross the road.

Kim noticed mailboxes every so often with no regularity. They were mounted on poles far off to the edges of the muddy gravel shoulders, probably to allow room for snowplows in the winter.

She'd been slowing as she approached each mailbox, giving herself a chance to read the names and addresses.

Which was how she found the rusted green steel box marking the edge of Kaplan's driveway. The driveway, barely wide enough for her SUV, had been cut into the heavy forest long ago when vehicles were smaller. Her SUV would be a snug fit.

On each side of the driveway, the owner had posted No Trespassing signs large enough to capture the attention of any intruder.

She turned into the driveway to allow her high beams to shine toward the house, but all she saw was more trees through the now raging storm.

Kaplan's home must have been deeper into the forest, which could be a small mercy.

Unless there was another approach, the sniper's sight line would be obstructed, too.

Kim called Smithers again. This time, the call failed. She tried Gaspar with the same result.

Cell signals out here were unreliable as hell anyway. The storm certainly didn't help.

If she couldn't call out, then no one could reach her, either.

She could try Cooper on the satellite phone, but she'd called several times already. She wouldn't beg him to talk to her.

She stopped pushing buttons and returned her full attention to navigating the narrow approach to whatever was at the end of the drive.

CHAPTER 40

Tuesday, June 21
Rural Vermont

JOHN DROVE NORA'S RANGE Rover through the worsening thunderstorm toward the old plant. She was nervous, angry, worried. The decrepit facility had been abandoned years ago and she avoided the place like a leper colony.

"Why does Makinde want to meet you at South Ridge?" John asked. "He knows how you feel about the place."

"You heard the message." Nora shrugged. "Privacy, he said. No one will be there. No cameras or devices or surveillance."

"Still think he didn't try to kill you before and he's not planning to finish the job now?" John asked, raising both eyebrows and casting a stern glare across the cabin.

"I believe it was Makinde in the woods. But I don't think he wanted to kill me. His entire future is tied to R2. I'm the only one who can give it to him. There's no benefit to him if I die," Nora said reasonably, again, as if the rationale gained strength every time she repeated it.

"People aren't always rational, Nora. Makinde's in trouble in Nigeria. I told you that. He may be looking to take the money and run at this point. In which case, killing you makes perfect sense," John warned as he turned off the dirt road toward the plant.

"Forget about Makinde. He wants more money. If I have to, I'll give it to him. The bigger problem is Mercer," Nora said, watching the woods as the Range Rover hustled past.

"What about the two guys who broke into your home? Makinde again?"

"I don't think so," Nora said slowly, as if she were still unsure.

"Did you search the house? Find anything they might have left behind?"

"I did. Personally. Found nothing amiss," John slipped the transmission into all-wheel drive and slowed his speed.

The SUV bounced over deep ruts in the abandoned road as it rolled along the reasonably flat ground. Vermont was the Green Mountain State, but there were valleys and flat land in this area.

The southside plant had been built on a farmer's field. The SUV was well equipped for the drive, even through the raging storm.

The clouds had effectively darkened the sky and eliminated all ambient light. Which wasn't a problem for Nora. When she was a child, her father worked here most nights while she played on the floor near his desk. She could have made the trip to the old plant blindfolded.

The place had held fond memories for her. Until the end. Since her father took his life here, she'd never been back. But she knew every inch of the place.

John was following the road, driving carefully, headed in the right direction. Nora let her mind wander.

What did Makinde do? And what did he want her to do now?

"When did you last meet with your team?" John asked. "Gunston, Zabrinski, Bamford, Soper, Kaplan. Have you talked to them about all of this?"

"Not since Tardelli died. I told them we had options, and we were working to finalize them. I wanted to develop a plan first," Nora replied.

"So they don't know what's been going on with R2 or Makinde or Mercer?"

"Not yet."

"Then why didn't they show up at your conference call tonight?" John asked. "That's unusual, isn't it? They normally participate when you ask them to do so, right?"

Nora was barely paying attention. Distractedly, she replied, "Yes, of course. We have a common goal. Everyone wants R2 to succeed."

"I know you want to believe that your team is loyal, but the facts suggest otherwise. Setting Makinde aside, Tardelli was the glue that held everyone together. Yet, someone killed her. Mercer is now threatening you. You haven't talked to your team in days," John said.

Nora straightened her shoulders and gave him a stare across the cabin. "What's your point?"

"The situation is not what you think it is. Not what you want it to be. You need to face that and deal with it," John said as he rounded the last curve in the old road.

Nora stared at the building straight ahead in the darkness. Only the silhouette of its hulking shape was visible in the distance. No vehicle was parked on the broken pavement. No one moved near the plant at all.

"Wouldn't Makinde have brought a flashlight, at least?" John asked reasonably.

"He's not here," Nora said, peering through the rain as if she could manifest him from the force of her will.

"You can't be surprised. Why are you so sure Makinde's reliable? Nothing we know about the man and nothing he's done to you supports that idea," John shook his head as he rolled the SUV closer to the building. "Makinde's lured you here for a reason. What is it?"

Before Nora had a chance to reply, a flash of light brightened the interior of the decrepit building.

The unmistakable noise of a gunshot rang out.

"What the hell?" John slammed the brakes and drew his pistol.

Nora reached into her bag to retrieve her weapon, too. A second muzzle flash and gunshot followed the first.

After that, a long silence, and a third shot followed by a startling clap of thunder loud enough to wake the dead. Another muzzle flashed through the darkness. If Makinde was inside, he was in trouble. John's hand moved to his holster, his eyes scanning the decrepit building.

"Stay in the SUV while I check this out," he ordered, his voice low and urgent.

"I'm going with you. I know the building. You don't," Nora replied as she reached into her bag for her weapon.

"Okay. But stay close." John peered through the rain-streaked window, straining to see any movement. "Ready?"

"Yeah. There's a side entrance on the left. Follow me," Nora said as she slipped out of the vehicle into the storm.

The old chemical plant, a relic of her family's past, loomed like a specter. Lightning illuminated the scene in stark flashes, revealing nothing of who or what might be going on inside.

The rain muffled their approach as Nora neared the building. John moved with the stealth of an experienced fighter behind her.

As they reached the side entrance, Nora's breath caught. The faint lingering smell of chemicals and decay was a grim reminder of her father's death. A time in her life she preferred to forget.

The side door was shut tight. John stepped forward to muscle it open, knocking rusty paint to the ground. Nora slipped inside to a muddle of discarded packing crates, corroded machinery, and tangled pipes.

Their stealthy footsteps seemed to echo loudly in the vast emptiness, even as the storm raged furiously outside.

"The muzzle flashes came from over there," John pointed as he signaled for quiet and moved to navigate the maze.

Nora's eyes adjusted to the darkness between flashes of lightning. Amid the bulky castoffs she caught a glimpse of movement ahead.

"John," she whispered. "Three o'clock."

Without warning, a shot rang out, shattering the silence.

John spun, pushing Nora behind a rusted container.

"They've got night vision. They can see us. Stay down," John whispered, his eyes scanning the shadows.

Nora, heart pounding, peered around the container. She saw them positioned across the room, guns trained in her direction.

John edged around the container, firing a controlled burst. One man held a rifle, but the other man fired back with his handgun.

The noise of the rapid gunfire exchange blasted through the plant and John advanced. He rounded a stack of old crates and disappeared from Nora's view.

Sporadic flashes of lightning from outside weren't enough. In the confusion, she heard shouts, the sounds of a struggle.

Nora crawled toward the noise, her heart in her throat. As she neared, a hand grabbed her biceps and jerked her aside. She jabbed her elbow out instinctively and made contact with hard flesh.

"It's me," John's voice hissed. "That's a wicked elbow you've got there."

"Sorry." Relief flooded her, but it was short-lived.

A flashlight beam sliced through the darkness, swinging toward their hiding spot. Nora and John held their breaths, frozen.

The light illuminated their faces briefly. Then flashed to a large dark shape on the floor before it flickered and died.

Nora heard a curse, then the sound of retreating footsteps. They were fleeing.

"Let them go," Nora said as she and John emerged carefully from their hiding spot.

"Look," John pointed toward the large body on the ground, a pool of blood surrounding him. "Makinde?"

They moved toward where he lay.

As they approached, Nora steeled herself. She had partnered with Makinde, respected him. Without his help, R2 would be nothing but a pipe dream.

She fished her phone from her pocket and turned the flashlight on the body, to be sure.

Seeing Makinde there, lifeless, a casualty in a fight she hardly understood, fueled a level of anger she barely recognized. She was a scientist, not a soldier. She wanted only to save lives, not take them.

"We have to stop them," she said, her voice steady.

"Are you sure you have no idea who these guys are?" John asked, his expression grim.

"What do you mean?"

"They seem to know a lot about you. Where you live. Where your father died," John let his voice trail off. "Seems like a vendetta of some sort to me. And that's usually personal."

Nora nodded. "Then why not stay and kill me now? They had the advantage. Why run off?"

"Come on," John said urgently, grabbing Nora's arm. "We've gotta get out of here."

"What about Makinde?" she asked, stumbling along between the debris field covering the corridor.

"They can't kill him twice, Nora," John said flatly.

Nora's eyes widened in recognition.

"Explosives," she whispered, the realization hitting her like a physical blow.

John pulled her forward and gave her a push toward the exit.

They ran flat out toward the side door.

As John burst out of the building behind Nora, the night sky was split by a fiery explosion that engulfed the chemical plant, illuminating the stormy night.

The shockwave knocked Nora off her feet. John pulled her up, his grip firm.

"We have to get to the main Ramsey Chemical plant," Nora said, her voice urgent. "That must be where they're going."

As they ran to the SUV, the storm raged on. John climbed in behind the wheel as Nora settled into the passenger seat. He whipped the transmission into reverse and floored the accelerator away from the burning building.

"We're heading into a bigger trap," John said. "You know that now, right?"

"Kaplan lives near here. He can help."

CHAPTER 41

Tuesday, June 21
Rural Vermont

KIM ROLLED THE SUV slowly along the wet narrow driveway deeper into the woods.

The drive was poorly graded. Big holes alternated with smooth patches and slippery gravel. A couple of washouts were filled with old and new rainwater.

The trip felt like the time she'd tried to ride a bronco out of the gate at the state fair rodeo. She'd had no control over that horse, and she had very little control now.

The SUV slipped and skidded and bounced along for half a mile. The SUV bottomed out at the dip in a particularly long downward slope, and she accelerated toward the next rise.

Over the hump, the SUV's headlights illuminated a cattle gate at the bottom of yet another hill.

The posted sign repeated the No Trespassing warning.

It also warned that the gate and the fence on either side were electrified.

"Electricity in the rain. Just great," Kim grumbled, trying to slow the rapidly moving beast against the pull of gravity.

The SUV's tires failed to grip the muddy hillside and began sliding fast down the incline.

Heart pounding wildly, Kim stood on the brake pedal with both feet and her full weight as the brakes locked and the heavy SUV planed all the way down, heading straight toward the electrified steel gate.

When the SUV hit a large boulder, it slowed enough to get traction. In one heart-swallowing thump it bounced high and down to stick the landing at the bottom of the hill. Briefly.

Then momentum pushed it to glide a few more feet on flat, muddy ground until its metal bumper slammed the rigid steel gate.

Like throwing a raw egg into a steel door.

The impact knocked Kim off her feet. Her seatbelt yanked her body backward into the plush upholstery.

Instantly, she covered her face with both arms and ducked her head, waiting.

"Small mercies," she mumbled when she realized she hadn't been punched in the face and chest by exploding nylon.

She'd been traveling too slow for the collision to deploy the airbag.

Now the SUV's bumper was mangled and hopelessly wedged between the steel gate's horizontal and vertical supports.

The gate was barely bent.

Which was another indication of how sturdy the gate was.

And an indication of the strength of the electrical current running through it.

Briefly, she thought everything might be okay.

She was wrong.

The electrified gate fought back against the assault with a strong electric jolt.

Sparks flew into the darkness like a magnificent fireworks display, temporarily blinding her vision.

Breathing hard, she managed to set the parking brake with her left foot before she collapsed into the driver's seat, legs and arms quivering with tension.

The windshield wipers were still slapping furiously from side to side while the rain pounded the SUV like an angry jackhammer that matched the cadence of her heartbeat.

Kim reached to turn the wipers off when she noticed, through the momentarily cleared space on the windshield, a flat bit of grass and the dark silhouette of a house a hundred feet beyond the gate.

The collision must have triggered an alarm inside the house.

Flood lights popped on, shining directly toward the SUV's windshield and blinding Kim.

She covered her eyes and blinked to regain her vision.

A moment later, a man opened the front door and stepped onto the porch holding a shotgun aimed in Kim's direction.

He fired a shot over the roof of the SUV, maybe a warning.

Or maybe he wasn't good with a gun.

Either way, the message was clear.

Get the hell off my lawn.

The silly thought caused her to giggle with relief.

"Glad to oblige," she said aloud to further control the tension as she slid the transmission into reverse and punched the accelerator.

The SUV's bumper and grille were wedged tightly into the gate's structure.

The engine was unable to pull the two apart.

The wheels were spinning in the mud, warming the sodden gravel and miring the SUV deeper. But the gate and the SUV were still engaged in their impossible embrace holding Kim hostage.

The man continued to point the shotgun from his porch, preparing to shoot again.

Rapidly, she ran through her remaining options.

She'd been called out to enough power line emergencies to know that she was protected from electrocution while she remained inside surrounded by the SUV's steel cage.

But gunshots could easily penetrate inside the SUV's cabin. Nothing on the vehicle would stop bullets except the engine block.

Which he might not know.

Safer, though, to assume the shooter knew exactly where to place his shots.

Shooting into the vehicle was certainly possible.

Meaning he could kill her, but she couldn't return the threat.

Shooting out of the cabin of any vehicle was problematic.

Difficult to control the trajectory of the bullet.

She might hit the shooter.

But given these conditions, she could just as easily miss.

Odds were against her.

Bottom line, she needed to get away as soon as possible and definitely before he started shooting again with a better aim.

But the options for a clean escape from an electrified vehicle were even worse.

Maybe she could break the electrical circuit to exit the vehicle without letting her body provide a path for the electricity to flow from the SUV to the ground. She'd need to jump at least eight feet before touching the ground.

The SUV was surrounded on all sides by muddy slopes covered with trees. The chances she could clear a wild leap like that were miniscule.

But if she could do it, then what?

The violent storm continued like an outraged toddler with none of its destructive energy dissipating.

Wandering lost in the woods in the storm presented its own dangerous challenges.

She was at least a mile from the road.

And the road itself was miles from everywhere.

Leaving the SUV seemed just as suicidal as staying.

She could tell the shooter she was a federal agent.

That piece of intel could push him either way. Many citizens had very little respect for law enforcement in general and the FBI in particular.

What about this guy?

If he knew her identity, would he ramp up the violence or stand down?

Another thought flashed through her mind with the next bolt of lightning.

Was this guy the sniper they'd been looking for? Was he alone in that cabin?

How long could she wait to find out?

A pair of headlights came over the hill behind Kim's SUV, aiming straight down into her vehicle. The driver must have been familiar with the approach because he descended slowly until he stopped a couple of feet behind her on the incline, boxing her in.

CHAPTER 42

Tuesday, June 21
Rural Vermont

KIM PULLED HER WEAPON and peered through the blinding headlights into the windshield of the SUV parked behind her. A man she didn't recognize was behind the steering wheel.

But she'd seen the woman's photo before.

In Gaspar's files.

Nora Ramsey.

Kim had known Sheryl Tardelli well enough to hope that Tardelli wouldn't knowingly befriend a killer. And everything she'd read about Nora Ramsey suggested the woman could be reasoned with, at least under normal circumstances.

And Kim had to take a risk.

Nora Ramsey was the least dangerous of the issues she was faced with at the moment.

Trapped in the SUV ensnared by the electrified gate. Kaplan, wary and armed, stood on his porch, his shotgun aimed straight at Kim. Nora's SUV was effectively blocking any potential escape.

She lowered the SUV's rear window, crouched behind the seat, and called out between bouts of thunder, "Nora Ramsey! I'm here about Sheryl Tardelli's death!"

Nora and the man exchanged a few words. He opened his door and stepped out of the SUV, weapon pointed in Kim's direction.

When he was in position, Nora climbed out into the pouring rain. She was also armed, but her free hand was raised in a gesture of peace.

Kim shouted again, "My name is Kim Otto. I'm here to help."

Nora moved closer to the open rear window of Kim's SUV. She stood a few feet from the bumper.

"Don't touch my vehicle. It's electrified by the fence," Kim warned, as the man kept his weapon trained on her.

Nora assessed the situation with a sharp eye, recognized the need for immediate action. "Kaplan. It's Nora Ramsey," she yelled, her voice battling the storm's howl. "Open the gate. Let us in."

Kaplan squinted through the rain, remaining suspicious, his grip on the shotgun tight. "Nora? John? What the hell is going on?"

"Turn off the gate's electricity," Nora shouted. "Let us in."

Kaplan, still hesitant, seemed to weigh the situation. After a tense moment, he disappeared into his house. Moments later, the buzzing sound of the electrified gate ceased, signaling he'd cut the power.

Tension that had been holding Kim's body taut as a bowstring since she'd hit the gate backed off a couple of millimeters. She waited to be sure the electricity had enough time to stop circulating through the SUV before she opened the door and stepped out into the icy rain.

"I slid down the hill. The bumper is stuck in the gate. I can't move the vehicle," she explained.

John holstered his weapon and grabbed a pair of bolt cutters from their SUV. He dashed toward the gate, his movements swift and determined under the relentless downpour.

The cutters bit through the metal and the gate was freed from the SUV.

"Okay," John said, pulling the gate aside manually. "Drive toward the house. We'll follow you."

Kim hopped into the driver's seat and prepared to move.

As soon as the gate was clear, she revved the engine and carefully maneuvered the vehicle free. She rolled along the muddy driveway and parked in front of Kaplan's house. John pulled up and parked beside her.

Stepping out, Kim hurried toward Kaplan, who had re-emerged onto his porch, the shotgun now hanging loosely in his hand.

"Who are you?" Kaplan asked as she stomped water from her clothes on the porch.

She raised her voice above the raging storm, as she displayed her badge. "Agent Kim Otto, FBI."

Nora and John exchanged glances.

"Nora, are you alright?" Kaplan asked, his expression a mixture of confusion and relief. "Let's get out of this damned storm."

They hurried inside and Kim followed quickly behind. Warmth enveloped her chilled body like a cozy blanket. Drenched and disheveled, they gathered around the fire burning in the fireplace.

Kaplan set his shotgun aside. "I've been trying to call you."

"Why?" Nora asked.

"You don't know?"

"Know what?"

"They called. There's been an explosion. At the plant. And a second explosion at your house," Kaplan said. "I've been frantically trying to find you."

Nora's wide-eyed stare was dumbfounded. She stumbled to the sofa and plopped down like a dead weight.

Then she struggled to stand. "We need to get back. John?"

"Nothing we can do right now. First responders will be at the scene. It's safer here. We'll go in a minute." John laid a calming hand on her shoulder and turned to Kim. "First, why are you here?"

Kim wasted no time getting to the point. "We're investigating a string of murders."

"Murders?" Nora repeated, eyes even wider.

Kim's gaze held Kaplan's. "We had reason to believe that you are the killer's next target."

All three spoke at once, their voices colliding into confusion.

"That's absurd," Nora said in a rush of fear tinged with horror.

"Me? Why would anyone want to kill me?" Kaplan asked, his voice quivering like a taut bowstring about to snap.

"Who are the other victims?" John demanded.

"The first victim was Sheryl Tardelli," Kim replied evenly. "The second, Matt Gunston. Harold Zabrinski was the third target, but the sniper's aim was off. Killed his son instead."

Nora had turned a sour shade of green and collapsed into a chair as if her bones had turned to water. This time, she made no effort to get up.

Kaplan's hands were shaking, so he stuffed them into his pockets.

John's frosty tone cut through the tension, sharp and insistent. "That's not the whole list, is it?"

Kim shook her head. "Sam Soper and Nadia Bamford were killed a few hours ago. We believed Drew Kaplan is the last target of the group. And now, it looks like they tried to kill Nora, too."

Kaplan cleared his throat. "The last of what group?"

"I was hoping you could tell me. Because we've found very little to connect the victims in a way that might make sense to a killer," Kim replied. "We need to find him. Before he kills anyone else."

Nora Ramsey dropped her head into her hands. "It's the connection to Ramsey Chemical, isn't it?"

"We believe so, yes." Kim gave her a hard glance. "Who wants to kill you and your team, Dr. Ramsey?"

John replied, "Iniko Makinde is the obvious choice. He's a Nigerian national who wants R2 to save his people from malaria. He's angry with Ramsey Chemical because Nora can't supply R2 until it gets governmental support."

"Which has been held up because of Congresswoman Tardelli's death, I gather," Kim said flatly.

Nora gave Kim a steady stare. "I had thought Makinde could be dangerous. He threatened me a couple of times. That's why John is traveling everywhere with me now."

"You don't think he's dangerous anymore," Kim said. "Why not?"

Nora's answer was swift and certain. "Because Makinde is dead. Someone killed him tonight."

"What?" Kaplan said, astonished, his voice a strangled whisper.

Nora gave John a quick nod.

"At the old Ramsey plant about five miles north," John said flatly. "That's why we headed here. If what you say is true, they are probably on the way here to deal with Drew, if they're not out there already."

"So you saw who killed Makinde?" Kim asked.

"We saw two men in the dark. No way we could pick them out of a lineup," John replied.

"Confirms our theory. That there are two men working together," Kim said. "Did you see a vehicle?"

John shook his head. "They parked on the other side of the building. We didn't even know they were there until we went inside."

"And Makinde? He was alone?" Kim asked.

Nora nodded and replied wearily, "We didn't see anyone else with him."

Kim moved cautiously toward the window, her internal threat meter on high alert.

"He could be out there, waiting for the right moment," she said, her eyes scanning the darkness beyond the glass.

Nora stood beside her, her body tensed for action, while John checked his own weapon, ready to defend if necessary.

Kaplan remained a step behind, peering over their shoulders.

"How did you know about the explosions at the plant and Nora's home?" she asked Kaplan.

"I got a call from the sheriff. He wanted confirmation that I wasn't there, and he was looking for Nora," Kaplan said.

"You have a land line?" Kim asked. Kaplan nodded. "Call nine-one-one. Tell them to send out two cars. Say the words 'active shooter.'"

Kaplan nodded. "They're overwhelmed. It's a small department. I don't know if they'll have anyone to send."

"Do it anyway," Kim said, and Kaplan hurried toward the phone.

CHAPTER 43

Tuesday, June 21
Rural Vermont

THE SHOOTER HAD COVERED the rifle and hoisted its cumbersome weight over his shoulder. They emerged from the abandoned warehouse into rain driven by winds that howled through the broken windows and gaping doorways.

He led the way, scanning the dark woods, alert for signs of pursuit or other dangers.

The driver staggered behind, one hand clutching his head, the other bracing against trees for support. A thin trickle of blood oozed from his ear on the side where Makinde had slammed his head into the concrete.

"Come on, we need to move," the shooter urged, his voice barely audible over the storm's roar.

The driver nodded weakly, his face ghastly pale. He stumbled forward, each step a monumental effort. Twice, he stopped to vomit.

The treacherous path to where the parked sedan was obscured by overgrowth and mud from the relentless downpour. The shooter slipped and righted himself, holding the rifle above his head to be sure it didn't land in the mud.

The driver's condition worsened with every step. He leaned heavily against the trees, his breaths coming in ragged gasps. Halfway through, he doubled over, retching violently. The sound was lost in the storm, but dizziness brought him to his knees.

"Hang in there. We're almost done," the shooter said because the injury was more serious than he had initially realized. He wondered briefly if he should just put the man down here and now.

They trudged on through the obstacle course of undergrowth and fallen branches in the darkness. The shooter's grip on the rifle tightened, its presence both a comfort and a burden.

Lightning illuminated the path in brief, eerie flashes revealing the rugged terrain.

Finally, they reached the clearing where they'd parked the sedan.

The shooter opened the back door to safely stow the rifle. Then he helped the driver stumble into the front passenger seat, noticing the driver's skin was cold and clammy to the touch.

The shooter quickly moved to position himself behind the steering wheel. His clothes were cold and soaked and clinging to his skin.

The driver's body slumped against the passenger door, his head resting against the window. Blood still trickled from his ear. His eyes were closed. He mumbled words the shooter couldn't decipher.

Teeth chattering, the shooter started the car and flipped the heat on full blast. He rolled the sedan forward, peering through the foggy windshield, focused on the muddy trail. Each twist and turn was a challenge, but he managed to keep the old sedan between the ditches.

The trail had been abandoned long ago. It led from the old plant through the property along the back side of Kaplan's homestead. Which was why they'd chosen it.

Drew Kaplan was almost a recluse. He worked odd hours of the day and night and lived alone. He traveled to work at Ramsey Chemical and then home again and went almost nowhere else.

Which was why the shooter had planned to kill him at home. Even under normal circumstances, his absence wouldn't be noticed for a good long time. After the explosion at the plant, they wouldn't know he was missing from the rubble for a good long time.

Kaplan's cabin was surrounded by four acres of undeveloped land. But it was only fenced on the front. Presumably because Kaplan's visitors were only expected to approach from the main road.

Across the front property line, Kaplan had installed a one-acre electrified fence and gate to keep people away. Only the most ambitious of unwanted visitors would attempt to go beyond the gate.

For all of these reasons, the shooter was expecting an easy kill with no surprises.

The shooter maneuvered the sedan through the dense woods through the storm's fury. Beside him, the driver slumped in the passenger seat, his head lolling with each jolt of the vehicle.

"Stay with me, buddy," the shooter urged, his voice tense. "Almost done. One more, and we're outta here."

The rain hammered against the windshield in a relentless torrent. Visibility was nearly impossible.

The driver groaned in response to every jolt of the sedan's exhausted suspension. He pressed his hand to his head but didn't open his eyes.

The shooter gritted his teeth and pushed the car harder. The back trail was rough and barely visible, but it was the only way to approach the house undetected.

The car's headlights barely cut through the darkness. The storm had turned night into an impenetrable shroud. Branches scraped against the sides of the vehicle, barely noticeable above the storm's howling.

The sedan bounced into a deep hole. The old suspension groaned, and the tires struggled to pull the weight out again.

The driver let out a stifled moan, his body convulsing slightly. "I'm gonna be sick," he mumbled, barely audible over the roar of the storm and the struggling engine.

"Just hold on a little longer." The shooter glanced over, annoyed. His grip tightened on the steering wheel. "We take care of Kaplan first. Then we'll get you some help."

As they neared Kaplan's property, the shooter squelched the headlights and navigated by feel and memory through the complete darkness.

They reached the trail at the back of Kaplan's property and the shooter slowed the car to a stop under cover of thick trees.

The shooter peered through the rain, trying to discern the outline of Kaplan's house in the distance. It was late. He expected the house to be dark, Kaplan unsuspecting.

But lights flickered inside. Shadows moved across the windows. Kaplan wasn't alone.

The shooter felt a surge of adrenaline as he was forced to adjust his plan. He reached for the gun.

"Looks like he's got company," he muttered, his eyes fixed on the house.

The driver, barely coherent, tried to focus, but his words were slurred. "Who's... there?"

The shooter didn't answer. Instead, he opened the car door. The storm greeted him with a violent gust, which he ignored.

"Wait here," he instructed. "I'll be back soon."

He stepped out, rifle in hand, slammed the door, and headed toward the house.

CHAPTER 44

Tuesday, June 21
Rural Vermont

THE SHOOTER MOVED STEALTHILY through the storm, the rain an incessant drumbeat against the foliage. He approached Kaplan's home from the rear. Through the downpour, the house lights glowed like a beacon.

He kept to the shadows, acutely aware of the risk. Without the safety provided by his warm, dry, comfortable sniper's nest in the sedan, he was exposed, vulnerable.

He couldn't afford mistakes.

As he neared the house, he saw people moving inside, confirming his suspicion that Kaplan was not alone.

His hand tightened around the rifle, his finger near the trigger.

"Precision. Surprise. One shot, one kill," he murmured.

Kaplan was his target. The others, a bonus.

The shooter circled to a spot where he could peer into the house without being seen. He crouched low, the rifle poised on the tripod, his gaze scanning the interior.

Inside, he could see Kaplan, along with another man and two women. One a tiny Asian woman he didn't recognize, but the other was... Nora Ramsey.

What? How could that be? She was always home or at the plant at this hour of the night. Ramsey should have died in one of the explosions.

But she didn't. She's here. So what are you going to do about it?

He hesitated, weighing his options.

Killing Ramsey in Kaplan's house was not the plan.

Stick to the plan was his mantra. But now, the plan wouldn't work.

Bottom line, Ramsey needed to be dead.

Two birds dead in one house?

"One at a time. Bird by bird," he whispered.

First, isolate Kaplan.

Then Ramsey.

Hell, throw in the others, too. Why not?

Movement caught his eye, but he let it go. Patience.

The wind howled as the shooter crouched in the underbrush watching through the scope. His breaths came in controlled puffs, visible against the cold air the storm had blown in.

From his vantage point, he had a clear line of sight into Kaplan's cabin, and he could afford to be patient.

He didn't need to wait long. He steadied his view through the scope, the crosshairs finding Kaplan's silhouette.

His finger caressed the trigger like a gentle lover, waiting for the perfect moment.

As the lightning flashed, he squeezed. The sound of the shot was swallowed by the thunder.

The window shattered, deflecting his shot and sending shards of glass flying like icy daggers across the room.

All four of them dropped to the floor, although the shooter knew he'd missed his target.

He couldn't hear them, but he could see well enough and imagine the conversations inside.

"Stay down!" the second man barked, crawling to the broken window to return fire. He sent a volley of shots into the dark, hoping to hit or at least deter the hidden assailant.

The shooter smiled.

The tiny Asian woman crawled to the other side of the room, her weapon ready. As if she knew he'd reposition and take a better shot.

Kaplan's home, she must have realized, had become a death trap.

The shooter made a silent bet with himself about what would happen next.

The other man looked like the type to play the hero.

In fact, he was already moving toward the back door. The lights inside the house were extinguished and he yanked the door open and stepped outside.

"John, wait!" Ramsey's voice was fraught with concern, but the man she'd called John was already moving, his resolve as unyielding as the storm.

Patiently, the shooter paused.

As John burst from the house, the shooter was ready.

Approaching headlights drew his attention to the driveway in front of Kaplan's house. The shooter's heartbeat quickened. Who could that be?

Stay focused.

"Slow, steady, methodical," he whispered with each heartbeat.

Follow the plan.

"Wait for it," he murmured.

John hustled down the back steps and landed firmly on the grass. Now, John was running through the darkness.

The shooter raised one hand and slipped his thermal vision from his head to his face. When he looked again, John had advanced a dozen paces.

The shooter focused on the rifle's scope. John's heat signature came into clearer view.

The shooter released a single shot, cleaner and sharper than the chaotic symphony of the storm.

Bull's-eye. A solid hit, center mass.

Half a moment later, John fell, his last breath misting in the cold air.

The shooter's chest swelled with pride. He was a ghost in the storm, orchestrating chaos. Inside the house, he had shattered the sense of security as thoroughly as the window.

Now, the storm outside was no match for the storm within.

The shooter slid the thermal vision up to his head again and pivoted toward the headlights in the driveway. A big man hurried from an SUV headed toward the house, weapon ready.

He must have seen the muzzle flash for both shots because he veered away from the house toward the shooter's location. He crouched to provide cover and present a smaller profile to his enemy and more stability because he planned to fire his weapon.

The shooter lowered his eye to the scope, watching the man approach.

The big man was wide open. No real cover of any kind, although he might be wearing body armor.

He was backlit by the headlights, which made him an easier target.

The shooter breathed evenly, waiting, allowing his prey to clear a stand of trees on the right.

And when the big man came around the trees into the open, crouched low, weapon ready, a momentary lull in the storm dropped a blanket of total quiet.

The back door to the house slammed.

Distracted for a fraction of a moment, the shooter's focus glitched.

He flinched and fired at the same time.

The big man fell sideways onto the grass and fired his weapon toward the shooter.

The shooter squeezed the rifle's trigger smoothly.

He heard a sharp "ooof" from the man as he hit the ground before the shooter whipped his rifle around to deal with the threat approaching from the back of the house.

CHAPTER 45

Tuesday, June 21
Rural Vermont

WEAPON DRAWN, KIM HAD watched as Nora posted herself at one of the windows with her pistol and Kaplan at another with his shotgun. The shooter was out there in the inky blackness, but where?

As soon as John was ready to open the back door, Kaplan flipped off the lights inside the house. Kim kept her gaze steady, and her vision began to adapt while John hustled outside and down the steps to the grass.

The lightning had shifted farther north, taking the brief slices of illumination and the sound of thunder with it. Otherwise, the storm raged on, a relentless symphony of wind and rain battering the landscape.

Kim scanned the shadowed lawn seeking to identify any sign of unidentified human movement.

Nora lowered her profile to a crouch, breathing shallowly as she watched John's silhouette merge with the night. Kaplan, meanwhile, had pressed his back against the wall near his window, breaths coming in sharp bursts Kim could hear from across the silent room.

The darkness inside the house was complete, which Kim hoped was a tactical advantage. But the truth was that if the shooter had good thermal vision, he'd be able to find them inside and out.

Her hand tightened around the grip of her weapon, her senses hyper-alert.

Outside, John moved deliberately, with calculated speed toward the back of the property where Kaplan had said an old lumbering road led to the abandoned plant where Makinde had been attacked.

Almost simultaneously, Kim saw the muzzle flash twenty yards in front of John on his left.

A crack of thunder masked the sound of the rifle as the sniper fired.

Nora's whispered plea, "No, no, no," was a futile lament.

The bullet found its target. John crumpled to the ground, his warmth spilling out onto the cold, wet grass.

A moment later, headlight beams strobed the house from the front driveway.

"Smithers?" Kim wondered aloud. She glanced at her watch, realizing he'd had time to reach Kaplan's place by now.

"Who is Smithers?" Nora asked quietly.

"My partner. We split up. He tried to warn Bamford, but the sniper got there first. Smithers was on his way here," Kim replied.

She hurried to the front window and peered toward the driveway. Smithers climbed out of his SUV, readied his weapon, and headed around toward the back of the house.

He must have seen the muzzle flash when John went down and accurately assessed the position of the threat.

Smithers wouldn't know the shooter had thermal vision, but he might have guessed.

"If I can see Smithers, the shooter can, too," she said aloud.

The last thing Kim wanted was Smithers laid out on the grass next to John. Even his body armor wouldn't keep him alive when the sniper fired the next shot.

Kim watched from the doorway, her resolve steeling.

"Stay inside," she instructed Nora and Kaplan on her way to the back exit. "I'm ending this."

A moment after Kim made it through the door, she heard another gunshot crack through the air.

Bile rose in her throat when she saw that Smithers was hit.

His body jolted with the impact as he fell awkwardly beside a stand of trees. Was he dead? She couldn't tell. Her view was blocked by the trees. But she couldn't simply leave him there alone.

A moment later, the sniper took a second shot, seeking to confirm the first. He wanted them all dead and so far, he was succeeding.

While the sniper was focused on Smithers, Kim stood still, allowing the darkness to swallow her whole, hoping the shooter was repositioning and might not see her immediately.

She knew exactly where he was now. She'd seen the muzzle flash three times from the same location nestled in the trees at the north edge of the lawn.

And he must be alone. Only one rifle and one shooter to contend with. Which was plenty.

But Kim had no time to waste. His thermal vision would spot her any moment now when he returned his attention to the occupants of the house.

She moved with the stealth of a shadow. Each step silent and deliberate as she closed the distance between them, seeking cover where she could find it.

The storm seemed to conspire with her, each gust of wind and lash of rain covering her movements. She allowed the storm to envelop her. She could feel the killer's presence, a malignant force in the darkness ahead.

A flash of lightning illuminated the backyard for a split second, revealing John's body and Smithers's, too. Her resolve hardened and fueled her determination.

She was completely soaked. Her clothes clung to her body like an icy shroud. Rainwater dripped into her face.

She ignored everything except the shooter. She knew where he was. So far, he didn't seem to have noticed that she was now stalking him.

She needed only a brief glimpse of him behind the rifle's scope. One quick look and she could take him out. She needed to draw him out. Make him show himself.

Kim knelt onto the wet ground, patting the mud until her fingers found a rock the size of her palm. She maneuvered the stone from the mud and let the rain wash it clean. Then she lifted it in her left hand as she steadied her weapon in her right.

She took a deep breath and tossed the rock as close to the shooter's position as she could aim. At the same time, she yelled, "FBI! Put down your weapon!"

She heard the rock thump against something harder than human flesh. A tree trunk? A boulder?

She'd had one chance, and she blew it.

But then she got lucky.

A weak lightning strike brightened the corner of the property where the sniper was nesting. For one quick moment, she saw him.

He looked like an alien being, with the night vision on his face and the rifle on its tripod in front of him.

Her luck was lucky for him, too. He saw her immediately.

She must have appeared like a specter of vengeance stalking in the night.

Quickly, she closed the distance between them.

He hurried to reposition his weapon, but before he could line up his shot, seeking to startle him, Kim shouted, "FBI! Stand down!"

Her words had little impact on him. He barely moved. He wasn't ready to shoot her, but he took the shot anyway.

The bullet whizzed past her a few inches to her right.

Instantly, Kim fired back.

Her first bullet found its mark.

The impact knocked the shooter away from his rifle. He screamed with pain.

He fell sideways, wounded.

But he reached for his rifle again, scrambling for the trigger.

"Stop!" she screamed over the raging storm.

He kept moving.

Kim fired twice more. Two solid hits.

He fell forward on top of the rifle and then rolled onto his face in the mud.

Adrenaline coursing through her body, Kim approached, weapon ready. She'd hit him three times, but she would empty her full magazine into the bastard if she had to.

She pulled her flashlight and shined it on his head as she flipped him over, ready to shoot him again. His face was a muddy, pulpy mess.

He didn't flinch. Life had ebbed away from him.

His plans, his focus, everything faded into the black rain that washed over them both.

Kim stood over the shooter, her chest heaving, the weight of the moment heavy on her shoulders.

A few moments later, Nora and Kaplan ran outside into the rain. They looked down at the dead shooter.

"He's just a kid," Kaplan said.

Nora sank to the muddy ground, the release of tension too much for her legs to bear.

"Kaplan, check on John," Kim said, running toward Smithers as two sets of flashing blue lights rushed from the long driveway toward the house and Cooper's satellite phone vibrated in her pocket.

CHAPTER 46

Thursday, June 23
Pound Ridge, New York

THE SPRAWLING GROUNDS OF Marilyn Stone's mansion in Pound Ridge, New York, looked like a feature from the old television show about lifestyles of the rich and famous. Stone wasn't famous. But, as Curry had mentioned more than once, she was very rich.

Briefly, Kim wondered if Stone would hire a new investigator now that Curry was gone.

Her rental glided smoothly up the long driveway and stopped before the grand entrance. Kim stepped out and took a moment to admire the expansive estate and inhale the scent of blooming flowers that filled the air.

She approached the ornate front door, footsteps echoing on the flagstone. The door opened before she could knock, revealing Marilyn Stone.

Stone exuded an aura of understated elegance. Her eyes, sharp and discerning, quickly appraised her visitor.

"Agent Otto. This is unexpected," Marilyn said, her voice a blend of warmth and caution. "Please, come in."

The interior of the mansion was as impressive as its exterior, with high ceilings and luxurious furnishings. Marilyn led her into a sunlit parlor overlooking the gardens. They settled into plush chairs, and Marilyn waited for Kim to take the lead.

"I'm here about Sheryl Tardelli," Kim began, her tone serious, revealing only what she'd come here to say. "We've identified who was responsible for Sheryl's death and the reasons behind it."

Marilyn's composure flickered, revealing a hint of vulnerability. "Sheryl's death... it was no accident, then?"

"You were right. Her death was murder," Kim confirmed. "It was connected to a larger, more dangerous situation she unknowingly became a part of. Just as you suspected."

"One of those protest groups?" Marilyn asked, dabbing tears from her eyes with a tissue. "I told Sheryl she was playing with fire. So many people were enraged about those chemicals and the impact they've had on people."

Kim nodded, waiting for Marilyn to process the truth. "And I wanted to offer my condolences. I'm sorry about Curry."

"I couldn't believe it. He called me after the accident. Said he was okay." Marilyn's eyes widened and she shook her head. "How could they just let him die like that?"

"What else did he say?" Kim asked. "Anything about Reacher?"

Marilyn stared out through the sunroom windows, enjoying the warmth of the afternoon. "We talked about how we met Reacher. He asked me about a list of names. I remembered them, of course. You don't forget a thing like that."

"Who were they?"

"Eight young soldiers. Seven of them died in a helicopter crash in Vietnam during the war. The eighth was Carl Allen," Marilyn paused while a long shiver of revulsion ran through her body. "Horrible man. A real psychopath if you ask me. He terrorized Sheryl and almost killed the rest of us."

"Almost killed who?"

"Me, Curry, Reacher. My husband, Chester. Jodie Jacob." She shivered again.

"What did Carl Allen do?" Although she had already pieced together some of it, Kim wanted to hear it from an eyewitness.

"He threatened to kill us. All of us. There's no question in my mind that we'd all be dead now if not for Reacher," Marilyn said, shaking all over now while keeping a white knuckled grip on her hands. "Allen shot Reacher, you know. Right in the chest. Hit him in the forehead with a nail gun, too. It was terrifying."

"But Reacher survived," Kim said flatly.

Marilyn nodded rapidly. "Absolutely. And he killed Carl Allen right there in front of us all. I remember it like it was yesterday. I'll never get over it."

She waited for Marilyn to regain control over her emotions, which didn't take long. Marilyn Stone was a strong woman.

Kim had learned that bad news was best delivered quickly, accurately, and without drama. A woman as strong as Marilyn could take it in and not be felled by it.

"The reason I'm asking about this now is I thought you'd want to know," Kim said. "Sheryl Tardelli's killer was related to Carl Allen."

Marilyn gasped and pulled the tissue in her fist toward her mouth. "What?"

"We've checked the DNA. And we have a witness. The shooter was Carl Allen's nephew," Kim said. "His name was Dax Allen."

"But why would he kill Sheryl? He didn't even know her," Marilyn said, eyes wide, bewildered. "Did he kill the others, too?"

"The witness is Carl Allen's brother, Ryan. He was seriously injured before Dax Allen died. We're hoping to learn the full extent of his motives. He has lawyers now, and we may never know the whole truth," Kim said as kindly as she could. "But the important thing is we don't believe you're in any danger. And I wanted to let you know that."

They sat in silence for a few minutes and then Kim rose to leave. Marilyn walked her to the door.

On the front steps, Kim turned back. "You've mentioned Jodie Jacob to me a few times. Do you know her?"

Marilyn smiled weakly and nodded. "You go through something like that with another person and I think it bonds you somehow, doesn't it?"

"I've been looking for her and haven't had any luck," Kim said. "You wouldn't happen to have a phone number for her, would you?"

"Reacher asked me that, too," Marilyn said.

"Reacher? When did you talk to him?"

"This morning. He came by to ask about Jodie. We had coffee together," Marilyn said. "Somehow, he'd been wounded out there at Kaplan's house, he said. Gunshot wound to his leg. He was okay. I cleaned it up for him before he left. I was trained as a nurse a long time ago, you know."

Kim shook her head. Knowing what questions to ask would always be an art and not a science. She'd never have considered that Reacher might have come here.

"What did he want?"

"He asked me to pass a message to Jodie, next time I connected with her. He wants to talk to her. He asked me to get her phone number. I told him I would."

Kim pulled a card from her pocket. "Would you ask Jodie Jacob to call me, too. When you hear from her."

"It could be a while. I haven't heard from her in months. But I'd be glad to," Marilyn said, placing a hand on Kim's arm. "Thank you for coming here. It doesn't bring Sheryl back. But it's good to know what really happened to her."

Kim walked to the rental and drove away, keeping an eye on Marilyn Stone in the rearview mirror. Half a mile down the lane, she grabbed her phone and placed an encrypted call to her boss. This time, Cooper picked up.

CHAPTER 47

Thursday, June 23
Pound Ridge, New York

"THERE ARE THINGS ABOUT Reacher that you don't want to know," Cooper said before she had a chance to complain about being kept in the dark again.

"So instead of letting me do my job, you ordered me to avoid Marilyn Stone because you were trying to protect my career?" Kim said calmly as if she'd accepted his excuse.

"I didn't expect Reacher to go back there. But I also wanted you to find the sniper before the press got wind of him and created a panic," Cooper replied reasonably. "You couldn't do both."

She was at the end of the long, winding two-lane that led to the county road she could take into the city to meet Smithers. She turned south.

Spring in upstate New York was similar to Michigan. New leaves, new flowers, cool days and cooler nights, lots of rain. But the sun was shining today, which reminded her of Key West and William Curry, spoiling the effect.

"We can't blame Reacher for Dax Allen's actions, you know," Cooper said, like a college professor.

"You're defending Reacher now?" Kim replied. "He killed Carl Allen. Which led Allen's nephew to kill at least six innocent people. Maybe more that we simply haven't connected to the kid yet."

"So you haven't heard the whole story, then."

"Meaning what?"

"Dax Allen probably killed his own family. He was a psychopath. There were questions at the time, but nothing was definitive, and Dax was just a kid. People figured he'd lost his whole family. They didn't want to pile on. So they said the father killed the family and then himself. Put it down to a murder/suicide. If they'd followed the evidence and charged the kid at the time, we wouldn't be having this conversation now," Cooper said with a weary sigh. "Fortunately for his victims, Dax wasn't as sadistic as his Uncle Carl."

"Dax Allen was a kid. Not more than twenty-five. What does any twenty-five-year-old know about anything?" Kim replied because she didn't want to believe in a world where depraved young psychopaths ran amok.

Cooper said, "Reacher did the world a favor when he dispatched Carl Allen."

Kim slowed her speed and merged into traffic. "That's what you want Reacher for? So he can do the world a few more favors?"

She fumbled in her bag for a pair of sunglasses and lowered the window to feel the spring breeze on her face and whisk the horror away.

"I'll send you the files on Carl Allen. You read them and then let me know if you disagree with Reacher's solution," Cooper said. "Meanwhile, you need a permanent partner. You like Smithers.

And he's agreed to serve. He'll be released from the hospital this afternoon and he'll meet you in the city tonight."

Cooper was placating her. And he knew she knew it.

Truth was, she did like Smithers. He was a great partner. She couldn't do any better. Being paired with Smithers was just fine with her.

She changed the subject. "What about Nora Ramsey?"

"In what sense?"

"Her friends were killed. Her life's work destroyed. What's she supposed to do now?" Kim asked.

"She'll start over. She's a brilliant chemist. She and Kaplan will be able to recreate their product. Away from the controversy of R1. Give it a new name. Package it as a preventative for malaria mosquitos. Uncle Sam will pay for it and send it to malaria-infested countries around the world. She'll make a fortune," Cooper said easily.

Kim said nothing, but she figured he was probably right. Nora was a survivor. She'd proven that several times over. She'd figure it out and take Kaplan along with her. She'd probably share the profits with the families of Allen's victims, too. Nora was that kind of woman.

"As for you, you have a reservation at the Conrad for tonight before you head out tomorrow. I've got to go. Check your secure server," Cooper suggested reasonably. "After you read the files, call me if you have questions."

He paused briefly to give her a chance to reply. When she didn't, he hung up.

No response was necessary, expected, or offered.

He was the boss.

She served at his pleasure.

There was nothing more to say.

Kim cleared her mind and focused on enjoying the drive, allowing the summer breeze to blow her worries away. She watched the scenery and permitted her mind to wander.

An evening at the Conrad Hotel on Cooper's dime didn't sound all that bad. One review she'd read described the luxury hotel with an astonishing art collection as an oasis in the chaos of New York City.

She imagined a leisurely dinner of amazing food and wine, followed by a good night's sleep on high-thread-count sheets, and maybe even a spa massage first.

Traffic grew increasingly heavy closer to the city and forward progress had stalled a couple of miles back. She was moving at the speed of a lazy turtle.

Thirty minutes from downtown, her personal cell phone rang.

"Kim Otto," she picked up through the head set without checking the caller ID.

"Agent Otto," Lamont Finlay said in his rumbling bass voice that could have been sweet-talking lonely women on late night radio.

"Finlay." Kim hadn't talked to Finlay in a while. Partly because Cooper hated the guy. Partly because Gaspar didn't trust him.

Mostly because she hadn't needed Finlay for anything since she'd leaned too heavily on his help with the Niagara Falls business.

She needed Finlay to be there when she called on him. He owed her nothing. She didn't want him to refuse to take her calls simply because he could.

"Seems like you've got time to talk." He chuckled in a way that reminded her of the reach of his influence.

"How can I help you?" she asked perfunctorily.

Anything Cooper could do, Finlay could do. The two were often at odds and both operated from hidden agendas. Neither man was wholly trustworthy where Kim or Reacher was concerned.

"I understand Reacher's been in New York again recently," Finlay said. "Be careful. Cooper has plans for Reacher that don't include keeping your career intact."

Tell me something I don't know, she thought. "You know what those plans are?"

"Cooper doesn't confide in me," he replied. "But if you don't find Reacher before Cooper needs him, then he might let this whole thing drop."

"So the classified job Reacher's being considered for is time sensitive?" She should have considered that herself.

Cooper had never pushed her to rush forward, so the thought hadn't occurred to her.

But it should have.

Finlay replied, cagey as ever, "You've been on the hunt for Reacher for more than eight months now. How much longer do you expect Cooper to wait?"

"Are you saying you're willing to help me out here? You know where Reacher is. Or you can find him. Somehow," Kim said. "Is that it?"

She heard people talking in the background of Finlay's call now. He'd had a few moments free, so he'd called. But his time was always short.

"Cooper is dangerous. He'll cut his losses if he runs up against his drop-dead dates," Finlay said. "I like you, Otto. I don't want this to end badly for you."

"We can both agree on that," Kim said, staring at the sea of taillights flashing ahead like hundreds of warnings all at once.

"We'll talk more," Finlay said. "Keep in touch."

FROM LEE CHILD
THE REACHER REPORT:
March 2nd, 2012

The other big news is Diane Capri—a friend of mine—wrote a book revisiting the events of KILLING FLOOR in Margrave, Georgia. She imagines an FBI team tasked to trace Reacher's current-day whereabouts. They begin by interviewing people who knew him—starting out with Roscoe and Finlay. Check out this review: "Oh heck yes! I am in love with this book. I'm a huge Jack Reacher fan. If you don't know Jack (pun intended!) then get thee to the bookstore/wherever you buy your fix and pick up one of the many Jack Reacher books by Lee Child. Heck, pick up all of them. In particular, read Killing Floor. Then come back and read Don't Know Jack. This story picks up the other from the point of view of Kim and Gaspar, FBI agents assigned to build a file on Jack Reacher. The problem is, as anyone who knows Reacher can attest, he lives completely off the grid. No cell phone, no house, no car…he's not tied down. A pretty daunting task, then, wouldn't you say?

First lines: "Just the facts. And not many of them, either. Jack Reacher's file was too stale and too thin to be credible. No human could be as invisible as Reacher appeared to be, whether he was currently above the ground or under it. Either the file had been sanitized, or Reacher was the most off-the-grid paranoid Kim Otto had ever heard of." Right away, I'm sensing who Kim Otto is and I'm delighted that I know something she doesn't. You see, I DO know Jack. And I know he's not paranoid. Not really. I know why he lives as he does, and I know what kind of man he is. I loved having that over Kim and Gaspar. If you haven't read any Reacher novels, then this will feel like a good, solid story in its own right. If you have…oh if you have, then you, too, will feel like you have a one-up on the FBI. It's a fun feeling!

"Kim and Gaspar are sent to Margrave by a mysterious boss who reminds me of Charlie, in Charlie's Angels. You never see him…you hear him. He never gives them all the facts. So they are left with a big pile of nothing. They end up embroiled in a murder case that seems connected to Reacher somehow, but they can't see how. Suffice to say the efforts to find the murderer and Reacher, and not lose their own heads in the process, makes for an entertaining read.

"I love the way the author handled the entire story. The pacing is dead on (okay another pun intended), the story is full of twists and turns like a Reacher novel would be, but it's another viewpoint of a Reacher story. It's an outside-in approach to Reacher.

"You might be asking, do they find him? Do they finally meet the infamous Jack Reacher?

"Go…read…now…find out!"

Sounds great, right? Check out "Don't Know Jack," and let me know what you think.

So that's it for now…again, thanks for reading THE AFFAIR, and I hope you'll like A WANTED MAN just as much in September.

Lee Child

ABOUT THE AUTHOR

Diane Capri is an award-winning *New York Times*, *USA Today*, and worldwide bestselling author. She's a recovering lawyer and snowbird who divides her time between Florida and Michigan. An active member of Mystery Writers of America, Author's Guild, International Thriller Writers, Alliance of Independent Authors, Novelists, Inc., and Sisters in Crime, she loves to hear from readers. She is hard at work on her next novel.

Please connect with her online:
http://www.DianeCapri.com
Twitter: http://twitter.com/@DianeCapri
Facebook: http://www.facebook.com/Diane.Capri1
http://www.facebook.com/DianeCapriBooks

Made in United States
Troutdale, OR
03/03/2024

18043313R00184